She had to stay focused

Paulina put a hand up to Gil's massive chest, feeling the powerful surge of his heartbeat and the depth of his love for the baby, which was like an aura radiating from his heart. She needed to be strong for Gil and not be rattled by the anxiety spiking through her or the compelling desire to stop thinking and just react to the situation by holding him in her arms, reassuring him that everything would by okay. Logic would find the little boy. She, a P.I. who specialized in finding missing children, knew that better than anybody. She couldn't be sidetracked.

ABOUT THE AUTHOR

Joyce credits her lawyer mother with instilling in her a love of reading and writing—and a fascination for solving mysteries. She has a bachelor's degree in criminal justice and worked several years as a private investigator before turning her hand to writing romantic suspense. A transplanted American, Joyce makes her home in Aylmer, Quebec, with her handsome French-Canadian husband and two casebook-toting kid detectives.

Books by Joyce Sullivan

HARLEQUIN INTRIGUE
352—THE NIGHT BEFORE CHRISTMAS

This Little Baby
Joyce Sullivan

Harlequin Books

TORONTO • NEW YORK • LONDON
AMSTERDAM • PARIS • SYDNEY • HAMBURG
STOCKHOLM • ATHENS • TOKYO • MILAN
MADRID • WARSAW • BUDAPEST • AUCKLAND

In loving memory of Anna Michelle Sullivan and the joy her short life and sweet smiles gave her family.

ACKNOWLEDGMENTS

I'm grateful to the following people for helping me turn an idea into a credible story. Any mistakes are my own.

Mark Batten-Carew, Software Architect, Entrust; Superintendent Gary Forbes, Kelowna R.C.M.P.; Sergeant Tyrus Cameron, Ottawa-Carleton Police; Detective Constable Mike Faulds, Ministry of Solicitor General; Susan Pranschke, Children's Aid Society; Lawyers Robert Lewis and Glenn Kealy; T. Lorraine Vassalo, Criminologist; Ken Blackburn, 3rd Dan Black belt, Tae E. Lee, Tae Kwon Do; Paul V. Polishuk, M.D.; Andy Awada, Performance Mazda; Barry Smith, Southbank Dodge Chrysler; Lewis Eisen; Jean Tremblay; Gilles David; Ed Sullivan; and Joan Kilby.

Special thanks to Elizabeth Batten-Carew.

ISBN 0-373-22436-2

THIS LITTLE BABY

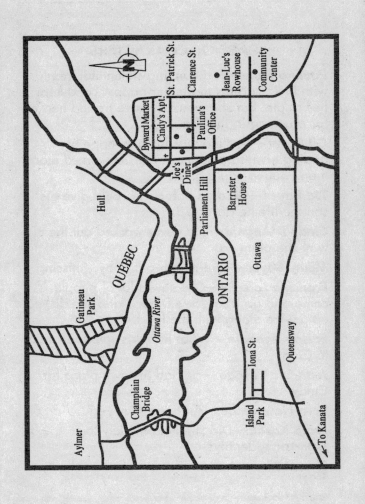

CAST OF CHARACTERS

Paulina Stewart—Reuniting stolen children with their parents made her happy…and kept her single. But she wouldn't have traded her job for anything in the world.

Gil Boyer—Paulina was his only hope of finding his infant nephew. But Gil wanted more than Paulina could give.

Ted Boyer—He died before he could give his son the life he deserved.

Cindy D'Angelo—Life never worked out the way she planned.

Mikey Boyer—Five-month-old baby…missing.

Francine Loiselle—She saw a lot of people come and go from Joe's Diner…and she dished up advice along with the food.

Edison Tweedie—What had this salesman said to Cindy?

Jean-Luc Deveau—He had his own plans for Cindy.

Vern Newcombe—An honest lawyer?

Lydia Kosak—Did she hold the key to Jean-Luc's identity?

Elva Madre—A counselor or a lawbreaker?

Prologue

Am I doing the right thing? The question rattled around in Cindy D'Angelo's head like a marble avoiding capture on a game board. She clutched the mug of black coffee firmly in her fingers and gazed down at her slumbering five-month-old son, Mikey. He'd fallen asleep in his stroller during the ten-minute walk through the Byward Market to Joe's Diner. His plump little arms framed his head as though he'd drifted off combing his wispy blond curls. He resembled a shining golden bee in his yellow-striped terry sleeper.

He sighed softly in his sleep and a spasm of longing started deep in Cindy's heart and shuddered through her. Her coffee splashed onto the gray-flecked Formica tabletop and she mopped it up with a paper napkin, her fingers trembling. Mikey really was a good baby. It wasn't his fault he couldn't sleep through the night yet. She just wasn't a good mother.

Cindy pressed her hands over her ears to block out the clink of plates and cutlery that sounded like her mother's jarring screech telling Cindy she was bad for getting pregnant. She was bad for cheating on Ted…and she was bad for wanting to live a little with Jean-Luc.

How had things gotten so confusing? Her mind reeled as she fought against a dizzying bout of fatigue. She hadn't slept much since Ted's death. There were too many decisions being forced on her. Too many other voices in her head talking all at once: Ted's...Gil's...Jean-Luc's... Elva's... Cindy just wanted to be free of the responsibility.

She reached down and tweaked Mikey's terry-covered toe. She wished he'd open his eyes, which were the same milky blue as her own. She wanted them to be together— today of all days.

Mikey made sucking noises and slumbered on. Cindy felt the tears spring to her eyes, clouding her vision. What was she going to do?

"That's a beautiful baby you have there, ma'am," a man said, stopping at her booth to admire Mikey. "You're right lucky."

Cindy nodded miserably, feeling the tears slide down her face. She hid them in shame. She'd felt lucky when Mikey was born and Ted had been so full of promises. Now she felt dispirited. How did she know whose promises to believe?

He touched her shoulder, his hand gentle and comforting. "Here now, what's this? You look like you could use a friend."

Cindy looked at him through the veil of her straggling bangs. His lined features suggested he'd endured a hardship or two, but his hazel eyes were kind and she felt reassured by the silver cross dangling at the open neck of his short-sleeved shirt. Maybe it would help to confide in a stranger. For the first time in over a month, Cindy felt a stabilizing calmness come over her as the man sat down and gestured for Francine to bring two more coffees.

THREE HOURS LATER...that silver cross was the last image in Cindy's mind as the life was strangled out of her.

Chapter One

Paulina Stewart pegged Gil Boyer for a man with a guilty conscience the second he strode into her office. She could see it in the anxious glint in his dark blue eyes and the tense ridge of his massive shoulders as he offered her his hand.

Guilty and handsome, she amended quickly, noting the lustrous gleam to his thick, dark hair and the chiseled planes of his face as she rescued her hand from his bone-crushing grip. The guy had the stride and muscular definition of a football player or a weight lifter. Judging by the bump in an otherwise perfect Roman nose, Paulina bet on football.

"Have a seat and tell me what I can do for you, Mr. Boyer," she directed, sitting down so she wouldn't feel quite so overwhelmed by the size of him. She picked up the gold pen her father had given her for a good luck charm and pulled a yellow legal pad from among the clutter of missing-children files on her desktop to make notes.

Somehow he managed to fold all that tense muscle and barely controlled anxiety into her standard-issue office chair. His gaze locked on her and Paulina felt a flicker of unfamiliar uncertainty deep in her belly. For some reason, she sat up straighter.

"I want you to find my sister-in-law, Cindy D'Angelo,

and my nephew, Mikey Boyer,'' he said forcefully. ''I
think she ran off with my nephew sometime last week.''

Paulina raised her eyebrows, growing steadily more in-
trigued. She'd seen all different types come into her office,
but no one with quite his puissance. ''Your sister-in-law?''

''Well, technically she and Ted weren't really married—
only common-law.''

''Are you hiring me for your brother, then?''

A storm front of pain froze his features, making her
almost regret the question.

''No. You don't understand.'' He flexed the fingers of
his right hand, then curled them into a tight fist. ''My
brother died six weeks ago in a hit-and-run accident.'' His
words came out in a rush, low and clipped, the forcefulness
ebbing for a moment, then resurging. ''I want to find
Cindy because I'm worried about her and the baby.
Mikey's only five months old. Since Ted's death I've been
going to their apartment once a week to see how they're
doing and drop off some money. You know, see if there's
anything I can do to help. She seems kind of lost—'' He
paused, his Adam's apple bobbing as he struggled to control his emotions.

Paulina had no doubt Mr. Boyer was feeling somewhat
lost, as well. Her heart went out to him, stirred by memories of her own loss. ''I'm sorry about your brother,'' she
said softly, thinking of her father. ''This must be a very
painful time for you.''

He nodded faintly, as though not wanting to acknowledge it. ''Um, anyway, I dropped by last Thursday and she
wasn't home. I've tried calling, but she doesn't answer.''

Paulina picked up her phone. ''What's Cindy's number?'' She punched in the number he told her and glanced
back at him again, aware that his blue measuring gaze had
never left her. Her pulse gave a sudden leap at the base of
her throat and fluttered down to settle in her abdomen.

Funny, she was five foot seven in her stocking feet, but he made her feel petite and undeniably feminine. No doubt he had the same effect on a lot of women. She turned slightly in her chair, shielding herself from his scrutiny as she cradled the receiver against her ear. She hung up after the seventh ring. "Maybe Cindy wanted to get away for a few days..." she suggested.

"I thought of that, but I think she would have told me. Our Thursday night thing is pretty regular. I take her and Mikey out to dinner, then I stay with Mikey while Cindy goes out for a few hours." His forearms braced against the chair's armrests as he laced his fingers in his lap.

Paulina wondered why his strong, square-tipped fingers trembled. She waited for him to tell her more.

"I called Cindy on Monday to confirm and she said we were on for Thursday night." He drew a ragged breath. The muscles in his arms contracted rigidly. "I can understand she might have decided to change her plans and blow me off, but she wouldn't have blown off the support checks I've been bringing to buy groceries and formula for Mikey. After Ted's funeral, I told her I'd take over paying child support for Mikey so she wouldn't have to worry about anything."

Paulina nodded thoughtfully, hiding her surprise and burgeoning respect as she jotted down the pertinent details. An uncle who wanted to pay child support; that was a new one for her files. She'd like to put Mr. Boyer in front of a group of deadbeat dads to lecture about responsibility. "Have you tried contacting her family?"

"She doesn't have any. Ted told me she's been on her own since she was sixteen."

"What about her friends?"

He shifted awkwardly, his massive thighs spreading. The steel-framed chair creaked in protest. "She's talked about some mothers she met at the drop-in program she takes Mikey to, but I don't know their names. Cindy's kind of a loner. She and Ted had that in common. They had each other—and Mikey. That's why I'm worried she's freaked out and gone off somewhere on her own.''

And if she was reading him right, Paulina suspected he probably felt guilty he hadn't done enough for Cindy.

Shadows of anxiety turned the deep blue of his eyes to indigo. "Can you help me find her, Ms. Stewart?"

"I can try. I'll require a five hundred dollar retainer before I get started. I charge sixty-five an hour, plus expenses.''

"No problem." He pulled a checkbook from the back pocket of his jeans and started writing out a check. "What do we do first?"

Paulina chose to ignore his use of the plural "we." She issued a receipt for the retainer and passed him some standard locate forms and a client-information sheet to fill out. "You give me all the personal data you have on Cindy. I'll get back to you as soon as I have something solid to report.''

Mr. Boyer put down his pen. "That's not good enough," he said quietly and firmly. "I want to help with the investigation.''

The stubborn insistence in his words and the sudden poised watchfulness in his massive body—like a bull preparing to charge—warned Paulina she had to handle the situation delicately. Why did people think hiring a P.I. was like buying a ticket to a murder-mystery dinner theater? You shell out a few bucks in exchange for the chance to play detective. She smiled reassuringly. "I appreciate your offer, Mr. Boyer, but really, the only assistance I require from you is the information in these forms. If I need more information, I'll contact you.''

His dark brows drew together ominously. "I insist. Cindy's in a fragile emotional state. I don't want her frightened by an overeager private investigator.''

And he thought *he* was a calming influence? Granted, the sheer size of him, accompanied by one of those frowns, could silence a roomful of people awfully fast. With practised skill, Paulina kept her smile from fading. ''I hardly think I'm the type of person who would frighten anyone. And if I may speak plainly, your presence would only be a hindrance.''

He returned her smile just as quickly, just as falsely, his tone cordial and businesslike, ''I believe that's for me to decide. I am, after all, paying for your services.''

''My point exactly, Mr. Boyer. You're paying me for my services—you're not paying me to drag you along.'' She glanced at his stonewashed denim jeans, his modestly priced blue knit shirt and Brooks running shoes. ''If you want that privilege, it'll cost you double. One thirty an hour. Your choice.''

A light gleamed in his eyes as their gazes locked again. Paulina felt the challenge from that light stoke her insides.

''All right, Ms. Stewart. Here's my counteroffer—I'll pay you one fifty an hour. The extra twenty is to compensate you for calling me Gil.'' His smile was sheer devilry.

She'd underestimated him and he was enjoying it.

For a moment, she considered showing him to the door. As much as she'd enjoy the experience, she decided it would be foolish. The case was a fairly straightforward locate, and ''Gil's'' extra fees would pay for a significant amount of gratis work she did for parents who couldn't afford to search for their missing children. There was one case in particular: a fourteen-year-old boy named Bryan Watson, whose mother hadn't seen him since he was two years old.

Paulina had recently discovered the father was living in Australia, but she didn't know which state—yet. Someday soon Bryan's picture was going to join the other children's pictures mounted on her Found display, which took up one wall of her office. What was a little baby-sitting compared to Brenda's joy at seeing her son again?

Paulina stuck her hand across the table. "You have a deal, *Gil*."

"I knew we could come to a mutually satisfactory arrangement." His large hand engulfed hers, his touch so unexpectedly gentle this time she felt a tickle of unease at the nape of her neck.

She struggled to conceal her discomfiture. He was only a client. She was selling her time, not her integrity. There was no reason to feel as though she'd sold her soul to the devil.

While Gil filled out forms, Paulina studied photos he'd brought of Cindy and Mikey. Cindy looked young and vulnerable. She wore her thin blond hair in a shoulder-length style with pouffed bangs achieved through teasing and hairspray. She played up her pale blue eyes with black mascara and blue eyeliner. Her bio information said she was twenty-two, five years younger than Paulina. Mikey was a butterball. Plump, dimpled and blue-eyed, with a soft crown of golden down.

Paulina started reading the forms and making notes. A glance at the client credit information section told her Gil owned a computer consulting firm and lived in Kanata, just west of Ottawa. Interesting. But then, she'd already begun to suspect a deceptively smart man dwelled in that powerhouse of a body.

Still, for someone who specialized in information processing, he didn't know diddly about his sister-in-law. Not even the names of her parents. She skimmed over the blank spaces on the forms to what little he knew: Cindy's former place of work and her address. Her apartment was located in the Byward Market on the two hundred block of St.

Patrick Street. It was the obvious place to start. They could walk over. She grabbed her purse and keys and informed Andrea, an intern student who worked for her part-time, that she was headed out for a while.

When they reached the street, Gil insisted they take his black Mazda Precidia.

"It'll be faster to walk," she assured him in case he was worried about his hundred and fifty dollar an hour bargain.

"You haven't seen the way I drive."

It wasn't worth arguing about. The meter was running and it was his nickel. Paulina only hoped as she settled into the passenger seat that she wouldn't have to battle him every step of the investigation. She was beginning to see why Cindy might have left for a few days without informing her brother-in-law. Gil probably would have had something to say about her travel plans.

If Gil had seemed overwhelming in her office, he completely dwarfed her in his compact sports car. At six foot three, he had a definite sense of presence that made a silent assault on her senses. She could scoot her body to the far side of the gray corduroy seat to avoid his arm brushing hers as he changed gears, but she couldn't avoid noticing his discreet masculine cologne or the smooth finesse with which he maneuvered the car in and out of the Market's brick one-way streets.

It was nearing the end of September—a perfect Indian summer day. Paulina felt flushed and uncomfortable despite the air blasting on the air conditioner.

The Market in Canada's capital city was vibrant with flowers, produce and shoppers. St. Patrick Street was duller, the closely spaced buildings casting the street in shadow. At the end of the street, the elegant silver spires of St. Patrick's Church beckoned the eye. Gil found a parking spot in front of a run-down apartment building that lacked the fine, albeit sagging architectural detailing of the neighboring row houses. Enclosed concrete balconies from a more modern era of design hugged the ugly brick building. Narrow concrete steps led up to a nondescript entrance.

Gil pressed his lips together and glanced uneasily at the beautiful, midnight-haired woman beside him. He felt as though he'd scored a major point just getting her to Cindy's apartment. He hadn't known what to expect when he'd made a few inquiries with the solicitor general's office about private investigators, but so far he wasn't disappointed. Paulina Stewart was competent and tough all right, and she had a keen intelligence in her starry eyes. She also drove a hard bargain.

He gestured toward the apartment building, ashamed to show her the dump Ted was raising his son in. "This is it. It's not exactly the Château Laurier." Hell, as soon as Cindy would agree to it, he planned to move them to a nicer neighborhood. He let Paulina go first up the steps, ready to steady her in case she stumbled on the caking concrete in her high heels. The interior of the building smelled of onions and browning meat. Cindy's apartment was on the first floor and faced the street. He knocked on the door loudly. "Cindy? It's Gil, open up."

They waited a few minutes to no avail. Gil shrugged his shoulders. The sick feeling he'd been harboring since Friday told him Cindy hadn't been home for days.

"So, what do we do now?" He tapped Paulina's navy leather purse. "Do you have some tools in there to pick the lock?"

Her gray eyes narrowed. "No. Let's get something clear between us, Mr. Boyer," she said coldly. "Private investigators don't have a license to break and enter. I operate completely within the law. If you can't accept that, then I'll be happy to return your retainer."

He held up his hands. Terrific. He'd offended the most

highly respected P.I. in the province. "I'm sorry. I guess I've been watching too much TV. What do you suggest we do next?"

"We get into Cindy's apartment." A trace of a smile flicked over her lips as she turned and set off briskly down the hall.

"What?" Gil's jaw dropped. He stood there, his chin all but scraping the floor, watching her walk away. The short skirt of her chic navy-and-white two-piece outfit revealed a great pair of legs. If it wasn't politically incorrect and she wasn't working for him, he'd even go so far as to admit she was sexy in a fascinating, irritating way. And bossy. Definitely bossy.

He charged after her. "But you said—"

She cut him off, talking over her shoulder. "Watch and listen. Don't say anything unless I give you permission to speak—or you're out on the pavement. Got it?"

He swallowed hard. "Got it."

She stopped suddenly at the door to the building manager's apartment. "By the way, you got any more checks on you?" she demanded, raising her hand to knock.

"Yeah."

"Good." She gave the door a discreet rap. "We're probably going to need one."

A grizzled old guy with a beer gut swung open the door. The sound of applause from a talk show floated into the hallway. "What can I do for ya?"

Paulina flashed a bright smile that probably made the old geezer wish he was thirty years younger. "Are you the manager?"

At the man's nod, she pulled her ID from her purse and introduced herself. "I apologize for taking you away from your program. We're here because my client, Mr. Boyer, is worried about his sister-in-law, Cindy, in apartment seven," she explained. "Gil, show him your driver's license."

Gil immediately complied.

"Boyer?" The manager's curious eyes scanned the license and gave Gil the once-over. "Is that your brother Ted who died?"

Gil nodded, trying to follow Paulina's instructions to the letter.

"Sorry."

Paulina put her hand to her breast and spoke in a low confidential tone, "Then you understand the situation, Mr....?"

"Just call me Max," the man replied.

"Well, Max, Cindy's naturally been very upset by Ted's death. She's in a fragile emotional state. Mr. Boyer was supposed to take Cindy and the baby out to dinner last Thursday, but Cindy wasn't home. And she hasn't been answering the phone. Would it be too much trouble for you to check her apartment—just to make sure she and the baby are okay? Maybe Mr. Boyer could leave her a note to allay his concerns?"

Max frowned. "Do you think she's run off? Tomorrow's the end of the month and she hasn't paid her rent."

Paulina cleared her throat. "It's possible. As I said, she's in a fragile state. And if that's the case, we're sure you and the company that manages the building would want to be informed immediately. Mr. Boyer would be more than happy to give you a check to cover October's rent. If Cindy has skipped out, you can consider this her thirty days' notice."

"Let's have a look, then," Max decided. Gil could have kissed Paulina as the manager stepped into the corridor, closing his apartment door behind him. She had that old guy wrapped around her finger, sweet as you please.

But Gil's fever of excitement was short lived. The barren closets of Cindy's apartment confirmed his worst fears. Cindy had left the furnishings, but she'd taken everything else that could fit into a suitcase—with the exception of the plushy caramel teddy bear Gil had given Mikey three weeks ago. Gil felt a tight band snap inside him as he lifted the bear from Mikey's crib and held it against his chest. It smelled of diapers and baby powder…and Mikey.

Oh, God, had Cindy left the bear behind as a subtle way of saying she didn't want him involved in her and Mikey's life?

Gil wasn't sure he could endure losing both Ted and Mikey. Ted was his only sibling. Regret and guilt burned like acid in Gil's heart. *If only I'd kept my opinions to myself and loaned Ted the money, then none of this would have happened.* Gil abruptly deleted the "if" statement from his mind, as though debugging a program. Mikey needed an uncle in his life as much as Gil needed to love Mikey. Somebody had to teach the kid how to play baseball and…

"Gil?"

He turned around to see Paulina framed in the doorway of the bedroom. He liked the soft and compassionate way she said his name; it was worth twenty extra bucks an hour. He gruffly swiped his eyes. Damn, the last six weeks had turned him to mush.

"I'll need the check now for four hundred dollars," she said. "Max has gone to get a copy of the lease on the apartment. Maybe Cindy listed some relatives on it, to contact in case of emergency."

Gil fumbled for his checkbook and saluted her with it. "I hear and I obey. Do you think Max would mind if I kept my friend the bear here?"

Paulina felt unprofessional tears sting her eyes. Beneath Gil's macho exterior beat a heart of marshmallow. "No. In fact, I told him you'd take care of removing Cindy's things so the apartment could be available for rent sooner.''

"Thanks. I appreciate that.''

They walked into the small living area of the one-bedroom apartment. A worn plaid couch faced a natural wicker shelving unit holding the television. Magazines and baby toys were scattered on the carpet. An infant seat sat on the black oak table in the eating area. Paulina had already checked the cupboards for baby bottles and formula. Cindy had taken it all with her.

"You wrote on one of the forms that Cindy doesn't own a car, but you mentioned Ted had a truck. Could Cindy be driving Ted's truck?" Paulina asked Gil, wondering why Cindy hadn't bothered taking some of the lighter furniture.

"No. The garage told me it wasn't worth fixing. I had to pay them to tow it to a salvage yard. I'm not even sure Cindy knows how to drive.''

Paulina frowned.

Max reappeared lugging a stack of cardboard boxes. He carried a sheet of paper between his teeth like a dog delivering a newspaper. Setting the boxes down, he removed the paper from his mouth and passed it to her. "Here's the rental agreement.''

Paulina gingerly avoided the teeth marks and spittle at the top of the page. She could feel Gil standing behind her, reading over her shoulder. The heat of his body radiated into hers, heightening her awareness of him. She made a determined effort to focus her attention on the sections of the contract spelled out in blue ink.

"Sorry, all it says is her next-of-kin is Gilbert Boyer,'' Max added helpfully. He scratched the gray bristles studding his double chin.

"That's me in the flesh,'' Gil responded. "Here's the

check for the rent, Max—and something extra for your trouble.''

Max's eyes lit up at the crisp twenty-dollar bill. Paulina shot Gil a warning look over her shoulder to remind him not to take any more initiatives without consulting her. Not that he had done any damage. The close proximity of their bodies forced her to tilt her head back, granting her an up-close-and-personal view of Gil's jaw. Not a millimeter of flesh sagged. The skin hugging his square chin was smooth, lightly tanned—and scented of him.

Paulina's mouth went dry. Her cheeks grew warm as she hastily glanced back at the building manager. "Yes, thank you, Max. We'll remove a few things and tidy up. Is it all right if we talk to the neighbors? Maybe one of them saw or heard something that might tell us where Cindy was headed.''

"Sure. Let me know when you're done so I can lock up.''

Paulina returned the rental agreement to him. After Max had gone, she tried to ignore the fact that Gil was in the apartment with her as she picked up Cindy's phone and pressed the redial button. She had a job to do. It rang twice before an answering machine kicked in. A man's voice with a French accent said, ''Allo, leave a message.''

''Hi, this is Louise,'' she ad-libbed. ''I'm a friend of Cindy D'Angelo. Could you please get back to me at 555-7012?'' She disconnected the line, then punched in the code *69. An automated voice told her the last number to have called Cindy's apartment. She repeated it to Gil. ''Does that sound familiar to you?''

''Yeah, it's my home number.'' He jabbed his hands into the pockets of his jeans. The fabric stretched taut across his lower hips. ''Who's Louise?''

''I've no idea,'' Paulina responded, averting her gaze from the locale of his impressive, male attributes. ''Every-

body knows at least one Louise in Ottawa, don't they? The
number I left is a private unlisted line to my office. If
someone calls back, I'll say I'm a mother from the parent
drop-in program. Don't just stand there,'' she instructed,
plucking the Yellow Pages phone directory from the kitch-
en counter and tossing it into one of the boxes. "Grab all
the wastebaskets in the apartment. We're taking the trash
with us—we'll sort it later at my office." She started peeling off the tape that held Cindy's calendar to the refrigerator door.

"Okay, you're the boss." He disappeared into the bathroom, where she heard him opening cupboards.

She fluffed her bangs from her sticky forehead. Heaven
help her, it was hot in here. Her suit top was clamped to
her skin. She added the calendar to the box and crossed
the living room to open the sliding-glass patio door. The
drooping beige drapes were partially drawn. They rattled
along the rod as she shoved them aside in search of the
door handle. Paulina froze. The door was open a crack.
Had Cindy forgotten to lock it?

Paulina ditched that theory when she glanced through
the window and noticed the narrow white plastic planter
that had obviously fallen from the ledge of the concrete
balcony. Pink and purple petunias and potting soil littered
the concrete floor. Paulina slid the door wider and examined the locking mechanism in consternation. Someone
had been up here—and it wasn't the wind. The wind
couldn't gouge fresh scratch marks in the door's aluminum
frame.

Someone had obviously broken into Cindy's apartment.
Who? Thieves?

Thoughtfully, Paulina leaned over the concrete balcony
wall. Cindy's apartment was one floor above the parking
garage. Low-growing junipers crowded a shrub bed bordering the building's cracked front steps. But a metal hand-

rail at the main entrance provided a convenient leg up to a would-be intruder with enough upper-body strength to pull himself over the balcony. Whoever it was had legs long enough to knock over the planter when they straddled the wall.

Crouching down, she examined a partial footprint in the potting soil. The letters of a word were clearly discernible; the shoe manufacturer's name spelled backward. *Brooks.*

Paulina rocked back on her heels and swore.

What the hell had Gil been doing up here?

Chapter Two

Tamping down her anger, Paulina collected her purse from the kitchen table and slung it over her shoulder. "I quit," she informed Gil as he deposited two plastic grocery bags filled with garbage alongside a large green bag he'd removed from the trash container under the kitchen sink.

His face paled.

"What do you mean you quit?" he demanded, taking a threatening step toward her. "You can't just change your mind like that."

"Yes, I can." She crossed her arms over her chest, holding her ground. "You're not being straight with me. Now I know why you seemed so certain Cindy had run off—because you broke into her apartment." She followed his glance toward the patio door. His cheeks flagged with sudden color, condemning him. She strove to keep her cool. "The only thing I don't understand is why you hired me."

His eyes met hers squarely, but it was impossible to guess what he was thinking. She only saw pain in his shadowed gaze. "I didn't break in. I only climbed onto the balcony Friday afternoon to look in the window and see if Cindy and Mikey were around."

She raised her eyebrows. "The marks on the patio door suggest otherwise. It's been jimmied open."

"Well, it wasn't open then. I know, because I tried the

door." His face turned an even shade of red, though he continued to meet her gaze. "I admit, one of the reasons I hired you was because I hoped you could get me inside. Then I'd know for sure if Cindy had gone. I had this sick feeling the other day—the apartment had such a deserted air to it." He wet his lips nervously. "How does that old saying go? 'Desperate times call for desperate measures?'"

Paulina didn't buy his pathetic excuse. Her mother had used the same expression to justify taking Paulina away from her father. "I don't break the law and I don't work for people who take the law into their own hands." She whirled around and headed for the door, her purse bouncing against her hip. "You'll get your retainer back in the mail, minus an hour's pay."

"Wait!"

The hoarse cry of pain resonating in his voice caused her to falter as she reached the door.

"You're right," he declared. "I didn't tell you everything. But it's hard to admit your mistakes out loud—especially ones that have tragic consequences."

Tragic consequences? What was he talking about? She paused, her hand on the doorknob, and told herself she was an idiot for sparing him even a second more of her time. But she couldn't walk away from him any more than she could abandon the children whose pictures plastered her office. "You have ten seconds to tell me what's eating away at you."

"I'm partly to blame for Ted's death," he said harshly, self-contempt riddling every word. "I didn't drive the car that hit him, but if I hadn't been such a selfish bastard his truck wouldn't have broken down that night. Ted called me a week before the accident to ask for a loan. He said he needed the money for car repairs. But I, uh, didn't believe him." Paulina heard a deep sob escape him. The air in the apartment grew thick with the weight of his anguish. Paulina kept her back to him, steeling herself to remain objective despite the tears gathering in her eyes.

After a minute, Gil continued, "I thought he was angling after poker money. He played poker once a week with his buddies from work and I thought he should be spending his free time with his family." His voice dipped, simmering with anger, "But Ted always shirked responsibility. He thought he loved Cindy, but he didn't want to marry her. He had a child and he didn't think about practical things like life insurance or putting money aside for emergencies. I should have known he'd go to the poker game anyway. His truck broke down on his way home. He got hit when he got out to fix it."

Paulina blinked away her tears and tried to keep a grip on her emotions as she turned to face him. He was carrying around a truckload of guilt that didn't belong to him. "You don't sound selfish to me. You sound like a caring big brother who tried to pass on sound advice to a sibling."

Gil laughed. The raw sound cut into Paulina's heart and made her want to open her arms to him. "Yes, well, my brotherly advice backfired with Ted, and it backfired with Cindy. I think I completely overwhelmed her by offering to pay support for Mikey. I honestly believe children need to be home with their mother when they're young—at least until they start school." He darted a look at her as though worried he might have offended her feminist principles.

He had.

But she remained silent as he planted his hands on his hips and stared at a *People* magazine lying on the gold shag carpet. "The last time we had dinner I offered to move them into a nicer apartment in Kanata—closer to where I live. My consulting firm is doing very well. I can afford to pay her to stay home with Mikey. All I asked for in exchange was reasonable visitation. I want to play an active part in Mikey's life. That little kid is all my parents and I have left of Ted.''

Paulina absorbed his words, listening to her heart. She didn't share his archaic views on child care—Gil sounded too much like her ex-husband. She wondered how Cindy had reacted. Gil's offer smacked of control, but Paulina respected the fact that he wanted to be more to his nephew than a signature on a support check. She didn't think he'd withdraw the support money if Cindy decided to work. The dark circles under his eyes and the lines of tension carved in his features broadcast his genuine concern.

He was telling the truth. She was sure of it. He'd climbed onto the balcony but he hadn't pried open the door, which posed the unsettling question—who did? And why?

With tentative strides he joined her in the narrow corridor, the bulk of his massive frame blocking the sunlight that filtered through the patio window from the living area. Wrapped in shadow, he gave the impression of a strong man trying to find his way in the dark.

"You're still here," he remarked quietly. "Does that mean you've reconsidered and you'll help me find Cindy and Mikey?"

Gil held his breath and prayed, waiting for her response. He didn't have a chance in hell of finding Cindy without Paulina. Why hadn't he paid more attention to the details of Cindy's life? He didn't even know her birthday. March something, he *thought*. He was more adept with recursive file searches than people searches, and a contact in the solicitor general's office had confidentially told him Paulina was the best.

Her expression was unreadable in the shadowy foyer. Did she find the idea of working for him that repugnant?

In his college days at Northwestern Gil had faced three-hundred-sixty-pound offensive tackles at the line of scrimmage and tenth-level wizards in role-playing games who hadn't intimidated him half as much. Those linemen and wizards didn't wear delicately scented perfume that reminded him of the wild lilacs blooming in the spring along his favorite jogging route.

"I'll continue working for you on one condition," she said, holding up her finger like a dungeon master laying out the rules of a quest. "From now on, we play by my rules and my rules only. Agreed?"

Gil blinked as relief flooded through him. "Yes, ma'am. Can I have a look at the door now? I haven't got a clue why someone would want to break into Cindy's apartment. But come to think of it, the place seems messier. I don't recall the magazines being on the floor."

"Be my guest. We'll let Max know so he can get it repaired. I just want a peek inside Cindy's dresser drawers, then we can try talking to the neighbors."

Gil noticed Paulina came back from the bedroom with her hands empty. He accompanied her out into the hallway. He had no intention of interfering with her investigative techniques any more than she would have tried to tell him how to customize a computer application to a client's needs. He just wanted to be part of the action. Sitting on the sidelines would drive him crazy.

He tried not to be discouraged when it quickly became apparent the neighbors didn't know anything about Cindy—not even her name.

Paulina gave him a sharp poke in the ribs as she moved on to a door at the end of the hall. "Stop glowering, it doesn't help."

He pasted a smile on his face.

"Now you look like you're on drugs."

"Half the people in this building look like they're on drugs." He wasted the smile though. No one was home.

"Let's try the apartments near the front entrance," Paulina suggested. "If we're lucky, there'll be a busybody in residence."

THE BUSYBODY WAS A scrawny elderly woman in a flowered housecoat. Her red lipstick rimmed her mouth as though it had been applied with a plunger. Either that or she'd had her mouth pressed to the door while she'd ogled them through the peephole.

"You look familiar, young man," the woman told Gil with a wink as she opened her door.

Paulina launched into her spiel and showed a picture of Mikey and Cindy. Her story found a sympathetic audience.

"That poor young woman having to raise her baby on her own. It's tough with all the welfare cuts the government has been inflicting these days. How are we expected to eat? You say her husband died?"

"Yes."

"That's a shame. I don't think I saw him more than a few times. That's a peculiar schedule her husband had, bringing him home in the afternoons." She winked at Gil again and patted her unnaturally orangish hairdo. "He was quite a handsome man, but then, I've always had a weakness for blondes."

Gil frowned. "Blondes?"

"Yes. My first husband was a blonde, but his hair started to recede. I divorced him when he went totally bald. His head was so unattractive. My second husband, Gerry, had a head of hair you wouldn't believe—"

"Excuse me…but is this the man you saw?" Gil opened his wallet to a family photo taken a few years ago and pointed to Ted, whose dark brown hair could never be mistaken for blond.

"Why, no! Though, come to think of it, he looks vaguely familiar. I thought this bloke lived up on the third floor. He struck me as the construction type."

Gil felt as if the woman had kicked him in the kidneys. *Who was the blond man Cindy was seeing?*

"You're remarkably observant," Paulina complimented the woman. "Could you tell us what the man you saw with Cindy looked like?"

"Well, he wasn't nearly as tall as this young buck you've got here. But five foot ten is tall for a woman of my stature. He had a good physique—very athletic. He hoisted the baby carriage over the front steps no problem."

Gil's insides churned. Ted was six foot one and lean. He wanted to blurt out a million questions at the woman but Paulina had shifted her body stance, positioning her shoulder slightly in front of him as though subtly telling him to back off and let her handle things.

"Long or short blond hair?"

"Long and flowing like the men on the cover of those books near the checkout counter in the grocery store."

"No wonder you noticed him. Blond men with muscles are a memorable combination." Gil saw the corner of Paulina's mouth curve into an appreciative this-is-a-woman-thing smile. "Can you recall when you saw him last? Was it recently—within the last week or two?"

"Now that's a tough one." The woman tapped a finger adorned with a peeling coat of plum polish on her lipstick-smeared lips. "Oh, I remember, it was Labor Day weekend. It was an evening, and quite hot and humid. The baby was crying in his carriage. I opened my door a crack and peeked out into the lobby to make sure everything was okay. I could tell they were tense with each other. He was hollering over the sound of the baby and asking where they were going. She hollered right back and said anywhere with air-conditioning. I got a laugh over that. Babies, they don't like the heat."

"I don't suppose in all this hollering you happened to overhear his name?"

The woman shook her head. "Afraid not. I closed the door as soon as I was sure nobody was being slapped around. I don't like to pry into other people's business."

Paulina thanked the woman and moved down the hallway knocking on doors. Numbly, Gil stuck close to Paulina's side, but his thoughts were far away.

Had Cindy run off with another man?

"ARE YOU OKAY?" Paulina cast a sideways glance at Gil as they emptied the garbage bags from Cindy's apartment onto the conference table in the back room of Stewart Investigations. He'd been awfully quiet since they'd found out about the blond man with muscles. Paulina didn't have to guess why. She'd been doing a little speculating herself.

"Yeah, I'm okay." He scowled fiercely. "I just wasn't expecting to find out Cindy was cheating on Ted."

"We don't know that for certain. I agree it's a possibility we should consider, but we don't have enough information to come to a conclusion like that yet. This man could be a friend of Cindy's or a friend of Ted's. Or a relative you know nothing about." She handed him a pair of surgical gloves. "With luck, the garbage will give us a few clues. Let's dispense with the disgusting stuff first. The diapers are making the room stink. Then we'll sift through what's left."

Paulina wasn't sure if Gil had ever actually changed one of his nephew's diapers. Probably not, if she was reading him right. That chore was probably mothers' work in his rule book. At least he didn't complain as he slipped on the gloves and combed the pile for dirty diapers, lobbing the white plastic bundles with unerring aim into the wastebasket she'd set on the table for that purpose.

"Believe it or not, this is very similar to what I do designing applications for my customers," he said tightly. Another diaper scored two points with a dull thunk. Paulina wagered he was working out a lot of pent-up aggression by the sound of those thunks. "During the analysis phase, I weed through a lot of bits of paper—and I've been known to pull stuff out of the trash—so I can figure out how their business operates and tailor a program to suit their needs. But, holy mackerel, I'll think twice before I take on contracts with day cares."

A laugh slipped out of her mouth before she could stop it. She glanced at him quickly, an apology ready on her lips. There was nothing laughable about the situation—a baby and his mother were missing. But Gil was on the brink of laughing himself, the tension in his face eased by a halfhearted smile. Paulina felt a tiny flutter like the brush of a butterfly's wings in her stomach. She hoped that faint smile of his lingered a long time. His fears about Mikey would return soon enough and chase the smile away.

Twenty minutes later she felt it safe to conclude—once they'd opened a window and were breathing fresh air again—that Cindy had a fondness for frozen dinners, bananas and fudge cookies. They'd also salvaged an eight-day-old Sunday edition of the *Ottawa Citizen*—which Paulina fervently hoped Cindy had bought for the free television guide and not the travel section—and a small pile of miscellanea including business cards, receipts and the odd bill, which suggested Cindy had cleaned out her purse before her departure. Paulina considered this pile a gold mine and hoped it would yield a nugget or two.

She handed Gil the Sunday paper and Cindy's Yellow Pages directory. "Pore over the airlines listings in the Yellow Pages and every page of the newspaper for handwritten notes," she told him. "Pay particularly close attention to the travel section. She might have circled some cheap airfares if she was planning a trip to visit family or a friend."

"I think she'd have mentioned some family or close

friends if she had any,'' Gil muttered, his jaw visibly stiffening. Tension shimmered around him like an impermeable glass dome.

Paulina knew his anger and frustration weren't directed at her. "Not necessarily. Cindy could have run away from a tough situation—and had a change of heart because of recent events."

"Well, I don't buy that, but I see what you mean." He bent his head over the Yellow Pages directory. Paulina let her gaze rest on his thick, dark hair for a moment. Gil wasn't just trying to find Mikey and Cindy, he was battling loss and disillusionment. Paulina had had her own run-in with those two nemeses and she'd survived. Gil would, too. With a small sigh, she started sifting through the pile of miscellanea awaiting her inspection.

The business card for the pregnancy counseling clinic raised a few questions in her mind, but now wasn't a good time to ask Gil about it. She fanned out the receipts, checking the dates. Three were for Joe's Diner, a popular Fifties-style diner in the Byward Market. All three receipts indicated Cindy had dined alone within the last month. There were grocery receipts dating as far as four months back and a two-week-old receipt for magazines from a pharmacy.

There was no doubt about it. Cindy had cleaned out her purse—the kind of thing a woman did before she went on a trip. Not the kind of thing she did before she moved in with a man in another part of town. Paulina let that thought unfold.

Across the table the newspaper rattled. Gil cursed under his breath. She looked up, careful to shield her thoughts. "Find something?"

"The travel section is missing—and I'm leaping to conclusions," he said darkly. He sent the paper flying across the room. Anger, hurt and confusion deepened the worry lines framing his mouth. His eyes teemed with unanswered questions. "Dammit, why is she doing this?"

He looked so lost and in need of reassurance Paulina couldn't stop herself from laying her hand on his arm. From trying to somehow ease the pain he was enduring, to share part of his burden. "I don't know, Gil. But I promise you, we're going to find out."

The moment she touched him she was conscious of the heat and tension coiled in the contoured muscles of his forearm. It pulsed up her arm and circulated through every cell of her body. Her breath caught in her lungs as though paralyzed by the strange phenomenon invading her body. She'd had hundreds of clients unburden their souls to her over the past six years. She'd listened and cared—always ready with a supply of tissues and sympathy—using her heart and her conscience as her guides. But none of their stories had affected her in quite this way.

She'd never made a promise to a client before. She could almost hear the cadence of her father's baritone as he advised her to always err on the side of caution. Some of her cases had taken years of painstaking follow-up on the slimmest of leads to resolve—and here, she'd practically promised Gil she'd find Cindy and Mikey.

Her eyes searched his handsome face as she tried to pinpoint the cause of her rash behavior. The answer she arrived at was so blatantly obvious—as evident and intimidating as the battle-scar bump on his nose—she was embarrassed to acknowledge it. *She was reacting to his classic handsomeness.* She'd never had a client before of the knee-knocking male-soap-opera-star caliber. She probably wouldn't again, if word got out she was making promises she couldn't keep.

She absolutely had more important things to do than stare into a pair of indigo eyes. Clearing her throat, she glanced down at the table and realized she needed her hand in order to examine the telephone bill she'd found in Cindy's trash, but her hand was quite occupied making circular stroking motions on Gil's arm. Fire rose to Paulina's cheeks. No wonder she still felt so warm and tingly!

As though sensing Paulina was about to snatch her fingers away, Gil's hand settled over hers, trapping her hand on his arm. His large fingers made a surprisingly gentle cage.

"Thank you," he said in a husky tone. "After seeing you in action today, I know if anyone can find Mikey and Cindy—it'll be you." His eyes lingered on her for a minute—a brightness entering their turbulent depths that reminded her of sunshine dancing on the Ottawa River. Her heart did a funny skipping pattern against her ribs.

"I suggest we get back to work, then." Paulina tugged her fingers free. Sexual attraction had already led her through one marriage and divorce. She preferred to learn from her mistakes rather than repeat them. She'd already made a lifetime commitment to missing children. "So, no notes in the newspaper or in the telephone book?"

"Not a one."

She studied Cindy's phone bill. "There are no long-distance calls registered. What day did your brother die?"

"August seventeenth."

"This bill covers the period from August 8 to September 5. Cindy didn't phone anyone long-distance to tell them about Ted." She set the bill aside and flipped through Cindy's calendar to the month of September. Weekly notations written in girlish round letters indicated Cindy took Mikey to a play group every Wednesday morning. And she'd had an appointment with a lawyer at 11:00 a.m. the previous Monday. Unfortunately Cindy hadn't noted the lawyer's name, phone number or address. "You know the name of Cindy's lawyer?"

Gil shook his head. "No. I offered to handle Ted's estate but she said she'd hire a lawyer, so I didn't pry."

Paulina nodded in understanding as she flipped through the remaining months, looking for phone numbers of friends or other acquaintances. A work schedule in the early part of the year made her pause. Gil had indicated on Cindy's background form that she'd worked at a ladies' clothing store in the Rideau Center. "Did Cindy ever mention going back to work at Fashion Sense after Mikey was born?"

"Ted didn't see any reason why she should work."

Paulina rolled her eyes. Ted and Gil had evidently attended the same male-chauvinist training camp. "Well, it's worth a shot to contact her former employer." She stood and went to the door, calling into the outer office for Andrea to bring her the telephone directory. She had an assignment for her.

Paulina gave her intern a smile as the slim Asian woman entered the room, the scent of vanilla wafting around her person. She explained what she wanted Andrea to say, then sat back to watch Andrea's efforts. Gil shifted uncomfortably in Paulina's father's favorite leather chair, which seemed better suited to his size. His dark brows knit together as he observed the proceedings, but he didn't interfere.

Andrea conducted herself convincingly over the phone, her youthful, unsure voice just right as Cindy's "younger sister," who'd unexpectedly dropped into town and hoped to get a glimpse of her new nephew. Paulina took pride in Andrea's performance. She had high hopes Andrea could be convinced to stay on once her internship was finished. It would be nice to have a partner again.

"The manager told me Cindy quit in April," Andrea reported when the call was finished, tucking her chin-length hair behind her ear. "She's brought Mikey by the store a few times to show him off...and mentioned returning to her job when Mikey was a year old. No one's phoned the manager to verify her work references.''

Paulina beamed at Andrea, wishing Gil weren't present so she could give her an unbusinesslike hug. "You did great." Andrea's cheeks turned pink. "Can you write up a report now while it's fresh in your mind and leave it on my desk? Mr. Boyer and I are headed out again."

Paulina scooped up the diner receipts, removed the pictures of Cindy and Mikey from the case file and tucked them into her purse. She waved at Gil, who was sitting in his chair as if in a stupor. Paulina wondered fleetingly how much sleep he'd had lately. Obviously not enough. "Come on, we're outta here."

"Where are we going?" he asked, rising slowly to his feet.

"To lunch. It's two o'clock and I'm starving." She patted her purse. "I have just the place in mind—one of Cindy's favorite hangouts. With luck, we can feed our faces and our curiosity at the same time."

Chapter Three

Paulina eased into a family-size turquoise-and-salmon booth and cast an appreciative glance at the decor. Joe's Diner served up the food, the tunes and the nostalgia of the Fifties, right down to the chrome jukeboxes on the tables. Richie Valens was currently crooning a dance invitation to a girl. But Joe apparently drew the line at poodle skirts and saddle shoes for the waitresses. His employees wore turquoise bowling shirts and jeans with short black aprons tied around their waists.

A woman in her mid-forties with ginger hair swept high up on her head in beauty-parlor curls and impossibly black eyelashes told them her name was Francine as she passed them menus. "Could I get you folks something cool to drink? How about a soda or a root beer float?"

Paulina didn't even glance at the menu. Memory and the colorful placards on the walls touting the availability of thick milk shakes, home-cooked meat loaf and blue plate specials had her stomach growling in anticipation. She hadn't been here for at least two years—not since her dad had died. It had been their Tuesday take-out lunch spot. "I'll have a chocolate shake and a BLT, please," she said.

Gil ordered the cheeseburger special and a vanilla shake and informed the waitress the bill would be going to him.

"This place is stuck in a time warp," he confided, his gaze flicking toward the old-fashioned counter where the milk shake machine whirred noisily. "Makes me feel like I'm on a date in high school. Kingston—the town where I grew up—has the same kind of 'other era' feel to it." He paused, a hint of red creeping into his features. "Sorry, I didn't mean to imply anything untoward there. I realize this is not a date. Far from it."

Paulina laughed, trying not to dwell on the implication of his words. "Forget it, no offense taken. I'm sure your significant other wouldn't take offense, either."

"There is no significant other." His blue eyes held hers for a moment and Paulina felt goose bumps rise on her flesh.

She rubbed her arms. Had air-conditioning existed in the Fifties? Joe was overdoing it.

Fortunately Gil took the initiative and changed the subject. "So, when do you start asking questions about Cindy and Mikey?"

"After we eat. I perform better on a full stomach."

Francine arrived with their lunch and the conversation came to an abrupt halt. By the time the waitress reappeared to clear their plates, Paulina was ready for action. She caught Gil's eye. "Really, sweetie, I don't understand what happened to Cindy. She said she'd meet us here for dessert at two-thirty and it's after three now. It's not like her to be late. I knew something was wrong when she didn't answer the phone." Paulina glanced at Francine. "Excuse me, maybe you can help us? Has a blond woman with an infant been in here in the last hour?"

Francine laughed and reached for the plates. "Sugar, we get a lot of women and babies in here all day long. I don't know one hour from the next when we're busy."

"Of course." Paulina pulled the photo out of her purse. "Maybe this will help. My boyfriend and I are from Hanover, and we're driving through to Halifax. We called Cindy a couple of weeks ago and made arrangements to meet here. I tried calling her last night and this morning to confirm, but there wasn't any answer.'' She touched the photo. ''And I was hoping I'd get to see her baby. I haven't seen him yet.''

Francine peered down at the photo. Paulina wasn't sure, but she thought a strange expression flitted over the waitress's face. Her black lashes hooded her clear blue eyes, reminding Paulina of a doll's eyes.

''Why sure, I know Cindy,'' the waitress admitted. ''She's a regular, but she hasn't been in today. Last time I saw her was last week—Wednesday morning, as a matter of fact. She probably just forgot your appointment.'' She paused tactfully. ''You know, things have been rough on her since her man died.''

''Yes,'' Paulina agreed. ''Losing Ted in that terrible accident was such a shock. Now she has to raise Mikey on her own.''

Francine collected their soiled cutlery and stacked the dirty plates. ''Well, it don't help none that Ted's brother is trying to get custody of the baby.''

Paulina nudged Gil under the table to keep him from responding and blowing her cover, but she was too late. Francine had already noticed the dark, rebuking frown on his face.

''Say, is that who you are—Ted's brother? I thought you reminded me of someone.'' The cutlery clinked as it landed on the plates. ''You should be ashamed of yourself, trying to take a baby away from its mother. It's no wonder Cindy isn't answering her door to you.''

With a haughty sniff, Francine departed. Two minutes later she came back and slapped their bill on the table. ''Don't bother leaving a tip.''

Paulina tried to salvage the situation. ''Please, you're

getting this all wrong. Gil doesn't want custody of the baby. We're here because Cindy's disappeared and—''

Francine rudely cut her off. "Save it for the judge. It's Cindy's life and her kid. It's a free country. She can do what she wants.''

Gil watched the waitress stalk away and felt as though she were tramping his hopes of finding Cindy into the linoleum. "Damn, I blew that,'' he admitted, finally daring to face Paulina. She was annoyed and trying hard to cover it. The fiery white gleam in her silver eyes gave her away. "I'm sorry.''

"Don't worry,'' she told him, kind enough to be gracious. "There are three other servers. If Francine knew Cindy, chances are the others did, too. Stay here while I ask around.''

Gil recognized he was being told to butt out. She made quick work of talking to the other servers, which meant Francine had probably blabbed in the kitchen. That fact was confirmed when a guy the size of a refrigerator approached their booth. "I hear you've been questioning my employees about one of my customers.''

Gil cast a glance at Paulina. She was talking to a waiter at the cash register. He'd have to handle this beefcake himself. Gil slid out of the booth and stood, offering the man a good look at his physical condition in case he had trouble on his mind.

"Are you Joe?'' Gil held out his hand. "Pleased to meet you. This is a great place you're running.''

The man ignored Gil's hand and folded his brawny arms across the white extra-large chef's apron covering his expansive chest. "Why are you bothering Francine?''

"I'm sorry if I upset your waitress, Joe, but I'm pretty upset myself. My brother was killed in an accident six weeks ago, leaving behind a wife and a five-month-old baby. My sister-in-law is so distraught that she's gone off

God knows where with the baby. I know Cindy comes in here a lot, so I was hoping someone had seen her lately—maybe talked to her the last time she was in.'' Gil squared his shoulders. "I don't know what Francine told you, but all I'm trying to do is honor my responsibility to my brother and his family. Surely you can understand that? If your sister-in-law suddenly disappeared with her baby, you'd be combing the woods for her, too.''

Joe, if that was even his name, appeared to be considering what Gil had said. His charcoal eyes, at least, seemed less hostile. Gil smiled uneasily at Paulina as she joined them. He introduced her. "This is a private investigator I hired to help me find them.''

Paulina flashed Joe a friendly smile and showed him the picture of Cindy and Mikey. "Francine said she was in last Wednesday.''

Joe nodded. "That's right. Come to think of it, she did seem upset.'' His eyes zeroed in on Gil suspiciously. "You sure you aren't trying to get her kid?''

Gil felt as if he were walking a tightrope. Sweat slicked his forehead. Was the guy going to tell them anything or not? "I'd like to lead a woman to the altar *before* I consider becoming a parent.'' He considered adding that he hadn't even met a woman worth booking a church over, but Paulina smoothly intervened.

"Are you sure it was Wednesday?'' she asked.

"Yeah, I'm sure, because she sat in the back section—where the stroller don't block the aisle—and talked to Ed for quite a while. Ed's some kind of salesman. He comes in on the second Wednesday of the month like clockwork.''

Paulina took a pen and a notepad from her purse. "Do you know Ed's last name—or what company he works for?''

"Sorry, can't help you there. I think he sells tools or hardware. Something like that."

Great, Gil thought, choking back a wave of frustration. There were probably fifty Eds working in tools or hardware across Canada.

Paulina looked up from her note taking, her gray eyes thoughtful. Suddenly her expression brightened and she gestured toward the door with her pen. "I noticed you have a fishbowl by the cash register for people to toss in their business cards for a free lunch. Mind if I have a look? Maybe Ed hoped he'd get lucky—"

"Be my guest," Joe said. "Just don't go calling all my customers."

They thanked Joe. Gil picked up the tab and threw a modest tip on the table, then cupped Paulina's elbow and led her to the cash register. "Thanks," he said under his breath, leaning his head close to hers. "You bailed me out—again." The fragrant scent of her shampoo filled his nostrils.

"No, I didn't," she whispered back. "You were doing fine on your own." She smiled up at him and he realized that beneath her toughness dwelled the soul of a compassionate and caring lady.

She plunged her hands into the fishbowl and pulled out the top two inches of cards.

A victorious smile lit her delicate features as she held up a white business card imprinted with a screw logo. "This has got to be it. Edison Tweedie. Sales rep. CW Hardware."

Gil's spirits rose, as did his respect for the woman beside him.

"They're based in Mississauga," Paulina added, writing the information down in her notebook. "We'll call from my office."

Gil nodded sharply and jerked the door open for her. If

their luck held, maybe Edison Tweedie would lead them to Cindy and Mikey.

CW HARDWARE HAD PUT HER on hold. Paulina nervously doodled figure eights on the legal pad on her desk. Gil was braced against the doorjamb of her office, his potent eyes boring into her. Her heart thrummed unsteadily, which seemed to be its normal pace since Gil had walked into her office this morning. What had she been thinking—making that ridiculous deal with him? She should have—

A woman suddenly came back on the line and told Paulina that Edison Tweedie was currently on the road and she didn't know why he wasn't answering his car phone. Possibly he'd already stopped at a motel for the night.

Paulina stifled a sigh of disappointment. "When do you expect to hear from him?"

"Well, I'm not sure." The woman hesitated. "He's already checked in for today. According to his itinerary, his next scheduled stop is with a Home Hardware in Winnipeg at nine-thirty tomorrow morning. I could give you the phone number of the store and you could try reaching him there—though you should keep in mind they're an hour behind our time zone. Other than that, I suggest you keep trying his car phone—or I can pass him a message to contact you the next time he calls in."

"I'll try to contact him first," Paulina decided. "What's the number of the store?" A few minutes later she thanked the woman for her help and hung up the phone.

"Let me guess," Gil said, rubbing the back of his neck. "Ed Tweedie's not available."

"Not until nine-thirty tomorrow morning. He's on the road to Winnipeg—"

"Well, then…" he cut her off. "Come hell or high water we're going to be in Winnipeg to meet him when he gets there." He glanced at his watch. "It's almost five. We shouldn't have any trouble catching a flight."

Paulina stared at him in amazement, not the least bit thrilled by the way he'd made the decision without asking for her opinion. Is that why Cindy ran away? Paulina wondered fleetingly. Gil was like a steamroller, charging ahead to get the job done. He was so consumed with guilt and his own good intentions he'd probably never stopped to listen to what Cindy had to say.

She rose and gathered her notes and Cindy's file into a briefcase. "*I* agree, going to Winnipeg is a good idea," she said, stressing who was in charge of this investigation. "Tweedie may be more helpful if *I* talk to him in person. I keep a bag packed upstairs in my apartment for occasions such as this. It won't take but a minute to grab it. Or would you prefer to meet at the airport?"

The corners of his mouth spread in a wide grin that revealed even white teeth. "No, I don't wear pajamas, and they sell shirts and toothbrushes at the airport. I'll wait— and we'll take my car."

She nodded, more disturbed by an image of Gil wearing nothing but that sexy smile than by his insistence that they use his car. "You might as well come up with me so Andrea can lock up," she said. He followed her into the reception area, where she gave Andrea instructions to check the post-office box for a reply on the Watson case. Paulina also told Andrea she could take a well-deserved day off tomorrow, since Paulina wasn't sure when they'd be back from Winnipeg.

Paulina tried not to be aware of Gil dogging her heels as she turned into the brick-paved carriageway between Stewart Investigations and the Mangia restaurant. A black wrought iron gate secured a tiled recessed stairway leading to her apartment.

Her living room felt stuffy with humidity, the receding

late-afternoon sunlight creating a pattern of light and shadow on the Devonshire cream walls. Her tastes ran toward the simple and eclectic. She'd taken the apartment when she and Karl split up, preferring its convenience to work. No more long drives into Ottawa from the suburb of Orleans. She left Gil in front of the antique pine cupboard that housed the collection of thank-you gifts she'd received from searching parents, to run a comb through her short hair and freshen her lipstick. Then she pulled her small overnight bag from the closet.

"Here, I'll take that for you," Gil offered, as Paulina returned to the living room, her heels clicking on the old pine floorboards. He reached for her bag, his fingers brushing innocently against her shoulder.

Paulina drew in a sharp breath as the sensation registered along her nerve endings like an electric shock. She backed away from him in alarm, experiencing an unaccustomed sense of panic.

Gil was getting too damn close to her for comfort.

THE FEELING ONLY intensified once they were on the plane. Gil had purchased first-class tickets, and despite the extra space and wide seats Paulina felt as though every atom of her body was attuned to Gil's powerful presence.

She slowly sipped her ginger ale and hoped Edison Tweedie could give them a clue as to where Cindy had gone. Paulina wasn't sure how much more of this case she could take. When had she last taken a vacation? Not since her divorce had been made final a year ago. She didn't dare dwell on how long it had been since she'd made love—not with Gil's sensual male charms so close by.

Gil's voice intruded into her thoughts. "I noticed a wedding picture in your apartment. How does your husband feel about you jetting off with clients?"

Paulina choked on her soft drink and started to cough,

becoming more flustered when he gave her a sharp pat on the back. She waved away his offer of assistance. The last thing she needed was him touching her. She knew the picture he meant. It was one of the few she had of herself and her dad together. Did he think she'd married a man old enough to be her father? The fact he seemed interested enough in her personal life to ask sent a wild thrill racing through her.

"He didn't mind when we were married," she said when she finally felt capable of speech. "That was my father you saw in the tux. My ex-husband is an RCMP officer, so he knew what investigations involve. He was more concerned with the fact that I was away—than whom I was with. It's difficult enough to plan a home and family life around a police officer's schedule, without trying to factor in the unpredictability of my job. Our expectations of each other weren't in sync with reality."

"That's too bad," Gil murmured. "But it's true, having a family requires an enormous amount of time and financial commitment. Ted sure wasn't ready to shoulder the responsibility. But at least Cindy was able to quit work and stay home with Mikey."

Paulina fell silent, aware of the drone of the aircraft in the background. Her father had introduced her to Karl, and she'd married him believing he of all people would understand her erratic schedule and her commitment to her work. Things had been great for a couple of years, until her father had died and Karl had started dropping hints that she should ease back on her workload—or better yet close the agency—so they could start a family.

She glanced sideways at Gil, wondering why someone who so easily shouldered family responsibility didn't already have a wife and three kids. She couldn't resist teasing him—if only to reverse the downward turn of his mouth. Were his thoughts slipping back to Ted again?

"So, what's stopping you from jumping into marriage and a family?"

"Me? I haven't found the right significant other yet." He was teasing her back.

Curiosity got the better of her. Surely there were plenty of attractive women out there who'd gladly take on the job of being Mrs. Gilbert Boyer.

"And?" she probed.

"And?" For a moment Gil didn't know how to respond. His eyes narrowed on her as he swirled his Scotch in the crystal glass. "You're good, you know that? Insightful." He set his drink down on the tray. "But I'll play the game, since I started it. I m not willing to take that step until I have everything a man should give a wife and children. Why make life harder than it has to be? My dad was a carpenter—a damned good one—until he fell and injured his back. I was nine and Ted was two. Our whole life changed."

Gil rotated the glass a quarter turn, not wanting to dwell too much on the irreparable damage the accident had inflicted on his father's self-esteem. "My mom got a full-time job as a cashier in a grocery store to put food on the table and Ted got left with a succession of neighbors. My mom did the best she could under the circumstances, but I've always wondered if Ted would have grown into a more secure, confident adult if Mom hadn't gone to work just then. Ted was a—" he paused, searching for the right word. "Drifter. He'd go from one job to another, from one girlfriend to another. He probably wouldn't have stuck around with Cindy if it hadn't been for the baby. His last job was laying asphalt."

Gil clamped his mouth shut. Paulina's head was slightly turned toward him on the leather seat back and she appeared to be listening intently. But he was certain he was boring her half to death. She probably didn't want to hear how he'd gone to Northwestern University on a football scholarship and had majored in computer science. His dad's accident had taught him it wasn't wise to depend on your physical abilities for employment. One stroke of bad luck and your future was wiped away. Gil was proud he had his own consulting firm by the time he was thirty.

A chime sounded in the compartment and the pilot announced they were making the final descent to Winnipeg. Paulina was just too darn attractive. Not to mention easy to talk to—and available.

That realization dominated his thoughts as they hired a rental car and found a steak house for a late dinner. Then they went in search of a hotel located near the hardware store. It was almost midnight when he walked her to her room. They'd spent nearly fourteen hours together, and yet he was reluctant to say good-bye. She was one sexy, competent lady, with a heart the size of Ontario when it came to finding kids. Was it really just a conflict of schedules that prevented her from having a family of her own?

She pushed the key in the knob and opened the door, reaching her hand inside the room to flick on the lights. She'd insisted on carrying her own luggage.

Her eyes were luminescent as she turned back to him and held out her hand, her expression solemn. "Well, good night, then."

Gil grasped her hand and drew it to his lips. Her fingers were strong, resisting him, her skin satiny soft. He knew it was her very opposition that made him savor the sweetness of her skin. "Thanks for everything," he said quietly, meaning it with all his heart. He waited a moment until she'd closed her door before going to his own room.

As he stripped off his clothes and slid between the sheets, his tired mind fiddled with the possibility that after Mikey and Cindy were found he might do something really unorthodox to celebrate…like ask one certain midnight-haired, starry-eyed P.I. for a date.

Not that she'd say yes, but Gil thought it would be worth asking just to hear her reason for turning him down.

THE PLEATED SKIN nipping together Paulina's feather-thin brows was not a good omen, Gil decided when he joined her for coffee the next morning at eight-thirty sharp in the hotel's restaurant. Nor was the forced nature of her welcoming smile. Maybe he'd gotten too familiar last night. Or maybe she was only thinking about the case, which is what he was paying her to do.

She'd definitely say no if he asked her out.

With a sigh, he ordered a black coffee.

"Okay, Gil, here's the game plan for Tweedie," she said briskly, immediately getting down to business. "Cindy's my best friend and you're my husband. I do the talking. And you—" she pointed at him "—try to keep the dark frowns off your face."

Gil nodded bleakly. "I know the drill." He watched her as she produced a gold wedding band from her change purse, which she slipped onto her ring finger.

"There, that should look convincing. Just don't tell my ex I'm recycling his jewelry."

Gil noticed she wore a simple blue print dress scattered with flowers over a long-sleeved white blouse and pearl studs in her ears. He was wearing an Ottawa Senators T-shirt he'd bought at the airport the previous day.

"If Tweedie seems reluctant to talk to me," she continued, "then you can try a man-to-man line such as, 'Please tell my wife what she wants to know, because if you don't she's going to drag me all over the country looking for her friend.' If that doesn't work, play it by ear like you did at the diner yesterday."

Her hand came to rest on his shoulder and Gil felt an

inexplicable lightening sensation in his chest. Her touch was the closest he'd come to comfort in a long time. "You're a good salesman. You'll do fine." A waitress came and placed two pancake specials in front of them. "By the way, I ordered for both of us," she explained with an apologetic smile. "Now, eat up. We've got to leave in fifteen minutes. We don't want to risk missing Tweedie."

Tweedie had already arrived at the Home Hardware store. When Paulina explained the reason for their visit, the manager kindly allowed them to talk privately with Tweedie in the back office.

Paulina shook Mr. Tweedie's hand, taking in the wrinkles on his tanned face, the shock of white hair, hazel eyes and a short-sleeved blue shirt tucked into neatly pressed gray slacks. A silver cross rested at the base of his throat.

"Oh, yes, I remember your friend," Tweedie remarked, studying the photograph Paulina had handed him. "We talked for quite a while as I recall. She had a troubled heart."

"That's why we've flown here to see you. Sometimes I think we tell strangers more than our nearest and dearest—especially during difficult times."

Gil's arm settled around her shoulders. "There, there, sweetheart, we're going to find her."

Paulina froze as his invading warmth and his almost palpable fear for Mikey and Cindy stole into her heart. Tears welled in her eyes. She knew firsthand how frightening the prospect of never seeing a loved one again could be.

Mr. Tweedie passed her a tissue from a box on the desk. "We're all family in the eyes of the Lord. I'm sure Cindy knows the value of your friendship."

Paulina dabbed at her eyes. "Thank you. But something

must be terribly wrong. It's not like her to abandon her apartment and not tell me.''

"I'll be glad to share what little I know. I stopped by her table because she looked sadly in need of a friend. She told me she'd made a big decision about her future and her baby's future…and she was scared. A man had given her an ultimatum—was trying to tell her what to do about the baby.'' Tweedie scratched his head. ''I was under the impression she might have to give up her son.''

"For heaven's sake,'' Paulina whispered, praying Gil wouldn't overreact. "Poor Cindy. I had no idea. She loves Mikey. No wonder she ran as far and as fast as she could.''

"Well, she was in such a state, I suggested she speak to a counselor. She told me she'd already done so—and she'd spoken to a lawyer, too.''

"Did she mention any names?'' Paulina asked, feeling Gil's arm tighten around her shoulders. She reached up and squeezed his hand, sharing his frustration and pain. "Maybe they'd have some idea where Cindy planned to go.''

"I believe the lawyer was Vern Newcombe. I'm usually quite good with names—being in sales and all—but you might want to check with Francine Loiselle at Joe's to be sure. Francine would know, because I understand she referred Cindy to this fella. He was a relative of someone or what have you. The counselor's name was Elva—no last name. I remember that real well 'cause it's my mother's name.''

"Did Cindy mention anything else that might suggest where she was headed?''

"No, sorry. After she'd let it all tumble out, I told her that when the time came the Lord would let her know in her heart what was the right decision for herself and the baby.''

Paulina glanced into his hazel eyes: they were calm and

unruffled like the waters of a clear rock-bottomed pond. "Thank you very much. We'll let you get on with your business now."

"It was no trouble. God bless you both."

Paulina noticed Gil couldn't get out of the store fast enough. "Tweedie certainly confirmed that I'm the one responsible for Cindy's taking off." The words exploded from him like sharp reports the instant his Brooks running shoes hit the sidewalk. His fists clenched.

Paulina grabbed his arm. "Don't be so hard on yourself."

His blue eyes blazed down at her. Every muscle in his face was taut. A faint white line rimmed the tight seam of his lips. "I swear, I never once suggested wanting custody of Mikey. I'd never do that."

"I believe you." Gil was a straightforward person to read. "So, look, we find Cindy and you can apologize. Then you let her draw up the rules, so she won't feel pressured by your desire to stay involved in Mikey's life. It's very common for people to overreact during times of great stress—particularly after the death of a loved one. I lost my father two years ago and I was an emotional mess for a year. It's still hard. It takes time to adjust. Give yourself a break."

Gil seemed to accept what she said; the rigidity of his shoulders eased. The fact they'd both lost a family member formed a common bond between them. Gil removed her fingers from his biceps and gave them a faint squeeze.

Paulina noticed he didn't talk much as they returned to the Winnipeg airport to catch the next available flight to Ottawa. But then, maybe he didn't want to break her concentration—except to remark that she needed a laptop computer when she pulled out pen and paper to write a report of their conversation with Tweedie while the details remained fresh in her mind. After a while he fell asleep, which was a relief because it gave her time to think—undisturbed. However, she soon discovered that Gil, even asleep, with a lock of dark hair drifting boyishly onto his forehead, still disturbed her.

It was three-thirty by the time the taxi deposited her at her Clarence Street office. At the airport, she'd insisted Gil go home and rest. She had other cases requiring her attention. She let herself into her office, dropped her bags and gathered the day's mail, grateful to be alone in her own domain. The red button flashed on her answering machine. She hit the playback button, hoping there was nothing urgent. She needed a couple hours of solitude to go over Cindy's file and plan her strategy.

The first message immediately caught her attention. "Ma'am, this is Max—the manager of the Market Apartments. It's one o'clock. The police just came by about Cindy. They found a baby stroller with her name and address on it. I told them about you and Mr. Boyer and gave them your phone number. I hope that's okay."

"That's more than okay, Max," Paulina said out loud, a thread of unease wisping down her spine. "Every little bit helps." *Since when were the police in the business of returning lost baby strollers?* The answering machine beeped and another male voice—this one instantly recognizable as authoritative—filled her reception area, requesting her to call a detective with the Ottawa-Carleton Regional Police ASAP. Paulina grabbed a pencil.

She didn't have time to make the call though. The door to her agency opened and two men sporting conservative suits, short haircuts and tough-cop expressions made an entrance. Paulina felt physically ill. This little visit wasn't about a stroller. She eyed them warily. "I'm Paulina Stewart. Which one of you is Detective Robbins?"

"That would be me, ma'am." The tall sandy-haired man removed his ID from the breast pocket of his tan tweed sport coat. His eyes were a cool dove gray, giving her a quick survey. She had no doubt he'd noticed her suitcase by the door and the wrinkles in her dress. He gestured toward his sallow-faced, thirty-pounds-heavier sidekick. "This is my partner, Detective Zuker." A web of fine lines appeared at the corners of Robbins's eyes as he smiled briefly. Too briefly. "Ms. Stewart, we understand you were asking questions yesterday about a Cindy D'Angelo at her place of residence."

"Yes, I was."

"May we ask what your involvement is with Ms. D'Angelo?"

"Certainly. I was hired by a member of Cindy's family to find her. She'd missed an appointment and wasn't answering her phone. Her brother-in-law grew concerned after several days and contacted me on Monday. We talked to the manager of her apartment building. It looks like she cleared out without paying her next month's rent. In fact, we just arrived back from Winnipeg, following up a lead."

"We?" Robbins was digging for information like a dog after a bone.

"My client, Mr. Boyer, and I."

"Is Mr. Boyer here with you?"

"No, he went home to rest."

"Did Ms. D'Angelo have a child with her?"

"Yes, her five-month-old son, Mikey."

"Was Ms. D'Angelo involved in a custody dispute over the child?"

Paulina ignored the question, tired of having dirt kicked in her face. "Perhaps I could be of more help if you told me what this is about, Detective."

Robbins didn't pull any punches. "We're with the major-crime unit. The body of a white female was found on the east side of town earlier today. We have reason to believe the woman is Cindy D'Angelo. Foul play is suspected.''

Paulina felt the blood drain from her face and a clamminess creep over her skin. Horror clutched at her heart at the news of Cindy's death, but a deeper, insidious horror invaded her body. A horror so profound she could barely get her mouth to function properly...to ask what needed to be asked. "Wh-what about Mikey?"

Chapter Four

"No ma'am, the body of an infant was not found at the scene," Detective Robbins gravely informed her.

Paulina was acutely aware both detectives were observing her reaction. Detective Zuker's black eyes scrutinized her like a wolf trying to spot a weakness in its prey.

"The woman had no purse or other ID," Zuker added. "We thought she might be another murdered prostitute, but then we found an ID tag on a brand-new pricey stroller in the same Dumpster. The woman matches the description the apartment manager gave us of Cindy D'Angelo."

Paulina closed her eyes and tried to blank out the image the detective's words painted in her mind. Poor Cindy! Worry needled Paulina's stomach with thousands of tiny painful pricks. What had happened to Mikey? Had he been murdered, too—or kidnapped? Then she remembered Gil. He was already close to the snapping point over his brother's death. This news would send him over the edge.

She forced her eyes open. Forced herself to think. Be businesslike. "I have a photo of Cindy in my briefcase. Let's make sure we're talking about the right woman." Her fingers trembled as she opened her briefcase and passed Cindy's photo to the detectives. "She's twenty-two years old, five feet four inches tall, 120 pounds."

"That's her," Robbins confirmed.

Paulina's last shred of hope evaporated. But there were questions she should be asking—for Gil. For Mikey. "Wh-when did it happen?"

Robbins seemed to be the lead investigator. He answered her questions. "Not sure yet. The autopsy will tell us that."

She reached for the legal pad that was on top of Mikey's file in her briefcase to take notes. "What was the cause of death?"

"Strangulation, though we'd prefer not to discuss any further details, ma'am, as this is a murder investigation."

"Of course." She carefully set the legal pad on her desk, knowing the page would remain blank. They were stonewalling her.

Zuker's curious glance drifted pointedly to her open briefcase and Mikey's case file. "We'll also need a description and identifying information about the baby if you have it. We'll have to move fast..." His comment trailed off unfinished.

Paulina focused on keeping her temper in check. "I'm fully aware that every second that passes takes the baby farther away from being recovered, Detectives. My client and I will cooperate with your investigation in every way." She removed several extra prints of Mikey's photo from the file and gave them to Zuker. "I'll just go down the hall to run off photocopies of Mikey's identification sheet. It'll take a minute for the photocopier to warm up."

Paulina heard the murmur of their voices conferring in the reception area over the hum of the photocopier, but she couldn't make out what they were saying. Should she try phoning Gil? Tell him about Cindy so he heard the news from someone more compassionate than Robbins? No, better to wait until the police had left.

She returned to the reception area and passed the still-warm photocopies into Zuker's waiting hand.

"Thank you, ma'am."

At Robbins's request, she gave them Gil's full name, address and phone number.

"We'll contact him immediately," he said. "Someone will have to positively identify the body at the Riverside Hospital morgue."

"Mr. Boyer is Cindy's only local relative," she explained. Her gaze shifted from one officer to the other. She knew that police procedure required them to pick up Gil, drive him to the morgue and then to the station to be interviewed. She wasn't going to abandon him to endure that alone—not if she could help it. She took a deep, bracing breath. "I'd like to accompany you to Mr. Boyer's home. I know you're well trained in compassionate duty, but I think it would be easier on him if I told him about Cindy."

"Didn't you just meet yesterday?" Robbins's question oozed with suspicion.

"Yes," Paulina admitted, feeling perspiration dampen her blouse. "I specialize in missing children investigations—mostly custodial abductions. People turn to agencies like mine as their last hope...when they've exhausted other resources. They need hand holding and emotional support, because you and I both know the leads are few and far between and it can take years to locate a child." She squared her shoulders. "Mr. Boyer and I spent most of the last twenty-four hours trying to locate Cindy. You discover a lot about a person in twenty-four hours. Life has been rough enough on my client lately. His only brother—Cindy's common-law husband—was killed about six weeks ago in a hit-and-run accident on the Queensway. That's why my client was so concerned about her."

Robbins and Zuker exchanged a glance.

Paulina didn't want to speculate what that glance meant. She was concerned about Gil. It wasn't fair that he was about to be told two people he loved had been murdered within six weeks of each other—and Mikey was still missing. "Please. You can be there with me. I just think it would be easier to hear from someone who isn't a complete stranger. Since time is of the essence, I suggest I call Mr. Boyer and tell him I'm on my way over with new information. Will that suffice?"

"All right," Robbins conceded.

"Thank you. I'll bring my file. I'm sure you gentlemen will have questions for me later."

Gil had disobeyed her order to go home and rest. She tracked him down at his office. She had a feeling he was trying to keep himself busy. He agreed to wait for her.

Zuker handed off Mikey's identifying information to another team of investigators who'd been sitting in the restaurant next to the office. It would be taken down to the station ASAP.

Paulina followed behind Robbins and Zuker's unmarked police car to a new office building in Kanata. The golden haze of the late-afternoon sun glinted off the copper-tinted windows. She parked in a spot beside them. Robbins informed her she could have ten minutes alone with her client as she locked her blue Toyota Corolla. They'd wait out in the hallway.

The reception area was sleek and high tech with surrealistic artwork spotlighted on the walls. The receptionist's desk formed a dramatic sweeping arc against a mauve wall.

"Paulina?"

She turned at the sound of her name and saw Gil standing in the hallway to her left. He'd been talking to a petite and very pregnant brunette. "Thanks, Renée, we'll finish this later," he said.

Paulina studied him carefully. Dark rings showed under his eyes. He'd been waiting for her. He'd said her name like a question. Tension emanated from him like an energy field. His office must be equipped with shower facilities. He'd showered and changed into a pair of tan cotton twill pants and a beige-and-white sweater.

"Hi," she said softly. "Can we talk in your office?"

"Sure."

She made certain he closed the door. His office was masculine and sleek, too. Jet black furniture, glass shelves, a black leather couch. A state-of-the-art personal computer sat on his desktop.

"Would you like a coffee?" he asked.

"No." Paulina wet her lips nervously. "Gil, sit down on the couch with me." When he'd joined her, she turned toward him, their knees barely touching. Her eyes met his. In the indigo depths, she saw fear.

"I don't want to hear this, do I?" Gil asked, his voice husky.

Paulina clasped his arm, trying to transmit some of her strength to him. "The police were waiting at my office to talk to me. I'm very sorry to have to tell you this, but they believe they've found Cindy's body." Paulina saw the shock register in his features and felt her heart constrict. Tears stung her eyes. "They don't know where Mikey is, but they're already working on finding him." She told him the few details she knew. Beneath her fingers, the muscles of Gil's arm grew rigid. His face had a white gleam of marble. He was looking at her, but Paulina knew he wasn't seeing her. He was seeing Cindy.

"I know this is a lot to take in, but I need you to listen," she said gently. "For Mikey's sake you can't fall apart right now." She calmly laid out the steps of what would happen next, finishing just as a brisk knock sounded on the door.

She introduced Detectives Robbins and Zuker. Gil handled the questions well. He asked if he could have a few minutes to inform Renée, his senior analyst, of the situation, then they left for the morgue. Robbins made it clear Gil was riding with them.

Paulina tailed them, drumming her fingers restlessly on the steering wheel. Apprehension snaked through her abdomen. She could see Gil conversing with the detectives. She knew darn well the police already considered him a suspect.

Good investigators never overlook the obvious. Paulina certainly didn't intend to. She switched on her flasher to change lanes and exit the Queensway. In fact, her first order of business toward finding Mikey was satisfying herself that Gil wasn't involved.

THE MORGUE AWAITED THEM. Paulina decided telling Gil about Cindy's death and walking this seemingly endless basement corridor of Riverside Hospital was one of the hardest things she'd ever done.

It was almost as hard as attending her father's funeral. She'd enjoyed four special years working side by side with her dad in his private investigation agency. There were all those other children out there missing a parent. Children who were left wondering—feeling unloved and unwanted—just as she had. Every child she found and reunited with a searching parent healed some of the hurt in her own life. Paulina and her mother were still caught in an emotional stalemate, which she hoped time and understanding would resolve. Now Paulina was keenly aware that Mikey could never be reunited with his parents.

The realization seeped like a damp chill into her bones. Paulina shuddered. It didn't help that their footsteps echoed off the walls of the corridor like the displaced heartbeats of the deceased who'd been wheeled down to the morgue.

"I hate this place," Gil muttered under his breath.

"Me, too." Paulina kept a secure hold on his arm as

they were shown into a room where a sheet-draped form was laid on a stretcher. She steeled herself to remain detached as the sheet was lowered. But she couldn't remain detached from the sight of Cindy's body—or from Gil's sharp intake of dismay. Cindy's face showed the violence of her death.

A rush of sympathy cascaded from Paulina's heart to her stomach. She squeezed Gil's arm to remind him he wasn't alone. That he had someone beside him who cared.

"Is this Cindy D'Angelo?" Robbins asked him.

Gil nodded. "Yes, it's her." His fingers trembled as he gently touched a lock of Cindy's blond hair. "I'm so sorry this happened to you, sweetheart," he said hoarsely. The rawness of his reaction brought a hot flow of tears spilling onto her cheeks. He turned away and Paulina slipped her arms around him as a sob racked his body.

THIS WAS A NIGHTMARE. Gil tried to keep his irritation with the police questions under control. How many times would they ask him when he last saw Cindy? Had they had an argument? What had he been doing in her apartment? What had he done with her things? Why had he hired Paulina? Why had he and Paulina gone to Winnipeg? Didn't he find it odd that his brother had been killed six weeks ago—and now his sister-in-law? Did Ted and Cindy have any enemies?

The questions spun around in his head like a giant wagon wheel. At its hub hovered the most crucial unanswered question of all: What had happened to Mikey?

Gil wanted to slam his fist a few hundred times into whoever had killed Cindy and taken his nephew. He just hoped that whoever had kidnapped Mikey had wanted him enough to take care of him properly. But there were too many sickos out there for that thought to bring much comfort.

He tried to follow Paulina's advice to answer the questions candidly. But for an *interview,* this felt a lot like an interrogation. The sickening realization that they thought he might be involved slammed into him like a shoulder in the gut. Nausea rose in his throat. Jeez, if they talked to that waitress, Gil figured his goose was cooked.

At least Robbins told him the police were scouring the area where Cindy had been found, knocking on doors and asking if anyone had seen her with Mikey. Mikey's picture would be plastered all over the six o'clock news. Hopefully, someone would call in with a tip. Gil had offered to post a reward for information, if Robbins thought it would help.

He wished Paulina were here, holding on to him, grounding him to reality. But she was in another room at the police station answering questions, too.

A uniformed officer entered the room and handed Robbins a piece of paper. Gil wondered what the hell was on the paper. Robbins read it with a great deal of interest. The skin prickled on the back of Gil's neck.

"Mr. Boyer, where were you last Wednesday afternoon?"

Gil had to think back. "I'm not sure I—wait a minute." He snapped his fingers. "I was installing a system for a client, Robert Fielding, a CPA in Vanier."

"What time did you finish?"

"I'm not sure—between five and six. The accountant's office should be able to verify I was there."

"What did you do afterward?"

"I went jogging along the Rideau Canal," Gil said cautiously. "Then I went home to shower and eat dinner. Why?"

"Based on the stomach contents, the autopsy report estimates Cindy died between noon and eight last Wednesday evening."

"Wednesday?" Gil felt as though the world had dropped out from underneath him. He was painfully aware that Vanier was a ten-minute drive from the Byward Market. Robbins was eyeballing him as though he had Mikey stashed somewhere. "Well, we know she had breakfast at Joe's Diner that morning," Gil said, trying to piece together Cindy's last morning. "That alley's gotta be a couple of miles from the Market. Was she killed there or just um…" he struggled to find a better word than *dumped.* Dumped sounded as if she had no value and that simply wasn't true. A tightness gripped his throat and wouldn't let go. "Or just left there?"

"She was left there. What color interior is your car, Mr. Boyer?"

Oh, God. They do think I did it. "Charcoal gray."

"Some burgundy carpet fibers were recovered from Cindy's clothes, which indicates she was transported in a vehicle. Can you think of anyone she knows who owns a car with a burgundy interior?"

"No," he said, battling off another siege of frustration.

"I realize these questions seem pointless, but most people are killed by someone they know."

Yeah, well, hell, Gil wasn't going to sit around while Robbins played around with possibilities that included suspecting him. "Does the autopsy report say anything else that might help pinpoint Cindy's killer?"

"She was strangled with a two-inch-wide ligature."

Gil's stomach heaved. Sheer pride and self-discipline kept him from spilling his guts in the wastebasket in the corner. The damn room was airless. Gil ran a shaking hand across his damp forehead. He dreaded going home and calling his parents in Kingston. Ted's death had struck them hard. This would—

Gil wasn't even aware that Robbins was still talking until the detective slid a business card across the table toward him. It took a few seconds to register he was being dismissed.

"My number's on the card, Mr. Boyer. Call me or Detective Zuker if you remember something you think could be important. Ms. Stewart is waiting for you out in the hall. She'll drive you home."

Gil practically sprinted for the door. He was reassured to find Paulina sitting primly in a straight-backed chair. The strength of her indomitable spirit gave her skin a soft pearlescent glow. She rose in an elegant fluid motion and looped the spaghetti strap of her purse over her shoulder.

"You hanging in there?" It sounded more like an order than a question of concern. He felt immeasurably better just being within touching distance of her.

He squared his shoulders. "Yeah." He fell in step beside her as she walked toward the exit.

Once they were outside, he took several reviving breaths of the autumn-crisp air. Then he told her about the interview and the autopsy report. But he couldn't tell her they thought he did it. The injustice of it was just too painful to acknowledge. What if she started wondering if he'd done it? She unlocked the passenger door for him. He put his hand on the door, to stop her from opening it as if he was an invalid. "So what do we do now?" he asked.

Her eyes were so serious.

"That depends." She crossed her arms at her waist. The dark print of her dress emphasized the swell of her breasts. "Do you want me to continue with my investigation or do you want the police to carry on from here?"

"I want you to continue. Hell, all the police want to do is ask me questions."

Her gaze flicked toward the police station. "You'd better get used to it. They're going to ask a lot more."

Gil slid into the passenger seat feeling as though his

stomach wanted to leap out of his body. Now what the hell did she mean by that?

GIL HAD TOLD HER to make herself at home while he went upstairs to change and call his parents. Paulina figured she had ten, maybe twenty minutes tops to scout out the house. She slipped out of her shoes and walked soundlessly in her stockinged feet over the pale polished *bois franc* floors. The house was enormous. Thirty-five hundred square feet, at least. *What more did he think he needed to provide a family?* She checked the kitchen first. There was no baby formula in the refrigerator. She peeked in the cupboards. No sign of baby cereal, canned formula or baby bottles.

No smelly diapers in the trash.

She quickly checked the downstairs guest bath, then walked through the formal dining room and scanned the family room and living room for baby paraphernalia. Gil's taste in furnishings ran to the exquisite. A fossilized stone dining table, pickled pine and buttery soft sage leather sofas.

Paulina glanced up the gracious curved staircase. The house had a central hall design. She counted six doors upstairs. The double door to the master suite was closed. The others were open. She quietly mounted the staircase, counting off the rooms. A guest bath. A guest bedroom appointed with a queen-size bed. An exercise room with weight-lifting equipment. Two bare rooms.

Reaching the top of the stairs, she heard the murmur of Gil's voice. He was still on the phone. Heart pounding with nervousness, she tiptoed across the plush sage carpet to the guest bath and eased open the cupboards. No diapers or other baby stuff. No baby smell lingering in the air.

Mikey had not been here recently.

Feeling reassured, Paulina suddenly realized she could

no longer hear Gil's voice. He was off the phone! The door to the master suite opened with a faint click.

She schooled her features to innocence. "There you are. I just came up to make sure you were all right. Did you tell your parents?"

"Yeah. I told them we could talk about the funeral in the morning. Mom thinks we should wait with the arrangements until we know what happened to Mikey. I asked her about Cindy's parents. She doesn't know their names either, but she thinks Cindy's from Edmonton originally."

"Well, that's a place to start." Paulina laced her fingers through his. The warm bond sent a shiver through her. She still hadn't grown used to touching him. "Come downstairs. I'll fix you a drink. Are you hungry? I could make you a sandwich or something. But I warn you I'm not much of a cook."

"A beer sounds good. I'm too worried about Mikey to eat. I was thinking I could have some posters run off tomorrow. Pay some teenagers to hang them all over the city."

"That's a good idea." They walked into the kitchen. Paulina let go of his hand and opened the refrigerator. She retrieved a bottle of beer and a vegetable juice. She had to drive home soon and do some work. She took a glass from the upper cabinet nearest the dishwasher.

"Hey, that's pretty good," Gil commented, twisting off the cap. "You already know your way around my house— or at least to what's important."

Paulina flushed. His remark landed a little too close to the truth.

They sat at the counter stools. The curtain of night stretched ominously beyond the picture window as though its inky folds deliberately concealed the name and face of Cindy's killer and Mikey's abductor.

"You never told me what we should do next to find Mikey," Gil said, after a few minutes of silence.

Paulina ran her hand through her hair. "That's because I'm still working on a plan. I need to go home and think about it. I just wanted to make sure you're all right first. We'll talk tomorrow. The police are doing a lot of leg-work, so everything possible is being done. They'll ensure Mikey's photo receives plenty of media coverage. I'll concentrate on a more personal angle, like discovering the identity of the blond-haired man with the athletic build." She set down her empty glass.

Gil glanced at his watch. "It's after nine o'clock. You should go home, then—and think. I'll walk you to the door. What'd you do with your shoes? You're barefoot."

"In the foyer. I didn't want to scratch your floors."

There was an uncomfortable moment after she slipped on her navy slingbacks, when she looked up at him to say good-bye. She knew he needed to be alone with his grief and she had work to do, but it was hard to leave him.

He reached out and touched her wrist. "Paulina?"

Her breath snared in her throat. He had the darndest way of saying her name—like a question. "Yes?"

His hands settled on her shoulders. Her heart started to pound with a dizzying beat. "Could I kiss you?"

Was he crazy? Yes, in a way, crazy with grief and worry.

"Gil," she said softly, shaking her head. This case was rattling her nerves. No, her client was rattling her nerves. It was up to her to keep a level head. "I'm the last kind of woman you should be wanting to kiss." She didn't know if she was trying to convince him—or herself.

"I know. I recognize a career woman when I meet one. But I still want to kiss you. I've wanted to since last night." His fingers lightly grazed her jaw.

Paulina bit her lower lip as a tremor shot through her body.

"Let me, just once."

She knew she shouldn't, and yet she felt her resistance crumble like a stone wall giving way to a strong and insistent wind.

"All right," she said, exasperated with herself—and him. And with the intuitive voice in her brain that taunted her to venture out on this dangerous ledge with him. "Just once."

She closed her eyes as Gil's lips swept gently over hers—as though seeking permission a second time for the kiss. She granted it, opening her mouth to the seductive forays of his tongue. He tasted of beer and honeyed heat. The taste of him invaded her, claimed her in a way she'd never thought possible. She meant the kiss to last only a second, but in the first searing brush of tongues time slipped away as a flood of dizzying emotion slipped loose from her heart and spiraled downward to her toes like a euphoric drug.

Her fingers raised to touch his face as though seeking confirmation that he was the source of the craziness spilling through her veins. His mouth shifted on hers, the shadow of his beard rasping against her chin. As the kiss grew more demanding his thumbs pressed into the hollows above her collarbone, as if her collarbone represented a line he dared not cross. Instinctively she leaned into him, a heavy ache settling in her breasts as she absorbed the hard contours of his body into the softness of hers. Felt his arousal press against the curve of her belly—making his wants known.

Paulina heard a moan of surrender escape her lips as she responded to the need building in his kiss with a primitive need of her own. Suddenly, she was aware that Gil—with this big empty house of his—wanted more from her than she could ever give. She started to pull back, but Gil's arms tightened around her. Heat shimmered between them like a wall of humidity on a blistering summer day. The inner voice Paulina had heard before dared her to tread farther out onto the ledge. Paulina melted into Gil, succumbing to the fluid golden euphoria for a few more blissful seconds. *I can't remember being kissed like this.*

Exactly, the voice crowed with a superior ring of smugness. Paulina broke the kiss and stepped back, shaking.

THE PICTURE OF THE BABY flashed on the television screen. The woman froze, recognizing the infant who slept in the crib in the spare bedroom. "What are we going to do?" she asked the man stretched out on the shabby vinyl recliner across from her.

"The same as we're doing now. Lay low. Trust me, the hoopla will blow over in a few days."

"But what if—"

"Don't worry. I know what I'm doing."

The cry of the baby pierced the evening air. The woman hurried down the hall to the spare room and scooped the infant into her arms. It was a warm evening—with the windows open someone might hear.

The baby quieted instantly, a smile breaking on his sweet, little face. She'd put him down for the night an hour ago and here he was wide-awake—and wet. She pressed a kiss on his dimpled cheek and laughed when his fingers tangled in her hair. This was a precious one, all right. Longing and impatience welled in her breast. *Oh, how she wanted this one to be hers!*

She heard footsteps in the hall. The man stood in the doorway and watched her with the baby. "You look happy with a baby in your arms," he observed. "It won't be long now. You'll be holding your own baby soon."

She smiled. He was right. She'd have to be patient a little longer. Soon, her own happy day would come.

Chapter Five

Paulina stared at the half-eaten meatball sandwich she'd bought for dinner on her way back to the office and tried to formulate her thoughts as she came to the tail end of the report she was writing to reflect her activities from three that afternoon, when Detectives Robbins and Zuker had walked into her office, to nine-fifteen when Gil had kissed her.

She never should have let him kiss her. Stray traces of elation lingered in her bloodstream like raindrops after a sudden storm.

She drew a cupid's bow and arrow on a scratch pad that she kept for doodling when she was thinking. She shouldn't be feeling this way. She was letting her purely feminine attraction to a handsome man get in the way of her good judgment. Turning back to the report, Paulina wrote the last few lines without mentioning the kiss. It was enough that she knew about it.

She put a question mark above the bow and arrow. Why had he kissed her? Simple attraction?

Or had her trusty inner voice been warning her of something else?

Gil's footprint and the jimmied patio door in Cindy's apartment irked her—not to mention his insistence that he shadow the investigation. She couldn't shake the vague, niggling feeling she'd been set up. She was hearing two distinctly different stories. One from Gil. The other from Francine Loiselle and Edison Tweedie.

Was it possible Gil had been feeding her a line all this time and that kiss was a calculated ploy to make her his ally?

Maybe he'd dropped by to see Cindy on Wednesday and discovered she was packing to leave with Mikey. Could he have killed her and staged Mikey's abduction? He had money aplenty to pay someone to care for Mikey. Would Mikey show up abandoned in a public place in a few days—or a few weeks?

Paulina groaned. The last drops of jubilant passion remaining in her system evaporated under a dry dose of disillusionment. *And she'd gotten Gil inside Cindy's apartment! She'd* provided the perfectly logical reason why his fingerprints would be all over the place. But she wasn't ready to convict Gil on the basis of an uneasy feeling and a four-alarm kiss. She sifted through her reports until she came up with the information provided by Edison Tweedie. He'd said Francine, the waitress at the diner, had referred Cindy to a lawyer. *Maybe the lawyer could confirm that Gil threatened to sue for custody of Mikey?* Paulina looked up Vern Newcombe's number and address in the telephone book. His office was on Elgin Street across from the law courts. She'd pay him a visit first thing tomorrow.

She'd also ask if the lawyer could put a last name to "Elva," the counselor Cindy had been seeing. Paulina opened the manila envelope that held the tidbits she'd fished from Cindy's wastebasket and dumped the contents on her desk. Hadn't there been a card for a pregnancy counseling clinic? Yes, she found it. Maybe Elva worked there.

Paulina tapped the pink business card on the desk, toying with an idea. Could Cindy have decided to leave town because she was pregnant? Possibly. Particularly if the baby wasn't Ted's. Gil's offer to support her might have made Cindy uncomfortable, especially if she was involved with someone else.

Paulina made a note to ask Robbins if the autopsy report indicated Cindy was pregnant. It was worth asking, even though Robbins wasn't exactly brimming with information.

She'd also conduct background checks on Gil and Edison Tweedie. Tweedie had been awfully helpful. Maybe too cooperative—remembering names. Paulina put two question marks beside his name on her to-do list for the next morning. How many people remember that much detail about conversations they have with strangers? Why had he sat down and talked to Cindy in the first place—unless he was a leech who preyed on lonely young women?

Was he some sort of wacko who followed Cindy out of the diner and killed her? Since Cindy hadn't been sexually assaulted, Paulina could only come up with two reasons why Tweedie would do such a thing. Either he and his wife desperately wanted a baby or he was involved in baby selling. His job was the perfect cover. He traveled all over the country.

She picked up the phone and punched in her ex-husband's phone number. It was after ten, Karl should be watching the news.

He answered on the second ring.

"Hey, what's up, Paulie?" he said, his gravelly voice rumbling in her ear.

"I'm working on something I wanted to bounce off you. Can you talk?"

"If you're asking if I'm alone, the answer is yes."

"That wasn't the question, Karl. We're divorced. It's none of my business whom you entertain or when."

He cleared his throat. "And there I was hoping you were going to sweet-talk me back into your bed."

"Right. I'm going to sweet-talk you all right, but it has nothing to do with sex." Paulina laughed. At least they'd managed to remain friends after their divorce. "Did you see the news report about the missing baby?"

"Yeah. The mother was found in a trash can."

"Well, I'm doing a background check on a witness who spoke to the woman a couple of hours before she was killed. He just happened to sit down next to her in a restaurant because she looked like she needed a friend."

"You don't sound like you buy that explanation," Karl observed dryly.

"That obvious, eh?"

"So, what are you driving at?"

"Well, I've done some checking. The witness works as a sales rep for a hardware supply company. He does a lot of traveling on a regular schedule from southern Ontario to Saskatchewan. I'm wondering how many stranger abductions of babies or young children have occurred in towns and cities along this guy's route in the last five years. Do you think the RCMP Missing Children's Center could check it out?"

Karl whistled. "Sounds like you're on to something, Paulie. Give me everything you've got on this guy and the region he covers and I'll get back to you as soon as I can. It could be a few days."

"That's fine." She gave him the info she'd amassed on Edison Tweedie. "Thanks, Karl. You have my undying gratitude."

"It's not your gratitude I want, Paulie."

Paulina knew exactly what he wanted. He wanted her to give up who she was and be something she wasn't—to make *him* happy. *What was it about the male psyche that made men think they made the rules?*

"Good night, Karl," Paulina said firmly and hung up the phone. Karl was a good RCMP officer—one of the best—and he deserved everything he wanted out of life. But Paulina preferred that some other woman provide it.

With a small sigh, she gazed at the pile of papers in front of her. Maybe she'd read over everything one more time before she went to bed…just to make sure she hadn't missed anything. She still wasn't any closer to finding the man with long blond hair and the athlete's physique.

Forty-five minutes later, her extra effort paid off. She found a lead worth following up while she examined the photocopies the police had made of Cindy's calendar in exchange for her giving them the original. Cindy took Mikey to a drop-in program for parents and tots every Wednesday morning at the Sandy Hill Community Center. Had she attended the session the day she died? Paulina stood up and stretched the tired muscles in her back. Even if Cindy hadn't attended, Paulina would bet a lot of talking went on in a place like that. Gil had even suggested Cindy had made friends with some of the other mothers.

Tomorrow was Wednesday. For the first time in her adult life Paulina wished she had a baby, so she could attend the session undercover. People tended to be more honest and outspoken among their peers. Bring a cop or a P.I. into the room and no one wanted to get involved. Meanwhile, a killer and a child abductor was roaming the streets. Paulina smiled grimly. Somehow she'd get the information as Paulina Stewart, P.I.

NEWCOMBE'S OFFICE WAS on the sixth floor of Barrister House, one of the most respected addresses of barristers and solicitors in the city. The massive plate-glass lobby doors were etched with the scales of justice. Elegant brown-and-white marble floors lent an air of quiet respectability and tradition to the lobby. At eight-thirty sharp, Paulina stood outside the cherry-stained French doors to Newcombe and Bullhauser and smothered a yawn. She'd jumped the gun. The law offices weren't open for business yet.

Fifteen minutes later when she'd grown tired of looking at the polished brass nameplates and doorknobs of the other offices, the elevator doors slid open and a slender, efficient-looking woman wearing a black-and-white houndstooth check suit dashed down the hallway toward Paulina. The woman carried a large, heavy briefcase. Her long, silver-blond hair, which she'd pulled into an elegant ponytail, twitched from side to side with the energy of her momentum.

"Hi, sorry I'm late," the woman said, fishing in the pocket of her suit for her keys. "Have you been waiting long? I'm Lydia Kosak, the firm's paralegal. Our receptionist must be stuck in Queensway traffic again."

Paulina assured her she'd just arrived.

Lydia opened the door and flipped on the lights. Then she hefted her briefcase onto the receptionist's desk and scanned the appointment book. "Did you have an appointment, Ms—?" she asked.

Paulina shook her head and removed her ID from her purse. "No, I don't. I'm Paulina Stewart. I'm a private investigator. I was hired by the family of Cindy D'Angelo to look into her murder."

Lydia's pale brows drew together. "Cindy D'Angelo. The name sounds vaguely familiar. Was she a client of the firm's?"

"Yes. She was seeing Mr. Newcombe. She was a recently widowed young mother with a five-month-old baby. She had an appointment ten days ago—Monday, 11:00 a.m."

The paralegal flipped back through the pages of the appointment book. Then her amber eyes widened with shock as she seemed to place Cindy's name. "Oh, *that Cindy*. I remember now. I held her little boy for a few minutes while she conferred with Mr. Newcombe. Cute baby. But she was murdered, you say. How terrible!"

"I guess you didn't watch the evening news last night." Paulina sketched out the details.

"For heaven's sake," Lydia exclaimed, hugging herself. "That poor woman. And the baby's missing. Is that why you're here?"

"Yes, I'm hoping Mr. Newcombe can answer a few questions about Cindy's life—the people she knew."

Lydia's expression became guarded. "Ms. Stewart, as a private investigator, you are aware that the conversations between a counselor and a client are confidential?"

"I'm very much aware of that." Paulina smiled and glanced pointedly at the appointment book. "When will Mr. Newcombe be in?"

Was it reluctance she saw in the paralegal's eyes as she scanned the day's appointment schedule?

"He should be in shortly. His first appointment is at nine-thirty. Given the circumstances, I'll try to fit you in before that. Why don't you make yourself comfortable? I'll get the coffee perking."

Paulina waited patiently as the paralegal bustled off with the coffee carafe in her hand. Lydia returned two minutes later with the carafe full of water and poured it into the coffee maker.

"I've worked with a number of law firms in the city," Paulina began conversationally. "But I'm not familiar with Newcombe and Bullhauser. Has the firm been established long?"

"Seventeen years," Lydia replied. "We specialize in family law. I've been working here for six years." The smell of coffee percolating filled the air. She turned as the French doors to the office opened and a gangly gentleman in a black wool suit and striking red tie entered. Silver wire-rimmed glasses framed his steely gray eyes. "That's Mr. Newcombe arriving now. Right on time."

Newcombe's gaze swept the reception area, then settled on Lydia. "Janine's late again?"

Lydia made a face. "Afraid so."

"Hmm, that's three times in the last two weeks."

"She'll turn up." Lydia gestured toward Paulina. "There's someone here to see you—without an appointment. A private investigator inquiring about one of our clients."

Newcombe glanced at his gold watch, then gave Paulina a curious glance. "Give me two minutes to get settled and I'll have Lydia show you in. Lydia, a coffee, as soon as possible, please."

Lydia sent Paulina a conspiratorial grimace as she poured a mug of coffee for her boss. "Whenever Janine's late, I get demoted."

Paulina followed Lydia down the hall to an office appointed with beautiful antiques.

Newcombe was ensconced behind a massive oak desk on which piles of files had been laid out with meticulous care. Paulina experienced the full impact of Newcombe's assiduous gaze as she handed the lawyer her business card and stated the reason for her visit. Golden freckles dotted his pale skin. His red-gold hair had been parted and smoothed in place with hair gel. "Ms. D'Angelo had an appointment with you two days before she died," Paulina said matter-of-factly. "I'd like to know the nature of her consultation."

Newcombe didn't blink. He readjusted his glasses on the bridge of his nose. "I'm afraid I can't help you, Ms. Stewart. Client-lawyer privilege prevents me from disclosing any information Cindy D'Angelo may have shared with me—or from acknowledging that she was my client.''

Paulina folded her hands together in her lap. ''Actually, Mr. Newcombe, that privilege died with Cindy. Now her killer is out there with her child. I find it difficult to believe Cindy would not want you to divulge whatever information might assist the police in arresting her killer and recovering her child.'' She paused. ''Of course, Counselor, anything you feel ethically bound to tell me, need not go further than this room. My interest is in finding the baby alive.''

''Hmm-mmm.''

''I would not be offended if you wished to contact Ken Mayheu, of Mayheu, O'Connor and Dingwald, or Sandra Radnoff, of Ferris and Radnoff, to inquire about my integrity.'' A faint speculative gleam in his eyes suggested he recognized the names of senior partners at two of the most respected firms in the city.

''I went golfing with Ken Mayheu at the Hunt Club two weeks ago.''

Paulina felt as though they were playing tennis and he'd skillfully batted the ball back into her court.

''Well, if you're on friendly terms with Ken,'' she returned, crossing her legs and trying to look relaxed, ''you know his granddaughter was abducted by his son-in-law three years ago. Ken hired me to find her, which I did, and his firm has kept me reasonably busy ever since.''

''Very impressive.'' Newcombe cleared his throat and turned on his computer. ''Let me have a look at my files and I can make a determination.''

Paulina breathed easier as the lawyer perused the computer screen. After a long moment, he said, ''Hypothetically speaking, I think that if any young widowed mother came to see me, I'd advise her it's highly unlikely a court would take a child away from its mother and grant custody to another relative—say an uncle, for example—even if the relative was considerably better off financially.''

A cold stone sank in the pit of Paulina's stomach. *Gil.* Just what she'd been afraid of. She thanked Mr. Newcombe and rose to leave, feeling numb as she made her way back to the reception area. A plump brunette with dark, expressive eyes had replaced Lydia at the reception desk. Was this Janine—the tardy receptionist?

The woman met Paulina's gaze, her face troubled. ''Please convey my sympathies to Cindy's brother,'' she said. ''They seemed very close. He always drove Cindy and the baby to her appointments with Mr. Newcombe.''

Paulina nearly tripped on the conservative blue-gray carpet. *Appointments?* Just how worried was Cindy that Gil would take Mikey away from her? Or was Newcombe helping Cindy probate Ted's estate?

''Certainly, I'll be happy to—if you could tell me which brother,'' Paulina said, recovering quickly. ''Cindy has three.''

The receptionist frowned. ''Oh, I didn't know that. I believe his name was Jean-Luc. His hair was a shade darker blond than his sister's.''

''Did he have long hair?''

''Yes. He's disgustingly gorgeous.''

Lydia came into the reception area carrying a stack of express envelopes for the courier. ''Oh, you're still here, Ms. Stewart,'' she remarked, her thin carmine lips not quite pulling into a smile.

''Just on my way out,'' Paulina replied, sensing Lydia was not pleased to find Janine gossiping when she should have been working.

''Hey, Lyd, what's the name of Cindy's brother?'' Janine demanded. ''You know, the hunk. You spoke to him the last time Cindy was in.''

''I tried to help him quiet the baby. That's not really

talking. But he had a French name—Jean something. I think they're half brother and sister, because Cindy doesn't—uh—didn't have an accent at all.'' Lydia's amber eyes narrowed. "Don't you know his name, Ms. Stewart? I thought Cindy's family hired you."

Paulina ignored the paralegal's blunt suspicion. "Her mother hired me," she said blithely. "The names of her half brothers didn't enter into the conversation. Thank you for your time, ladies." Paulina waited until she was alone in the elevator before she raised her arms in a victory salute. She was one step closer to discovering the identity of the blond man in Cindy's life.

GIL KNEW WHEN HE WAS being given the runaround. "Where is Paulina, Andrea?" he barked into his car phone, tired of the intern's vague explanations.

"She's out of the office working on a case. Now, if you would care to leave a number, I'll have her return your call the moment she steps in."

"If she's working on my case, I want to know where she is and what she's doing. Now," he insisted.

"You'll have to discuss that with Ms. Stewart. I have a call coming in on the other line. Would you like to hold or leave a message?"

Gil gritted his teeth. "Here's my car-phone number. Tell her I've got an important meeting today until noon. I want to hear from her then." He slammed down the phone, braking suddenly as a traffic light turned red.

He'd never felt so out of control in his life. He hadn't slept most of the night. It was still sinking in that Cindy was dead and Mikey was God knows where. The harsh reality of the situation bore down on his shoulders like bone-crushing hundred-pound weights. He'd spent two hours on the phone with his parents after Paulina had left the previous night—reassuring them that everything possible was being done to find Mikey and capture Cindy's killer.

First thing this morning, Gil had ordered thousands of fliers bearing Mikey's picture to be made up. He'd hired the eighteen-year-old son of one of his consultants to find reliable teenagers to post the fliers all over the city. Then he'd phoned the funeral home to make an appointment to arrange Cindy's funeral.

Gil blinked back the horrible image of Cindy lying on that stretcher and tried to still the angry voice roaring inside his head for him to do something. His eyes felt as though they were shrinking into his skull. He wasn't up to doing this demo, but the client was too important and there was too much money riding on the deal to cancel. With all the uncertainty of Mikey's disappearance, it would be easier to get the meeting over with than try to reschedule. But damn, as soon as it was over, he was finding Paulina.

PAULINA GLANCED UP as Andrea walked into her office, a pink message slip in hand.

"He phoned again, boss. He's pretty upset," Andrea said, tossing the slip onto the two others on the desk. "He's out at a meeting and will be back at noon. He expects to hear from you then."

Paulina winced. "Don't take it personally. He's the 'give orders' type. I promised I'd phone him, but I have to finish these background checks first. The drop-in program at the community center starts at eleven-fifteen, which gives me less than an hour to figure out whether or not Gil's on the level. Andrea, you're a computer whiz. Call Gil's company and have them fax you a list of references. Make up a story that you're interested in having them design an application for your father's import business. Gil will be mad if he finds out we're checking up on him, but I'll deal with that when the time comes."

After Andrea had left, Paulina scanned the list of Tweedie's neighbors she'd gotten from a librarian in his hometown library. Thank God for city directories. She tried one of Tweedie's next-door neighbors first. A child answered the phone. Her mind scrambled for a story while she asked to speak to an adult.

"Mrs. Breckenridge?" Paulina quickly introduced herself as Pamela Willet. "I was put up for adoption when I was a baby and I'm searching for my birth parents. Would you mind if I asked you some confidential questions about one of your neighbors?"

"What kind of questions?" The woman's voice was wary but curious.

"Well, I'm trying to narrow down my search. I know my birth father's first initial was E and his last name was Tweedie. He was twenty-three when I was put up for adoption. That would make him forty-six now."

"Gee, I don't know how old Mr. Tweedie is exactly. He's active and young at heart, but I'm sure he's closer to retirement age. He's a nice man. Very quiet."

"Do you know what he does for a living? My information said he was a garage mechanic."

The woman laughed. "It's hard to imagine Mr. Tweedie getting greasy. He's very tidy. Most of the people on the street wonder how he manages to keep his yard immaculate when he's rarely home. This Mr. Tweedie sells hardware."

"I see. Just in case I decide to approach him, could you tell me if he's married and has children? I'm wondering what kind of reception I'd receive."

"He's a bachelor. If he has children I've never seen them, but frankly I think you've got the wrong Mr. Tweedie."

"I think you're right." Paulina heard a child's cry over

the phone. "Sounds like you have to go. Thank you for your help."

She quickly dialed another neighbor, careful to use the same story. She promptly got the phone slammed in her ear. On her fifth call, an elderly lady with a feeble voice answered the phone. Paulina gave her spiel.

"You say you were adopted? And you believe Mr. Tweedie to be your father?" Mrs. Eccles made a sympathetic clucking sound. "I'm sorry, dear, but I don't think that likely."

"Why is that, Mrs. Eccles?" Paulina experienced a twinge of alarm. Had the woman seen through her story?

"I've known Edison Tweedie for twenty years. We attend the same church—First Methodist. And I can tell you, I've rarely met a man of his fine moral caliber. He's dedicated his life to the church in the service of others—always the first to volunteer a hand to those less fortunate than himself. When he's not on the road, he spends much of his free time helping out at a local mission for the homeless."

"He sounds like an admirable individual. But we all experience moments of weakness in our lives. Do you think he'd mind if I phoned him? Would it upset his wife—or his children—for him to receive a call from me?"

"His wife died long ago and he's remained true to her memory. They had no children. Now, young lady, I would urge you to speak to Ed directly about this matter. I shudder to think of you making further indiscreet phone calls at the expense of his reputation. You've nothing to fear from him. God has filled his heart with goodness." The woman hung up before Paulina could ask another question. Mrs. Eccles clearly thought Edison Tweedie should be next in line for sainthood.

Paulina tried two other numbers without success, then

Andrea came in with a fax listing references for Gil's company. Paulina grabbed the list eagerly. She'd already checked out Gil's financial status. He'd worked hard to get where he was at; he was thirty-one years old and owned his home free and clear. "Did you finish talking to Gil's neighbors, too?"

Andrea grinned. "Yes, I told them I was a reporter doing a story on the missing baby. I didn't find out much. Gil works a lot. Doesn't seem to date much, either. But definitely no steady girlfriend around who might want to take care of a baby. The only female who regularly enters his house is a cleaning lady who arrives Friday afternoons. He goes jogging just about every day. Sometimes in the morning, sometimes in the evening. No set routine."

So it was reasonable for him to decide to go for a jog the day Cindy was killed because he happened to be working in the vicinity of the Rideau Canal. And he had no steady girlfriend. Paulina felt markedly more at ease. She couldn't imagine Gil giving up his work-heavy bachelor's life-style to care for Mikey on his own. But instinct told her to keep digging. Cindy had been worried enough about Gil getting custody of Mikey that she'd consulted a lawyer. There was more to the story somewhere.

"Thanks, Andrea. I'll call those references now." Paulina took a deep breath to clear her mind, then picked up the phone again, her pen poised to take notes. Thirty minutes later, she had six comments listed on her notepad—all of them repeated over and over by the company representatives she'd spoken to. *Hardworking. Competitive. Professional. Delivers on time. Willing to go the extra mile. Personable.* They all painted both Gil and his consulting firm in a positive light.

Another saint.

No, not a saint. A hardworking man who lived by the same code of ethics he worked by—and wasn't above admitting his mistakes. She felt reasonably certain Gil was being honest with her.

A heady wave of relief pulsed through her body. It was always nice to know your client wasn't a criminal, she thought wryly.

Yeah. Particularly handsome clients who've perfected the art of kissing, her inner voice piped up.

Paulina tuned it out. Sometimes, having a finely honed sense of intuition could be a pain. She shoved the file into her briefcase and grabbed her purse out of the bottom drawer of her desk.

"Andrea," she called as she sailed out of her office at a dead run. "Get hold of Gil. His office will know where he is. Tell him to meet me at the Sandy Hill Community Center as soon as possible. We've got a lost piece of a puzzle to find."

Chapter Six

"Ms. Stewart wishes me to assure you that anything said to her today would be kept in the strictest confidence," the director of the community center told the group of twenty or so parents sitting in a conversation-inducing circle. His voice rose over the shrieks of the toddlers crashing push toys and Big Wheels together in the rear half of the room. "She's not with the police. She's working on the behalf of Cindy's family." He gave her a nod and left the room.

Paulina searched the sea of shocked faces turned in her direction for indications that at least one of the parents nursing a disposable cup of coffee had shared confidences with Cindy. "Could someone tell me whether Cindy came to the group last Wednesday?" she asked.

"No, she didn't come last week," a young woman wearing a pink T-shirt and gray sweatpants volunteered. Her light brown hair was roughly shaped into a mushroom cut. She glanced at the olive-skinned woman beside her, whose long, dark, riotous curls were kept reasonably in check by an elastic secured in the region of her shoulder blades. "But she came fairly regularly over the summer and she attended the first three weeks of September."

"Thank you. If you don't mind, I'd like to circulate around the room and talk to each of you individually. Why don't you continue chatting and I'll start at this end of the circle?''

They were nervous, Paulina could tell. Though some people resumed their conversations, she was aware that others were listening in. So much the better. Maybe someone would want to get involved and feel compelled to add something that hadn't been said. She tried not to be discouraged when one attendee after another said they knew who she was, but they hadn't talked to her. Still, Paulina culled snippets of information. Someone had offered Cindy advice on how to get a baby to sleep through the night. Cindy had bottle-fed Mikey because the breast feeding wasn't working. An emaciated woman with dark smudges under her eyes told Paulina that Cindy had it quite rough— being a single mother and all.

"We swapped stories about life on the streets. It was hard, but Cindy said it was a picnic compared to the crap her parents laid on her." The woman rolled her eyes suggestively.

A strong surge of pathos and indignation for Cindy rose in Paulina's chest. It seemed horribly unjust that Cindy had escaped an unhappy family situation only to die a violent death. Paulina thanked the woman and kept circulating, finding it odd that no one seemed to know about Ted—or that he'd died recently. A man wearing a blue Expos cap discreetly informed her that Cindy usually talked to Kathie, the woman who'd spoken up earlier, and Danielle, the woman with the dark, curly hair.

Paulina progressed farther along the circle and had just said hello to Kathie and Danielle when Gil strode into the room. She had little doubt every female eye in the room took in the breathtakingly masculine way he filled out his dark gray suit. His crisp blue shirt and red-and-blue paisley tie added suave sophistication to his sheer brawn. A little girl with a pacifier bobbing in her mouth cut in front of him, tripping over a pile of cardboard bricks. Gil helped her up and charmed away her tears. Paulina noticed the way his large fingers gently patted the child's head.

She swallowed hard, watching him. An unfamiliar feeling—part desire, part longing—nudged at her heart. When he rose and made eye contact with her, the stark vulnerability that flashed in his indigo eyes for an instant touched her to the core. Then he hid it away. She pressed her hands together to keep herself from reaching out to him.

"Oh, good, you're here, *John,*" she said, hoping he'd catch on that she didn't think it prudent to introduce him as Cindy's brother-in-law. "Come join me—I'm conducting interviews about Cindy. John's my partner," she explained to Kathie and Danielle.

"Hi, ladies." Gil flashed them a smile that oozed sex appeal.

"Are you two married?" Danielle asked.

Paulina felt Gil's gaze sweep over her red crepe dress, warming her.

"They've found us out, sweetheart," he said, a hint of amusement in his tone.

To her embarrassment, she felt her breasts tingle with a heavy warmth and the heat of a blush rise to her cheeks. She, who prided herself on keeping her emotions under control. "I'm not even wearing my ring today," she replied tartly. "How did you know?"

Danielle waved her hand. "Oh, puh-lease. It's obvious the way you two looked at each other just then."

Paulina felt disconcerted. Was her attraction to Gil that apparent? She didn't like the idea at all. Could Kathie and Danielle tell the tantalizing masculine scent of Gil's cologne was making a slow assault on her senses?

"It was just like that with Cindy and Jean-Luc. Cindy tried to pretend she wasn't interested in him, but Kathie and I noticed the way she hung around the front desk before and after the drop-in program.''

"I take it Jean-Luc works at the center here?" Gil said.

Paulina knew the pains he took to feign disinterest and admired him for it. She liked a man who could think well on his feet and react fast.

"That's right," Kathie confirmed, in a soft voice. "I didn't see him today. He's probably not here because of— well, you know." Her velvety brown eyes shone with sudden moisture. She pulled a tissue out of a diaper bag and swabbed at a tear streaking her cheek. "We knew things weren't going well between Cindy and Ted. She mentioned their relationship had been rocky even before Mikey was born. But she got some counseling and Ted convinced her they could make it work. And she found it hard to take care of Mikey. She was very unsure of what to do. I suggested she ask her mom for advice, and Cindy said her mother had pretty much ignored her as a child. Then Ted died and Cindy felt even more overwhelmed. I kind of hoped maybe Cindy and Jean-Luc would hook up eventually."

Paulina made a determined effort not to look at Gil. She just prayed he didn't have a censorious frown marching across his forehead. "Do you know anything else about Jean-Luc?" she asked. "How long had Cindy been seeing him?"

"You don't think he killed Cindy, do you?" Danielle said, obviously horrified by the idea.

"We honestly don't know." Gil inserted himself back into the conversation with swift ease. "That's why we're so appreciative of *anything* you can tell us about her life."

Danielle twisted a thin gold ring on her pinkie. "Well, we took a twelve-week preparation course for new mothers here at the community center from January to March.

Cindy was friendly with Jean-Luc even then, but I don't know how involved they were.''

Which meant Danielle didn't know whether Cindy had even known Jean-Luc before the course started. Paulina wondered if Gil was thinking the same thing.

''I didn't finish the course, because my daughter came three weeks early,'' Danielle continued, pulling the ring off her finger. ''I think she was seeing him in July because she asked me for a lift to a row house near the University of Ottawa after the drop-in program one day when it was raining. I could be wrong, though.''

''Do either of you know his last name?'' Paulina asked.

Both women shook their heads.

''Would you mind if I took your names so I could call if we come across something in the investigation that you might be able to shed some light on?''

Paulina noted obvious reluctance in their eyes.

''Please,'' Gil said, emotion creeping into his deep voice. ''For Mikey's sake.''

''Okay,'' Kathie finally agreed.

Danielle nodded.

Paulina made a note of their names and telephone numbers. ''Is there anyone else here you think we should talk to?''

''Not really,'' Kathie said. ''The three of us got friendly straight off.''

Still, Paulina resisted the temptation to leave immediately. There might be someone else who could tell them something important. Twenty minutes later, she thanked everyone for their cooperation. Then she and Gil approached the front desk and asked to speak to the director.

''Are you finished, then?'' the director inquired, glancing at the clock. He removed the cap of a pen dangling from a cord around his neck and made a notation on a schedule secured to a clipboard.

"Yes, it's been very helpful." Paulina leaned against the counter. "But there's one other person I'd like to talk to. I understand Cindy was a friend of one of your employees. I believe his name is Jean-Luc?"

"That would be Jean-Luc Deveau."

"Is he here today? Could I talk to him?"

"That wouldn't be possible." The director gave Gil a long, appraising look. "Is he with the police?"

"No. He's my partner. If you could tell me when Jean-Luc's scheduled to be in next, I'd be happy to come back."

"You don't understand, Ms. Stewart," the director explained. "Jean-Luc won't be back. He quit last Tuesday. He didn't even give two weeks' notice."

Paulina frowned. "Have you got a phone number or an address where I could reach him?"

"I'm sorry, that's confidential information."

"Of course."

Gil stirred restlessly at her side, then politely excused himself. She tried to gauge what was going on with him in the brief look he sent her before he dug his hands into the pockets of his gray slacks and paced toward the elevator near the rear entrance. Maybe all the talk about Cindy's involvement with another man was getting to him. Paulina hovered between a compassionate urge to follow Gil and the compunction to complete the interview. She decided to stick with the director. Recovering Mikey was her top priority.

"You said Jean-Luc quit without notice," she remarked, trying another tact. "Did he give you any reason?"

"No. He just came into my office at the end of his shift last Tuesday and announced he was quitting. I asked why and he said it was none of my business. He told me to send him his last paycheck." The director put the cap back on his pen and scratched the bald spot on top of his head. "He probably found a better-paying job."

Paulina had other ideas—none of them good. "Well, thanks again for the help." She turned and headed in the direction in which Gil had gone. What had come over him? She took the elevator down and walked out to the parking lot. She found Gil's black sports car, but there was no sign of him. Had he gone for a walk around the block to vent some steam?

It didn't work, telling herself that her concern was purely professional. She was worried about the man. Not her client. Which was going to get her into trouble if she wasn't careful enough. Stifling an exasperated sigh, she returned to the rear lobby and picked up a pay phone. While Gil was cooling off, she might as well call Karl and see if he could get her an address on Jean-Luc Deveau.

Karl, as always, was happy to oblige her request. Paulina scribbled Jean-Luc's address onto her notepad. Finally, they were making progress in this case. Now, if she could just find Gil.

GIL FELT THE TENSION winding tighter in his body. He'd hoped one of the employees at the community center would have Jean-Luc's home number or would know where he lived, but he'd come up with a big fat zero. A male fitness instructor had told him Jean-Luc kept to himself. The only thing he talked about was his 1969 Mustang.

Somehow that didn't make Gil feel more relieved. How many lunatics out there kept to themselves?

He found Paulina standing on the sidewalk near the parking lot, her slender hand shielding her eyes from the sun as she gazed toward the park backing the community center. Her red crepe dress made her look smart and professional and very, very sexy. His body throbbed with an insatiable curiosity to find out if she wore lacy red underthings beneath it.

"Looking for someone?" he couldn't resist saying.

She whirled around, her expression a mixture of relief—and annoyance? She was probably mad about that married reference. Hell, he'd read all her signals and knew there was no way her life could be in sync with his—even though that kiss the other night had been spectacular. He was just having trouble convincing the rest of his body parts that she was not his type.

"There you are," she said. "Where were you?"

He told her.

"Well, it was worth a shot. I should have thought of it myself." She grabbed his arm, dragging him toward her car. For a slender woman hampered by high heels, she had a considerable amount of power.

He pulled his mind away from wondering if she was this assertive when it came to lovemaking. Why was he torturing himself with never-gonna-happen fantasies? Probably because he was focusing on Paulina's beauty to keep himself from going stark, raving crazy about Mikey. Thanks to one of those ladies inside, Gil now had another worry to add to his growing list—just who the hell had fathered Mikey?

"Come on," Paulina urged. "We don't have time to waste. I've got Jean-Luc's address."

For a moment he was dumbfounded as he tried to process what she'd just said, then questioned his surprise. Paulina Stewart seemed capable of anything. "How'd you get it?"

She shook her head, her short black cap of hair gleaming in the sunlight. "Can't tell, it's a trade secret."

"Damn woman," he muttered under his breath, half hoping she'd hear. She jammed a key into the lock of the passenger door. "Why are we taking your car?" he demanded. "I'll drive."

"Because it's not far and you have too much on your mind. Get in."

He obeyed her. She turned onto East Somerset and zipped up to King Edward Avenue.

"So," he began, "I was thinking about what Cindy's friends told us." He cleared his throat, afraid to say what was poisoning his thoughts. But he'd never run away from a problem in his life. In the long run it was easier to face up to things right from the start. "It got me wondering if Mikey is Ted's child." His fingers splayed on his thighs. Bitterness coated his tongue. "I used to tease Ted and say, 'Isn't it fortunate Mikey doesn't look anything like you?' Mikey's got pale blue eyes like Cindy—and his hair is blond. Ted had dark hair like me. Isn't dark hair dominant?" A fierce anger cut his guts to ribbons. It was killing him to think Mikey wasn't Ted's flesh and blood.

Paulina laid her hand on his left thigh, covering his hand with hers. Gil closed his eyes, overwhelmed by how good it felt to have her there to talk through this madness. To touch her and be soothed by the calm strength of her satiny fingers.

"Gil," she said firmly, "lots of kids have blond hair when they're babies and it becomes darker later in life. Try not to jump to conclusions."

He laughed abruptly. He knew she meant well, but he'd already taken a long flying leap. "You mean like don't assume this Jean-Luc character killed Cindy because he learned Mikey is his son and she'd tried to conceal the fact from him?" Gil realized his jaw was trembling with the effort of trying to keep himself together. "You know, it all makes sense in a sick kind of way. He quit the day before Cindy died. Was he making plans to kill her and run off with Mikey?"

Paulina didn't answer him. She gave his thigh a comforting squeeze, then returned her hand to the steering wheel so she could pull over to the curb. She pointed at a low two-story brick building down the street. "That's Jean-Luc's address."

Gil tensed, studying the decaying building. A marked difference in the color of the redbrick indicated where a grander front entrance had been replaced during the building's conversion to a row house. Now, a simple colonnaded porch painted Quebec blue-and-white sheltered two private entrances. A cornice across the top of the building ended in corner brackets detailed with French fleurs-de-lis. Jean-Luc's prized olive green Ford Mustang sat in the right side driveway.

Gil climbed out of the car, ready to draw blood.

The row house was ominously silent.

"Let me do the talking and keep your fists in your pockets," Paulina told him as they walked up the uneven concrete path to the porch. "You'll be no help to Mikey if you're thrown in jail for assault causing bodily injury."

Gil's heart started to pound. He rang the doorbell, hearing it echo in the abode. There was no sound of answering footsteps. Gil leaned over the porch railing to look in the living-room window. Paulina stepped in front of him for a look, too, her soft body brushing against his. Her fresh lilac scent tantalized him, despite his red-hot urge to throttle Jean-Luc on sight. The open layout of the row house allowed him to see straight back to the eating area—and the legs of a man sprawled on the floor. The man wasn't moving. Gil's heart sank with dread. Then he noticed a blue-and-red diaper bag on the table. *Mikey's* diaper bag.

Gil swore under his breath, fear and anger colliding head-on in his chest. He plied his shoulder to the door as a wild surge of adrenaline kicked into his system. The frame groaned in protest. "We've got to get in there. Mikey could be inside."

"Wait, Gil!" Paulina admonished him, tearing at the

gold clasp on her purse. She pulled out a tissue. *She wanted him to wait so she could blow her nose?*

Gil drew back for another lunge. He was getting inside. Now. He surged forward, caught by surprise that the door opened so easily. He'd barely touched it. He stumbled as he charged inside the narrow foyer, realizing to his embarrassment that Paulina had opened the door by turning the knob.

Paulina grabbed on to the back of his suit jacket, slowing him down. "Try not to touch anything," she cautioned as they wove through the furniture in the living room to the jean-clad figure lying on the speckled vinyl flooring.

The smell of death pervaded the house. Horror gripped Gil's heart and wouldn't let go. The fear that his gaze might fall on Mikey's lifeless body at any moment made his limbs quake. Paulina hunched down on her heels near the man's body, her expression grim. The man's shoulder-length blond hair and muscular build told Gil it had to be Jean-Luc. Blood surrounded a hole at the base of his head. A gun was clasped in Jean-Luc's right hand. Had he shot himself after he'd killed Cindy?

By sheer strength of will, Gil forced himself to glance around the room. Would they find Mikey here with— He couldn't think the worst. Gil strained his ears, listening for signs of life in the quiet house.

Paulina rose to her feet. "He's probably been dead a few days. We'll search the house for Mikey before we call the police." She handed Gil her tissue and pulled another out of her purse. "Just watch what you touch. Robbins will give us hell for disturbing a crime scene."

"Okay, okay. Let's go."

The row house was hot and the smell turned Gil's stomach. Sweat dripped down his face as they raced from room to room, searching for some sign of Mikey. Gil felt the air trap in his lungs every time they opened a cupboard or a door to one of the upstairs rooms. They found a pile of disposable diapers in the bathroom cabinet and a baby toy that must have rolled on the uneven pine floors to a low spot under a gliding rocker in the living room.

Where could he be? Gil wondered as they trudged downstairs to the cramped foyer. The diaper bag proved Mikey had been here. Cindy's name and phone number were written on it in permanent marker.

Paulina explored the narrow hallway that ran straight back to the kitchen, skirting the living and eating areas. "Gil, there's a door to the basement under the stairs," she said, her face white and pinched.

They went down together. Gil led the way on the narrow, rickety stairs, glad for the reassuring feel of Paulina's hand on his back. He was too tall to stand upright as they entered the gloomy cavern illuminated by a single bare bulb. The space was used to store a bicycle, hockey gear and homemade beer-brewing equipment. They methodically looked everywhere. To Gil's relief, the concrete floor revealed no signs of having been disturbed.

Paulina took a deep breath of cool basement air before they returned to the living room. She'd seen a phone on a student-type desk there. She put a call through directly to Detective Robbins. He instructed them to get out of the house and wait for his arrival.

She hung up and relayed Robbins's message to Gil. Then she looked thoughtfully at the red light flashing on Jean-Luc's answering machine. Her tissue-draped finger hovered over the button. "Shall we?" she asked Gil.

"Push it," he said, his face tight.

Paulina's own voice floated into the high-ceilinged room. There were no other messages. "Evidently, Jean-Luc was the last person Cindy called from her apartment," she observed.

"Evidently," he repeated.

Paulina pressed the redial button and listened to the phone ring, her gaze landing on a black metal-framed photograph of Jean-Luc that hung on the cracked plaster wall above the desk. His intense brown eyes hinted at a passionate personality. She wondered what he'd been passionate about in life—Cindy? But pictures of the dead don't speak.

A recorded message came on the line and informed her she'd reached Canadian Airlines. A customer-service representative would be with her shortly. Paulina shared the information with Gil.

Gil carefully picked up an envelope lying on the desk by the answering machine. Paulina used her tissue to pull out the papers inside.

"Oh, no," Paulina whispered, seeing two airplane tickets to Reno. The flight was for the previous Wednesday evening. She met Gil's troubled gaze. "Something obviously went horribly wrong between Jean-Luc and Cindy. It still doesn't explain where Mikey is, though." She checked the itinerary the travel agent had provided. "They planned to be away for two weeks. Maybe they meant to elope."

"I'll try not to be offended by the lack of an invitation," Gil bit out. "Or the fact my brother's been dead only two months."

Paulina slid the tickets back into the envelope. "We should get out of here before the police arrive."

They stood in the driveway, their fingers tangled together for mutual comfort, staring at Jean-Luc's Mustang. He'd kept the car in mint condition right down to the mag wheels. The paint looked brand-new. The doors were locked but there was nothing visible on the olive green leather seats. Not even an infant car seat.

"Mikey's obviously not here," Gil said, hope clinging to his voice. But his inner fears were telegraphed from every harsh line drawn around his handsome features. "I was thinking maybe Jean-Luc put him in the Dumpster with Cindy and a stranger heard him cry and rescued him. Maybe this person always wanted to have a child but couldn't..."

Paulina put her free hand up to his massive chest, feeling the powerful surge of his heartbeat and the depth of his love for Mikey, which was like an aura radiating from his heart. She needed to be strong for Gil and not be side-tracked by the anxiety spiking through her or the compelling desire to stop thinking and just react to the situation by holding him in her arms and reassuring him everything would be okay. Logic would find Mikey.

"Gil, we haven't actually determined Mikey's not here. There are two places we haven't searched. The yard and the trunk of Jean-Luc's car."

"I'll go inside and get the keys—"

Paulina gripped the lapels of his suit to stop him from charging off. "No, Gil." A hot lump wedged in her throat. "If he's here, it means he's..."

She saw the understanding dawn in his eyes. "Oh, Paulina, I want to take care of him. Ted thought he was his son and that's good enough for me." His face crumpled and Paulina slipped her arms around his waist and held on tight.

Hugging Gil was like embracing an elm tree. To see a man of such sheer muscular strength reduced to tears over a baby made a sizable impression on Paulina's heart. Her own tears slipped down her cheeks, saturating his shirt. "I don't want you to lose him, either," she said slowly, each word more painful to form than the last. "I'll be right here with you. No matter what."

He nodded, his damp cheek brushing hers. "You know, Paulina Stewart, you're one hell of a woman," he said thickly.

"Thank you." She tried to smile, but gave up. Right now she felt like one hell of a bad detective. "I'll take that as a compliment. But I don't hold a candle to a nice guy like you." Someday he'd be a good husband to some lucky woman—and a good father to some lucky kids. He deserved that much out of life.

Paulina turned her head at the sound of tires squealing in the street. The police had arrived.

GIL PUNCHED IN the security code of his house, feeling as though he'd been pushed through the wringer on the old washing machine his mom had kept for laundering his football uniforms. She'd been so proud of her new machine, she didn't want to soil it with grunge from the field.

He ran his hands through his hair. At least he still had hope. The police hadn't found Mikey. They had found suitcases when they opened the trunk of Jean-Luc's car.

"Gil?" He felt Paulina's hand on his shoulder. "How about I make us something to eat and we can talk?"

He blinked, realizing he'd been staring blankly at the keypad. It was probably a good thing Paulina had insisted on driving him home, though he hadn't liked leaving his car in the community center's lot. "Sure." He moved through the central hall to the kitchen, turning on lights.

The house had never felt so damned empty. He promised himself that when he found Mikey he'd make a home for him here. He'd also find the right significant other; someone who loved kids and wouldn't mind jumping right into motherhood. Gil would make it work somehow. He glanced at Paulina, who had washed her hands at the kitchen sink and was rummaging through his refrigerator as if it were her own. He'd never been so glad for company.

She pulled out packages of cold cuts, cheese, pickles,

lettuce and tomatoes, plopping them on the granite island. "Are sandwiches okay?"

He nodded and passed her a loaf of eight-grain bread, then set out clean plates, chips and soft drinks. Paulina made him two enormous sandwiches. By the time he'd finished the second sandwich, he felt his strength rebounding. Paulina had been quiet during their meal, her black winged brows drawn together, her silvery eyes narrowed in concentration. He knew her well enough by now to realize she was deep in thought. He hoped that sharp mind of hers had come up with something brilliant. He poured them each a snifter of brandy before they settled onto the living-room couch.

"So what do you think happened to Jean-Luc?" he asked, as her slender fingers closed around the crystal snifter. "He had a gun in his hand. Do you think he killed himself?"

"I honestly don't know, Gil," she murmured. "We'll have to wait for the autopsy report. My guess is he's been dead for several days but not a week. He probably died over the weekend."

Gil gulped his brandy, hoping it would erase the stark image of Jean-Luc's body from his mind. The brandy burned a warm path to his gut. "Maybe he killed Cindy and couldn't live with himself afterward."

"It's possible, but Robbins told you Cindy had been transported in a car with a burgundy interior. Jean-Luc's car has a green interior." She curled her legs beneath her. "The luggage in Jean-Luc's car suggests they planned to leave Wednesday night as scheduled. Cindy had to have given Jean-Luc their luggage Tuesday night or Wednesday morning. That could have occurred in several ways." She held up a finger. "One—Jean-Luc could have helped Cindy clear out of her apartment Tuesday night. It's easier to vacate in the middle of the night. Then he dropped

Mikey and Cindy off at the diner for breakfast Wednesday morning while he did errands—maybe he went to the bank for travelers' checks. But the distance between his row house and the diner bothers me. Surely there are restaurants closer to where he lives.''

''What if Jean-Luc spent Tuesday night at Cindy's apartment and took her things over to his place early Wednesday morning while she took Mikey out to breakfast?'' Gil suggested, seeing what she was driving at.

''That's my second option.'' She gave him an approving smile that made his heart stumble against his ribs. ''Maybe Jean-Luc had other errands, as well. It's possible they agreed to meet later, but Cindy never showed. Jean-Luc got worried. At some point he checked the airlines and tried to reschedule for a later flight—or maybe canceled the tickets. The police can corroborate that. But the big thing is…eventually he's frantic enough to break into her apartment. You said you climbed onto the balcony Friday afternoon and the door was locked, right?''

''That's right,'' he affirmed, relieved to know she'd believed him when he'd told her he hadn't forced the door open. Too bad the police weren't as perceptive of his veracity. Robbins had asked him a lot of questions about Jean-Luc and those tickets to Reno. Gil was certain Robbins hadn't believed him when he swore he hadn't even known Jean-Luc existed until the busybody in Cindy's building let the cat out of the bag.

Paulina's voice intruded into his thoughts. She was still hypothesizing. ''It's possible Jean-Luc noticed something in Cindy's apartment to indicate she'd deserted him, and he took his own life. If the autopsy report supports that theory we need to look more closely at Edison Tweedie, because he's the last known person to see Cindy alive.''

Gil stared at her in shock. ''Why would that old guy

kill Cindy?'' His hand shook as Paulina shared her theory about the hardware salesman.

''Some people are willing to pay big bucks for a child,'' she said. ''Tweedie could be working on his own—or be part of a ring. I asked my ex-husband to check with the RCMP's Missing Children's Center to find out how many infants or toddlers have disappeared in stranger abductions along Tweedie's route in the last five years.''

Gil drained his snifter. Numbing rage took hold of his body. The thought that Tweedie could have preyed on Cindy—because she seemed alone and vulnerable—sickened him. He'd tried to be there for her. But he'd failed Cindy as he'd failed Ted. *Please God, I don't want to fail Mikey, too.*

The brandy slowly dispersed through his body, its warmth and comfort a poor artificial remedy for the desperate craving he had for human contact and comfort. Paulina's sweet-scented warmth beckoned him. Irresistibly. Gil's fingers crept along the back of the couch, seeking the heat of her body. Unable to stop himself, he slipped his arm around her shoulders, needing to hold someone. No, not just someone. Paulina.

He inhaled deeply, breathing in her lilac scent as if he were drawing her essence into his soul. Her heat, soothing and feminine, seeped into his bloodstream.

To his gratification, she didn't pull away. Gil lost himself in the succor her body offered from the living hell that had started the day Ted died—and wouldn't end until Gil held Mikey in his arms again. Gil refused to consider he might have to lay Mikey to rest beside his parents. He swallowed hard, his throat aching with the effort of keeping himself together. ''If Tweedie took him, what are the chances of getting Mikey back?''

Her chin jutted up so she met his gaze squarely. ''That depends on whether or not Tweedie kept records and if he talks to the police. Even if he doesn't talk, the records might indicate who Mikey was given to—but sometimes they're encoded. Of course, this is all assuming the police can convince a judge enough reasonable grounds exist to get a search warrant.''

Not the most reassuring of answers.

''And if Jean-Luc killed Cindy and left Mikey there for someone else to find—?'' His voice cracked, reflecting his uncertainty.

She hesitated, and Gil's heart caked with ice as Paulina diverted her gaze to the green marble fireplace. She'd been brutally honest with him so far. Now, he counted on her honesty. He needed it.

He touched her cheek. ''Paulina, is finding Mikey hopeless?''

''No, Gil. Moments arise in this business when you have to be realistic and acknowledge possibilities. I won't lie to you. Statistically, the odds of recovery on stranger abductions are slim. But with a lot of media attention we may get lucky. Someone, somewhere, might notice a couple suddenly has a baby. The investigation is still in the early stages. I don't see any reason for us to give up hope that Mikey won't be recovered.''

Paulina leaned into the touch of Gil's hand and wished there was more she could do to remove the shadows of pain from his eyes. The rough feel of his fingertips on her skin stirred desires she hadn't let herself experience in a long time. What was it about Gil that affected her so?

''I don't tell all my clients this,'' she said very softly, ''but I wasn't quite five when my mother decided my father shouldn't have the right to see me. She packed our suitcases and told me we were going on holidays to the States. That holiday lasted sixteen years, most of those spent in Hartford, Connecticut. I thought Hughes was my last name until I was twenty-one years old and a man showed up at our house claiming to be my father.''

Her lips trembled. "I didn't believe him at first. When I was eight my mother told me he'd died, so I'd quit asking about him." *And quit hoping he'd show up one day and tell me how much he'd missed me. How much he loved me.* "But he had pictures of the three of us together. And the name Stewart had stuck in my head, but I thought it was my father's first name." She realized she was blabbering, but at least she was distracting Gil from thinking of Mikey.

"To make a long story short, he was my dad. And you know, he never gave up looking for me. He never stopped believing he'd see me again. He'd been a lawyer, but he'd turned to private investigating in order to find me and help other searching parents find their children." Hot tears slipped down her cheeks. Lord, she wanted Gil to have a happy ending with Mikey.

Gil wiped away her tears with his thumbs, capturing her face between his large palms. Paulina felt as though Gil was holding her heart in his hands and decided the brandy must be altering her perceptions. The warmth of his solid, muscled body spread through her, magnetic and overpowering. "Is that how you got into this racket?" he asked huskily.

She nodded. "I moved here to live near him. We had four great years together before he died of a heart attack."

"I'm sorry." His thumb caressed her cheekbone.

"Don't be. I'm grateful for every day we had together. He gave me unconditional love and a greater purpose in life—finding these kids. But the point is, he didn't give up hope—and neither should you." She smiled up at him, realizing that what made Gil a special man was his capacity to care. "We'll find Mikey, whether it takes a week, a month or years. Okay?"

"Okay." A faint determined smile tugged at his mouth, and Paulina felt her heart expand and contract. "What about your mom? Is she still alive?" he asked.

"My mom?" Her throat suddenly ached with tightly reined emotion. "She's still in Hartford, but that's another long story. Let's just say she isn't happy about my living in Ottawa and my choice of profession. She didn't even come to my wedding. Not that my marriage lasted long. I'd hoped Karl would understand my commitment to missing children because he was a police officer. He knew before we were married that I wasn't prepared to have children and he didn't take me seriously."

Gil frowned as though perplexed. "Why wouldn't you want to have children? You obviously love them."

Paulina lowered her eyes. "I do love kids. But the thought of being responsible for a child's upbringing terrifies me. I'm so afraid of making a mistake that'll leave emotional scars. There's no way to predict whether a marriage will last. People say that having children is supposed to bring couples closer, but just the talk of having a baby was driving Karl and me apart. I know it sounds selfish, but I just couldn't agree to have a child. In my heart, I knew I couldn't give Karl what he wanted and still be there for my missing kids."

"Selfish is not a word I'd use to describe you, Paulina. Ever," Gil said brusquely.

Paulina smiled, appreciating the accepting warmth of his fingers on her cheeks. The mood shifted subtly between them as her gaze rose to linger on the shadows hovering in his eyes. An insane and crazy desire to kiss him flared through her. His mouth hovered inches from hers. She wet her lips, the temptation so strong it pulled at her with invisible strings. It would be foolish. Stupid even. Her heartbeat tripled. She'd already conducted an experimental foray into that danger-laden zone.

Yet, her hand slowly slid over the muscled plateau of his chest to cup the back of his neck. She knew it was his love for a little boy that defeated all the logical, rational reasons why she shouldn't kiss him right now. His eyes shuttered closed as she planted moist, featherlight kisses on her brow, his lashes and his firm, supple lips. Something splintered in her as their tongues met in a tentative embrace. Fear and desire, passion and need passed between them in a heartbeat.

Paulina felt a sense of urgency stir within her as Gil groaned deep in his throat and slanted his mouth more firmly against hers, deepening the kiss. His fingers fanned over her back, creating a field of sensuous friction between her skin and the filmy fabric of her red crepe dress.

"Paulina," he whispered in a ragged tone, breaking their kiss to run a trail of wet, hot kisses along her jaw. "Is it hopeless for me to want you to spend the night?"

"No," she murmured, forcing him to recline on the sofa. Her nervous system went haywire with need as her breasts and pelvis came into glorious contact with his male counterparts. She knew they weren't talking about a relationship. They were both feeling vulnerable and were reaching out for comfort and moral support.

She sought the heat of his kiss, rotating her hips against his groin as his fingers slid under the hem of her dress and caressed her thighs. She gasped and braced her hands on his chest as whorls of sensation pulsed toward the core of her femininity. The light from the table lamp illuminated Gil's face. The sheer perfection of his features made her muscles clench deep inside her. Sometime she'd have to ask him how he acquired that perfect, rugged bump on his nose. But not now.

She moaned as he traced circles up her thighs, his fingers brushing higher and higher. Her nails dug into his shoulders in anticipation when he reached the lacy border of her panties and—stopped? Her eyes flew open in disappointment. She lifted her mouth from his and stared into his questioning indigo eyes.

He was waiting for her lead. Her invitation. She licked the tiny indentation in his chin, tasting his skin. "I'm a little wary of marriage and raising children, Gil. Not sex. Would you like to give me a tour of the master suite?"

Chapter Seven

Gil didn't require a second invitation. Admittedly, Paulina didn't quite fit the mold of the *significant other* he'd envisioned meeting someday, but running his fingers over her silk-clad legs ranked as one of the greatest pleasures he'd ever known. He had a feeling that sharing more intimate caresses with her would rank even higher.

Settling his hands around her slender middle, he rose to his feet, loving the way she was forced to clasp her legs around his waist to keep from tumbling to the floor. He had no intention of letting her fall, but the seductive feel of her moist heat pressed erotically against him had the blood thundering in his ears.

He carried her into the marble-tiled foyer and headed up the staircase. Paulina wasted no time. She loosened the buttons on his shirt and rubbed her fingers over his nipples, making him rigid with pleasure. Then she nipped his right pec with her teeth. Gil's blood pressure skyrocketed. Damn, even his ears were buzzing. It was all he could do to concentrate on climbing the oak steps without stumbling. He slipped his hands under her dress and kneaded her buttocks through the thin, silky layers of her panties and hose. She was wet for him. His thighs trembled. Hell, they might not make it to his bed.

She lifted her head, exposing her creamy white neck to

his lips. Gil eagerly ran his tongue over the tender spot below her jaw. "Wait, Gil, I think that's your phone," she said breathlessly. "You should answer it. It could be the police about Mikey."

Mikey. Anxiety pierced his lust as he set her down and pounded up the stairs to the bedroom extension. "Yeah?" His heart hammered wildly in his chest.

"Gil, honey? This is Mom. Is there any news about Mikey yet?" The grief rife in his mother's tone sent Gil crashing back into reality. He pulled the open flaps of his shirt together.

"Not yet," he replied. "But the P.I. I hired has uncovered some promising leads." *Oh, God, how am I going to tell her about Jean-Luc and Cindy?* Gil glanced toward the door, wondering if Paulina had followed him. She hadn't.

"Good. You can tell us all about it when we get there."

"You're coming here? Mom, that's not necessary. Dad hates not being at home. I've got everything under control."

"It's too late, honey. We're already on the road."

"On the road?" Gil croaked.

"I'm calling from a pay phone about twenty minutes away," his mother explained. "A neighbor was coming to Ottawa and offered us a lift. We want to be there to plan Cindy's memorial service. I tried calling your office this afternoon, but your secretary wasn't sure if you'd be coming in again. Can you put us up?"

"Of course, Mom. You don't have to ask."

"We just want to be near. When the police find Mikey, he'll need his grandma." Her voice broke.

It occurred to Gil that it had been a long time since he'd heard his mother laugh. "I'll see you soon, Mom."

He slowly hung up the phone. Maybe it was for the best

they were coming. They could learn the truth from him before the media televised the sordid story.

He walked into the upstairs hall. Through the oak railing he saw Paulina waiting near the front door, her purse slung over her shoulder. Her eyes were wide and wary as she gazed up at him.

"I heard," she said succinctly.

"My mom and dad are coming to stay with me for a while." Gil tapped the newel post twice, uncertain what to say next.

"It'll be good for you to have them around. Besides," she added, giving him a reserved smile as he descended the stairs, "they probably saved us from making a big mistake. You *are* my client."

Gil clamped his jaw tightly. There she went, pushing him away again. He hadn't imagined the way she'd touched him. His body ignited at the memory. He shoved his hands into the pockets of his slacks. "I could stop paying you."

"Nice try. Meet me for coffee tomorrow at nine in my office?"

He nodded.

This time she didn't offer him her hand in that charmingly assertive way of hers. "I'm going home to think."

As Gil watched her walk to her car, he refused to believe that sleeping with her could ever be a mistake. It would have been good to hold someone. And Paulina Stewart was a woman worth holding on to—even if it couldn't be forever.

FEELING SAFE UNDER THE protection of the night, the woman carried the crying infant out into the living room and settled into the maple rocker, where she could gaze out the window at the slumbering neighborhood. She could never be too careful.

The baby's cries increased.

"Hush, little one," she crooned. The chair made a rhythmic, soothing noise on the carpet. "It won't be long now. You'll meet your new mother and father soon. I promise."

And the next baby would be hers.

SHE'D ALMOST SLEPT with him. Worse, it was five minutes to nine and she was monitoring the clock for him. Paulina ran her fingers through her still-damp hair, realizing she was trembling with nervousness. She'd stayed up too late, going over the file and thinking about what almost happened with Gil.

Well, almost meant just that—*almost*. It didn't happen…and wouldn't *almost happen* ever again. She'd make darn sure of it. He was her client for heaven's sake. But that didn't stop her pulse from kick-starting when she heard Gil talking with Andrea in the reception area.

"Hi," she said far too happily, when he strolled into her office holding a mug of Andrea's fresh brew in his hand. He was dressed casually today, in denim jeans and shirt with the sleeves rolled up to his elbows. The top two buttons of his shirt weren't fastened, giving her a tantalizing glimpse of the dark hair feathering his chest. She told herself he could not have selected that shirt for any reason other than it was hanging in his closet. "Did your parents arrive?" she asked, determined not to inquire how he slept.

"Yeah, my dad's already complaining that the ramp I had built for his wheelchair isn't the right slope and the doorway into the dining room is too narrow."

Paulina smiled too brightly and fought the urge to hug him. "Sit down, I want to run a few ideas by you. It's been bugging me that Jean-Luc quit the day before their trip to Reno. Why would he do that if he was only going on vacation?"

"Maybe he'd already used up his paid vacation time and his employer wouldn't have given him the time off if he asked?" Gil suggested.

"Perhaps. Still, I find the timing interesting. It's quite possible their only motive was to give Cindy a change of scenery. She had been under a lot of stress. Cindy may not have told you because she was worried about your reaction to the fact she'd found someone else so soon. Or they were running off to get married, because they were worried about you legally seeking custody of Mikey. I asked Robbins last night if Cindy was pregnant, but the autopsy report said she wasn't, so we can rule out that possibility." Paulina glanced at her notes to keep from dwelling on every distracting detail of his appearance.

"Not to change the subject," she said faintly, "but do you remember seeing either Mikey's name—or the word *infant*—typed on Cindy's airplane ticket?"

He sipped his coffee, his brows knitting together. "I don't think so. Is it important?"

"It makes me curious. Infants don't need a ticket, but they're still required to be on the passenger list."

"Maybe Jean-Luc bought the tickets and didn't know he was supposed to mention it."

Maybe. Maybe not. But a hunch in the form of a knot in her stomach told her now was one of those times she should act on instinct. She jumped to her feet and tapped Gil's knee as she rounded her desk. "Come on, coffee break's over. Those tickets were bought at the travel agency in the Rideau Center. The mall will be open by the time we get there. It won't take long to check it out."

THE TRAVEL AGENCY KNEW exactly who had sold the tickets to Jean-Luc and Cindy. A homicide detective had just phoned, requesting the same information and the peppy heavyset agent was clearly enjoying the attention. Her flamboyant red-and-black silk kimono and flair for accessories suggested a predisposition for being center stage.

"I've never met a P.I. before," the travel agent confided in a voice loud enough for everyone in the office to hear as she carefully examined Paulina's license. "Do you know self-defense?"

"Yes. Could you tell me if the tickets were bought by phone or in person?"

"Why, in person." The woman rested her elbows on her desk and leaned forward. "The couple came in with their baby—a darling boy. He looked a lot like my son, Roger, at that age." She pointed toward a row of school photos tacked to her cubicle. "That's Roger now. He's nine."

"He's very handsome," Paulina murmured politely. "Was the infant put on the mother's ticket?"

"Oh, no. I asked if the baby would be accompanying them and she told me her mother would be watching him."

"Her mother?" Paulina's heart skipped a beat. Gil looked stunned. Cindy supposedly hadn't been in touch with her family for years.

"Yes. This was going to be an adult-only getaway." The agent lowered her booming tone. "I thought they were lucky to have a grandparent willing to baby-sit for two weeks. The most my husband and I ever got out of our parents was an evening. Not even a weekend!" Her expression grew suitably solemn. "Of course, they aren't lucky now, with both of them dead."

Paulina tapped her gold pen on her notepad. "Did Cindy mention anything else about her mother? Like her name or where she lived?"

"No. I told Detective Robbins the same thing. It's very strange. How could her mother have the baby and not come forward?" The agent toyed with a silver heron suspended from a chain around her neck. "Do you think people can have premonitions that something bad is going to happen? The baby's mother seemed so anxious about being away for such a long period. She had her arms locked around the baby the whole time they were here. Her husband reassured her everything would be okay, but now I wonder if her maternal instinct was warning her something terrible would happen. That happened with me once with Roger.'' Before the woman could relay her story, Paulina asked what date the tickets had been purchased.

"August twenty-seventh. They booked three weeks early, to get a cheaper fare. He came in and picked up the tickets. He paid cash."

Paulina thanked the woman for her time.

"What do you think?" she asked Gil as they cut through the mall toward the street exit.

"I don't know whether to feel more worried or relieved," Gil replied, shaking his head. "How could Cindy's mother have Mikey? She didn't keep in touch with her parents. Could they have meant Jean-Luc's mother?"

"That's what I was thinking. People don't always recall conversations accurately—they relate the gist of things and they embellish to make the telling a little more interesting."

They stopped at a crosswalk and waited for the light to change. The sky was overcast this morning. A chilly breeze swept down the narrow brick street and ruffled the skirt of Paulina's dress. She hugged her arms across her chest and took an unconscious step nearer to Gil's warmth. She wanted desperately for Mikey to be safe and sound in the care of Jean-Luc's mother.

"If they left Mikey with Jean-Luc's mother, why was the diaper bag still at Jean-Luc's?" she asked Gil. "And why was the stroller found with Cindy?"

"Hell, I don't know," he muttered grimly in her ear. "But I get your point."

The walk signal flashed and Paulina felt Gil's guiding hand rest on her back as they merged with the crowd crossing the street. How could such an insignificant gesture send sparks of awareness showering through her?

Paulina hopped onto the sidewalk. If she walked fast enough, he wouldn't be able to keep up with her, much less act like a gentleman. To her irritation, he moved to the curb, no doubt protecting her from reckless drivers. "Well, Robbins talked to the travel agent before we did," she said, growing breathless from her relentless pace. "You can be sure he and the other major-crime-unit detectives are contacting Jean-Luc's next of kin and tracking down Cindy's parents. They can find the information faster than I can. We'll call Robbins as soon as we get to my office. Maybe he's received the autopsy report on Jean-Luc."

At least once they got back to her office Gil was on the other side of the desk from her. A safe distance. Paulina put Robbins on the speaker phone so Gil could join the conversation. Robbins informed them the Edmonton police were searching for Cindy's parents. The coroner wouldn't have the autopsy results ready until later in the day. And they'd obtained Jean-Luc's mother's name and telephone number in Quebec City from his personnel file at the community center. Investigators were closing in on the address. He promised to call the moment he had news.

"So what do we do in the meantime—sit here and wait?" Gil asked, rubbing his forehead. His features were taut with tension.

Paulina tossed him her file. "Start reading this for inconsistencies. It could give us a new lead. I'm going to call that pregnancy counseling clinic. I never got around to it yesterday." She punched in the number.

"Hi, this is Mandy Steinberg. I have a message to call an Elvira—or Elva it looks like...at this number. Sorry, I can't make out the last name. My secretary's handwriting is terrible.''

The receptionist laughed. "You must mean Elva Madre. She's one of our counselors.''

"Great, could I book an appointment with her today?''

"I'm sorry, she's full this morning. She's taking a half day off and is leaving at noon. She has an opening October tenth in the afternoon.''

"Don't you have anything earlier?''

"Sorry, she's going away on holidays. Shall I pencil you in for the tenth?''

"No, thank you. She has my number. I'm sure she'll be in touch.'' Paulina hung up and glanced at her watch. It was eleven-thirty. They'd have to hurry to catch Elva before she left. She pushed back her chair and opened the bottom drawer of her desk. "Gil—''

"I know, let me guess. We're going somewhere.'' He was already on his feet.

She wrestled the drawer for her purse. The darn strap was caught on something. "How did you know?''

"I've been hanging around a P.I. and I'm getting good at interpreting her signals.'' He had the impudence to grin.

Paulina yanked her purse free, rattled by the sexy confidence in his smile. Lord help her if it was true. She just hoped he'd received her signals about what *almost happened* last night—loud and clear.

PAULINA WATCHED THE minutes tick away as Gil maneuvered through lunch-hour traffic to the counseling clinic in the Glebe. Thanks to his expert driving skills and several close shaves on yellow lights, he dropped her at a bus zone with seconds to spare before noon, then raced off to find a parking spot. Paulina hurried into the clinic.

With unfeigned breathlessness, she told the receptionist she was a friend of Elva's. "I was hoping to catch her before she went on holidays. Please don't tell me I've missed her?''

"No, she's still here. Her last appointment just left. Her office is the third door on the right. I'll buzz her if you like?''

"That's not necessary. I want to surprise her.'' Paulina flashed the receptionist a grateful smile and cleared out before the receptionist asked for her name. A woman of medium height and heavy around the hips was locking the door of the office Paulina was seeking. Her mousy hair, liberally laced with gray threads, was cut short. She wore a calf-length flowing dress and a crocheted ecru cotton vest. She turned when Paulina asked if she was Elva Madre. Her thick lenses made her blue eyes appear enormous.

"I'm Elva.'' Her soft, compassionate voice suited her occupation.

Paulina dug into her purse and showed her ID, explaining the details of Cindy's death and Mikey's kidnapping. The counseling center probably had strict rules about confidentiality, too. But Paulina hoped Elva would bend the rules under the circumstances.

"I'm aware of the woman's death,'' Elva admitted, moving down the corridor. Paulina thought she saw an uneasy flicker magnified in her eyes. Or was it the glare from the overhead fluorescent lights? "I saw the news last night. Have the police found the baby yet?''

"No. I know Cindy talked to you when she was pregnant with Mikey. One of Cindy's friends told me you worked with her.''

"What a shame,'' Elva said sadly. "After all Cindy's indecision and worrying it would come to this—a murder-suicide. You'll really have to excuse me, Ms. Stewart. I'm running late—and I don't see how I can help you, anyway. The clinic has a stringent confidentiality policy.''

Paulina kept stride with the counselor. "I understand

your policy,'' she replied with equal equanimity, lowering
her voice as they crossed the waiting room. ''But I'm trying to assist Cindy's family in finding her baby. It would
help my investigation if you could confirm when you last
spoke to Cindy?'' Was it the exercise of pushing the lobby
door open or the cool wind brewing outdoors that suddenly
turned the counselor's cheeks red?

''Excuse me,'' Elva said in a dismissive tone, turning
south down the street.

Paulina doggedly followed her. ''Ms. Madre, the like-
lihood of finding Mikey diminishes with each passing second. I know for a fact you spoke to Cindy recently. Did
she tell you she was leaving town with her boyfriend Jean-
Luc? Or mention who she planned to leave Mikey with?
Her mother? Another relative? A friend?''

''Really, Ms. Stewart. I'd like to help, but I can't.''

''I don't believe that. How can you live with yourself,
knowing that your deliberate silence may be preventing an
infant from being reunited with grieving family mem-
bers?''

''I have no comment.'' Elva's lips pressed tightly together as she darted into a pay lot and let herself into a
rusty blue Volvo.

Paulina memorized the license plate number as Elva
drove off, her brakes squealing and her muffler rattling
ominously. Damn! Why did she have the feeling Elva
knew more than she was telling? It would take a subpoena
to get that woman talking, and meanwhile the clock was
ticking.

Paulina recorded the plate number and Elva's name in
her notebook, placing a question mark beside the surname
Madre. She'd be very interested to know who that car was
registered to. She'd worked on a case in Mexico once, and
if memory served correct, *madre* meant mother in Spanish.
Paulina didn't believe in odd, little coincidences.

She looked up at the sound of a horn blaring. Gil's car was blocking traffic. He must have seen her leave with Elva and had followed. He rolled down the passenger-side window and called for her to hop in.

Paulina glanced down the street and sighed. Elva's Volvo was nowhere in sight. They'd missed a perfect opportunity to follow her. She climbed into the car. "I didn't get anything out of Elva," she confessed, trying not to let her frustration show. Gil needed her to be strong and optimistic. She flashed him a brief smile. "Maybe the autopsy results will be available when we get back to my office."

Gil nodded, his attention on the road. "I was thinking about the diaper bag and the luggage in Jean-Luc's car. We should ask the police whether the suitcases contained Jean-Luc's stuff, or Cindy's and Mikey's, too."

Paulina dropped her hand to his knee. "Good..." The instant her fingers made contact with his firm thigh, her voice trailed off. She'd told herself she wasn't going to touch him, wasn't going to get near him, and here she'd instigated the contact. She pulled her fingers away quickly as though she'd touched hot coals. Gil, blessedly, didn't seem to notice.

He used his car phone to check in with his parents. Paulina found herself wondering what they were like. Did Gil take after his mother or his father—or both?

When he'd finished, she directed him to a burger place for food to go. They could eat at her office. A growing sense of urgency pressed at the base of her spine, and experience had taught her not to dispute it.

Andrea informed them, when they arrived, that Robbins hadn't called back yet.

"Why don't you go on your lunch break now?" Paulina suggested. "We'll be in for a while." She grabbed a breaded chicken sandwich from the bag, then told Gil he could pull his chair up to her desk to eat, while she hunted down a couple of books.

She found a Spanish dictionary and a baby name book in the reference library, which was an avoidance term for her dad's old office. She still hadn't got used to her dad not being around, but at least she felt his presence with her like a guardian angel looking over her shoulder, guiding her in the right direction. She hoped he was exerting a little heavenly intervention now. She needed his patience and wisdom to find Mikey. And to keep her from making a fool of herself with Gil.

Gil glanced up when Paulina entered the room as if she were running a race. Didn't the woman ever stop? Not that he wasn't grateful for her single-minded devotion to Mikey's case, but he wouldn't be upset if she sat down for five minutes to eat her lunch. He'd already downed one of his two double-decker burgers.

"What are those for?" Gil asked, eyeing the books in her hand.

"I wanted to look up Elva Madre's name, to satisfy my curiosity." The pages of the baby book crackled crisply as Paulina hunted down the counselor's name. "Aha," she nearly crowed, her eyes gleaming like silver moonlight. "Elva means good counselor." She picked up the smaller book, which appeared to be a dictionary, and thumbed through the pages, her dusky pink lips pursed in concentration.

Gil couldn't budge his gaze from her mouth, remembering the way she'd bared his chest last night and licked his pectorals. And *bit him*. He stiffened instantly. The air turned thick, making breathing difficult. The soft, clinging knit dress shot with metallic gold thread that Paulina wore shimmered suggestively when she moved. The dress showed every luscious curve and hollow he'd been denied last night.

She tapped a page with her index finger, pulling him sharply from the lustful bent of his thoughts.

"There it is. *Madre* means mother in Spanish. I knew that name had to be a fictitious name."

Gil didn't question how she knew it. He merely accepted her gift as amazing.

The phone rang, startling them both. Anxiety stole Gil's appetite as Paulina reached for it. Was it the autopsy results?

"Hi, Karl. I was hoping you'd call."

Gil frowned at his French fries. Wasn't Karl Paulina's ex-husband? He glanced away to give her privacy, but not before he noticed the color seeping into her cheeks. For some reason that blush rankled him. Was she still in love with Karl? Gil hoisted himself out of his chair to leave the room, but Paulina waved at him to remain seated.

"You've got what?" Her voice rose with excitement. She grabbed a pen and started writing furiously. "Where? When? That's fabulous. Thanks, Karl. I owe you big-time."

Gil ground his teeth and squirmed in his chair, hoping the creaking leather would drown out the details of whatever they were arranging. Gil didn't want to know what Karl had said that made Paulina's eyes glow with satisfaction, nor did he want to speculate what Paulina owed Karl big-time. Gil absolutely did not want to dwell on the possibility that Paulina's legs had ever been wrapped tightly around another man's waist, especially not when her slightest touch—or one look at her soft lips—made Gil hard with wanting her.

She hung up, beaming. "The RCMP Missing Children's Center has found out that one child was the victim of a stranger abduction in a town along Tweedie's work route."

Gil stared at her, confused. She hadn't been arranging a date with her ex-husband? His momentary sense of relief was replaced by the sobering awareness that Paulina didn't want the home life Gil had spent years carefully planning.

"How old was the child?" Gil asked.

"Nine months old. He was taken from a stroller during a church picnic. Now, it could be a coincidence," she cautioned, "but it's a promising lead. It may indicate that Jean-Luc found Cindy's body—maybe they'd arranged to meet somewhere—and took his own life in his grief. Damn, we need those autopsy results."

As if on cue, the phone rang again.

Gil felt his heart twitch when Paulina put her hand over the receiver and mouthed Robbins's name. He gripped the edge of the desk waiting for Jean-Luc's autopsy report. But to Gil's disappointment, the conversation was short and sweet. Paulina agreed to a meeting at the police station in half an hour.

"Why do they want us to go there?" he asked when she'd terminated the call. "Do you think they've found Mikey?"

"No. If they'd found Mikey they'd tell us or come see us—particularly if the news was bad. My guess is the autopsy results are very interesting," Paulina mused.

Gil abandoned his lunch, feeling distinctly ill at ease. The way she'd said interesting, made him think interesting was definitely not good. Hell, was Robbins planning on interviewing him again?

ROBBINS'S EXPRESSION didn't give anything away, Paulina thought as she and Gil were shown to seats in an interrogation room. Detective Zuker looked slightly more relaxed as he offered them a drink.

"Have you received the autopsy results?" she asked Robbins, impatient with his intimidation ploys. He was seated at a large wooden table, his hands folded neatly on top of a tan file folder.

"Yes, we did, Ms. Stewart, but we'll get to that all in due time," he replied calmly. His tone intensified the discomposing jingle of alarms sounding in her head. She knew darn well that Robbins had something major to report or he wouldn't have summoned them. "First, the Edmonton police have interviewed Cindy's parents. Apparently, they haven't heard from her in years. They didn't know she had a baby. And I'm sad to say they frankly didn't care." Robbins cleared his throat.

Paulina mentally crossed that possibility off her list and glanced anxiously at Gil.

"We got a report from the GRC in Quebec City. They searched the home of Jean-Luc's mother. There's no sign of an infant. Madame Deveau claims she hasn't seen or talked to her son since Christmas."

"What about Jean-Luc's father?" Paulina asked.

"There's no contact there. The father deserted the family when Jean-Luc was three years old." Robbins opened the file on the table and an uncomfortable silence multiplied in the room as he scanned the top page as if reacquainting himself with the information. "As for the autopsy report, I have some disturbing news." Robbins raised his cold gray gaze from the autopsy report and zoomed in on Gil.

Dread clawed at Paulina's skin. She saw what was coming like a lob pitch. Instinctively, she reached for Gil's arm.

"The coroner concludes Jean-Luc Deveau was murdered," Robbins stated in a deceptively factual tone. "Would you happen to know anything about that, Mr. Boyer?"

Chapter Eight

Before Paulina could stop him, Gil bounded out of his chair like a panther in pursuit of a meal. Anger radiated from him as he leaned over Robbins, the muscles in his neck standing out like thick ropes. His massive fists looked capable of splintering the table and Robbins's smug expression in a single blow.

"Listen here, Detective. I didn't do it," he said, barely controlling his contempt. "So, why don't you stop wasting the taxpayers' money and look for the person who did?"

Zuker put a restraining hand on Gil's arm. Gil had the good sense not to shrug it away.

Paulina stood. "Detective Robbins," she said coolly. "If you're prepared to lay charges against my client, then inform him of his right to counsel and caution him. You may not have any worthwhile leads to pursue, but we do. In fact, we're prepared to share that information with you, in the interests of finding Mikey as expediently as possible."

Robbins's irises narrowed to pinpoints. He gestured with his hand. "Sit down, Mr. Boyer, and keep a lid on your temper."

Gil's jaw hardened into a granite ledge, but he resumed his seat. Paulina breathed an inward sigh of relief. *Men and testosterone.* "When was Jean-Luc killed?" she asked, flipping to a blank page in her notebook to jot down the specifics.

"Saturday night. A neighbor saw him arrive home about nine-thirty. The autopsy report indicates Jean-Luc was left-handed, but the gun was found in his right hand. The location and the angle of the entry wound make it extremely unlikely the injury was self-inflicted. The forensics lab is determining whether the strap of the diaper bag was the ligature used to kill Cindy."

Paulina raised her eyebrows in surprise, puzzling over the information.

"What about the luggage you found in the trunk of Jean-Luc's Mustang?" Gil asked, his voice hopeful. "Were Mikey's belongings there?"

"Actually, no," Robbins admitted. He extracted a list from the file and ran a finger down it. "There was clothing for a man and a woman. But the only items suitable for an infant were a rattle and one newborn-size outfit. Of course, there were diapers, a bottle of juice, two cans of baby formula and such in the diaper bag." He passed them a copy of the list.

"So whoever has Mikey has his clothes," Gil commented as Paulina held the list where they both could see. He pointed at the description of the outfit—a baseball uniform with a matching hat. "Ted bought that the day Mikey was born," he said quietly.

Paulina glanced up at Robbins. "It says there was a packet of photos. Of what?"

"The baby mostly. Newborn stuff." He gestured at his partner. "Zuker, get the photos."

Zuker left the room and returned almost immediately with several sheets of bristol board on which the photos had been mounted. He laid them on the table.

"There were none of Jean-Luc, the murder victim, but

we'd like to know who this man is." Zuker's beefy finger indicated a man bearing a strong resemblance to Gil.

"He's my brother," Gil said, his Adam's apple bobbing.

"And he died about two months ago?" Zuker inquired.

"Yeah."

Zuker nodded, his black eyes opaque. "Look at the pictures carefully, Mr. Boyer. Were any of them taken at places you're not familiar with or with people you don't recognize?"

Paulina noticed there were several photos of Ted holding Mikey. Gil identified his parents—Gil had inherited his size from his dad and his indigo eyes from his mother—and explained three of the photos were taken at their residence in Kingston. The rest were taken at the hospital or Ted's apartment.

Robbins seemed disappointed. "I've had a team of investigators combing the location where Cindy was found, but so far we've drawn a blank. No one saw anything. We've had a few calls about possible sightings that we've checked out thoroughly. But there's been nothing solid. However, forensics found some carpet fibers in the doormat at Jean-Luc's place that matched the fibers found on Cindy's body. So, it's likely the same person killed them."

"Have you had someone interview Edison Tweedie, the salesman we talked to in Winnipeg?" Paulina asked.

"Yes, I spoke to him by phone. He told me basically what he told you in your report. Why?"

"I think we should delve deeper into Tweedie's background," Paulina replied. "He was the last person to see Cindy alive." She told him her theory that Tweedie might have abducted Mikey to sell him. "I've learned from the RCMP Missing Children's Center that a nine-month-old boy was abducted July third of last year from a stroller during a church picnic at a park in Swift Current, Saskatchewan, which is along Tweedie's route. It shouldn't be too hard to find out where he was that day. He follows a regular schedule.'' She crossed her legs. ''It's possible Tweedie killed Cindy and Jean-Luc and planted the diaper bag in Jean-Luc's home to throw off the police.''

Gil leaned forward, his hands on his thighs. ''Cindy talked to Tweedie for quite a while that morning. She told him all about her problems, maybe even mentioned the trip she and Jean-Luc planned. She probably made it easy for him. They were leaving town, anyway. Who would miss them? Is it possible Tweedie helped himself to Mikey's clothes while he was at Jean-Luc's?''

Robbins rubbed his narrow jaw thoughtfully. ''Maybe. But that still doesn't explain the three-day time delay between Cindy's murder and Jean-Luc's.''

''Unless it took three days for Tweedie to locate Jean-Luc,'' Paulina suggested. ''He'd been seen at the diner talking to Cindy. He knew he'd be suspected. He probably jimmied the patio door of Cindy's apartment, thinking Jean-Luc lived with her.''

''I'll put some manpower on this right away,'' Robbins promised. ''Was there anything else?'' He looked at Paulina expectantly.

''Actually, I've found out the name of a counselor whom Cindy spoke to recently. This woman may be the only person who knows what was going on inside Cindy's head—and about her relationship with Jean-Luc. She works at a private counseling clinic. I tried to talk to her earlier today, but no dice. She *was* aware that Mikey was missing and Cindy and Jean-Luc were both dead.''

''Let's see what she has to say to me. Have you got the clinic's number?'' Robbins reached for the phone.

''Yes, but she's gone for the day—supposedly on holidays. I do have her license plate number.'' Paulina felt a blush graze her cheeks. ''I happened to have a pen handy when she drove away from work. It might save time if you contact her directly at home." She read him the number from her notebook. "By the way, you might want to run a criminal-records check on her. I'm fairly certain Elva Madre isn't her real name. I looked it up in a book and it means 'good counselor to mothers.'"

Robbins whistled. "Could I offer you a job, Ms. Stewart?" he said.

"No, thank you. I already have a job," she replied crisply. Though, it never hurt to win a little respect. Maybe Robbins would be more forthcoming now.

"Zuker, don't stand there with your mouth hanging open. Do as the lady says. Run the plate and get me the woman's home phone number."

Paulina snuck a glance at Gil; he was smiling at her. She smiled back, feeling a giddy warmth bubble in her chest. The admiration in Gil's eyes meant a whole lot more to her than Robbins's grudging acceptance.

"Could I have a look at Cindy and Jean-Luc's autopsy reports while we're waiting?" she asked.

"Sure." He passed her the documents.

She and Gil were still reading when Zuker hustled into the room several minutes later. Perspiration shone on his broad forehead and formed rings on his white shirt under the arms. "Looks like Ms. Stewart is on to something," he puffed. "The Volvo's registered to a Karen Louise Jamieson, who was convicted of forcible confinement in Vancouver five years ago for holding a pregnant woman against her will. She served three years' probation."

"Sounds like Ms. Jamieson changed her name and came to Ottawa for a fresh start," Paulina observed.

Beside her, Gil suddenly snapped his fingers. "I admit this is a stretch...but could Elva Madre be the mother Cindy was referring to?"

Paulina sucked in her breath. She hadn't thought of that.

She was going to have to stop charging Gil extra if he kept making brilliant suggestions like that.

Robbins stood up. "Under the circumstances, we'll pay Ms. Jamieson a personal visit."

"Mind if we tag along?" Paulina asked, rising with the detective.

He gave Paulina, then Gil a long, measuring gaze. "No. Just don't get in the way."

Paulina wouldn't dream of it. She recognized a privilege when it was handed to her. She just hoped Elva hadn't cleared out of town with Mikey.

KAREN JAMIESON LIVED in a faded white cottage on Broadway Avenue just off Bronson. A scarlet-leaved ivy obscured the front screen porch and made it difficult to tell if anyone was home—particularly from their vantage point down the block. Gil tightly gripped the steering wheel of his car, feeling knots of tension cramp in his biceps. Robbins could have let them park closer to the action. Gil watched as a team of officers wearing police vests crawled through the overgrown shrubbery like beetles and surrounded the house.

"Do you have binoculars in your car?" Paulina asked, fidgeting. "I don't see Elva's Volvo, but it might be parked in the back lane."

He shook his head, trying to ignore the fact his stomach felt as though someone wearing cleats had kicked him in the gut. Was Mikey in there? "Who keeps binoculars in their car, anyway?"

"I do. And I thought you might. You probably have season tickets to the Rough Riders' games."

He flashed her an unsteady grin. "You're half right. My tickets are on the fifty-yard line. You like football? You don't strike me as the type."

"My father was a Buffalo Bills fan. I rooted for the

opponent just to bug him.'' A wistful expression appeared in her silvery eyes, making Gil wonder if she worked so hard just to keep the loneliness from gnawing at her—the way he did. "What's your team?" she asked.

"Northwestern's my alma mater. Other than that, I'm a Chicago Bears fan.'' Gil straightened and broke into a cold sweat as Robbins opened the screen door and entered the porch.

A moment later, Robbins reappeared. His arm movements suggested he was ordering the officers to peer in the windows for movement inside the house. Gil tried to fend off a crushing sense of disappointment.

"She's not home,'' Paulina said decisively. "Look, he's dispatching officers to go door-to-door. Maybe one of the neighbors noticed something. The houses are close together. The cry of a baby would be easily heard.''

Gil nodded.

Minutes passed at an excruciating pace. Five. Ten. Twenty. *Had Robbins forgotten they were here?* Forty minutes later, as dusk settled over the street, Robbins approached their car. Gil let out an explosive sigh of relief.

The detective rested his hands on the open window. "Here's the situation. Karen's not in the house. A neighbor across the back lane spotted her around two this afternoon, loading her car with luggage. No sign of an infant. The neighbor to the east says Elva—that's what she called Karen—notified her she'd be going out of town for a week and asked her to keep an eye on the house. That neighbor also said Karen had visitors on Sunday last—a man, a woman and a baby.''

Gil's jaw shot up as hope welled anew in his heart. "Do you think the baby was Mikey?''

Robbins wet his lips. "Hard to say. The witness couldn't provide a description because the infant was wrapped in a blanket. All we got on the couple is the husband looked like a university professor—tall, skinny, receding hairline. Hair light brown or blond. Wire-rimmed glasses. The woman is medium height, shoulder-length red hair. We're doing everything possible to find out where Karen Jamieson went. We've got reasonable grounds to obtain search warrants for the house and the files of the counseling clinic. But it'll take a few hours. We've got someone working on the Tweedie angle, too. Why don't you go home and get some rest, Mr. Boyer? We'll keep you posted.''

As the detective walked away, Gil dropped his chin to his chest and banged his fist against the steering wheel. *Damn, so close.* And yet, Mikey still felt woefully out of reach.

''ARE YOU SURE YOU don't want to come to my place?'' Gil asked, taking Paulina's hand in his after he swung his sports car to the curb outside her Clarence Street office. The glow from the streetlight illuminated his fatigue-ridden features. Paulina's heart squeezed with empathy as she stroked the back of his hand with her thumb.

''Robbins might call with news,'' he continued, ''and, I'd like my parents to meet you. It's only seven-thirty. I could drive you home later.''

Paulina waffled, torn between her common sense and an irrational desire to be with him. They'd stopped for pizza, but neither of them was hungry. Paulina could smell the sausage and mushrooms in the box on the back seat. It was strange sitting in the car with him, with the engine humming impatiently as though urging her to make a decision. But she knew there was more to Gil's invitation than hand-holding support. They'd come perilously close to sleeping together the previous night—not that there was any chance of that happening tonight with his parents occupying the guest room.

But meeting his parents would be another step toward the intimacy she was trying to avoid. She already knew too much about Gil—liked too much about him. She didn't want to be in the position of knowing what his parents were like. Didn't want his mother sizing her up as prospective daughter-in-law material. If Cindy's friends could pick up on the attraction humming between her and Gil, then Gil's mother could, too.

Paulina decided it would be best for both her and Gil if they didn't get any more involved than they already were. They were holding hands now, for heaven's sake, and her insides were melting to honey.

"Robbins probably won't phone till tomorrow," she said softly. "They'll search Elva's house with a fine-tooth comb and that takes time. The same applies with the counseling clinic's files." She lifted her free hand and stroked his cheek, achingly aware of the contrast between the sandpaper stubble and the soft fibers of his hair at his temples. His breath stirred on her wrist. "Besides, your parents are waiting for you and you're running on empty. You need to rest."

"You're probably right."

She heard the hesitation in his voice. His eyes were dark, unreadable. She sensed he was holding back too, pretending the need rising between them wasn't real. Didn't exist.

"Good night, Gil." She severed the contact between them and fumbled for the door latch. She would have watched as he drove away, but she knew he'd wait until she was safely upstairs in her apartment with the lights turned on before he drove off. He was that kind of man— considerate and caring.

With a small sigh, she headed straight for the shower, hoping the pulse of hot water would relieve some of the tension flowing through her. She towel dried her hair and slipped into an oversize T-shirt before crawling into bed. Exhaustion settled in her tired limbs, but her mind refused to succumb to her body's need for sleep. The awareness that she could have invited Gil in dominated her thoughts. He could be sharing her bed with her now. She rolled over and smoothed the spare pillow on her queen-size bed.

She'd made the right decision, hadn't she?

Yes, she had. Gil would make another woman very happy someday.

Firmly, she nudged her fantasies aside and redirected the flow of her thoughts toward Mikey. And Elva. If she couldn't sleep, she might as well work.

Why would Elva agree to look after Mikey for two weeks? Had she duped Cindy by offering to baby-sit, with the intention of abducting Mikey and disappearing? Maybe Cindy got nervous and tried to back out of the arrangement and Elva killed her and Jean-Luc. Elva could have planted the diaper bag in Jean-Luc's apartment. Maybe Elva didn't think Cindy was a suitable mother. But would a family counselor commit murder—twice?

Questions started coming at her fast and loose. Paulina scrambled out of bed and grabbed her briefcase, which she'd left in the living room. She took it back to bed with her and pulled out her pen to make notes as she reread the file in search of a new set of answers. Had Cindy met Elva for lunch that fatal Wednesday?

An hour and a half later, she picked up Tweedie's statement. As far as Paulina was concerned, he was still a suspect. She flipped through the pages. What had he said about Elva?

The buzz of the doorbell suddenly broke Paulina's concentration. It was half past eleven. Who could it be at this hour? The police?

Wary, she hurried to the front door and pushed the button on the intercom that allowed her to screen her visitors. "Yes?"

"It's me. Gil. I noticed your light was on. Can I come up?"

She closed her eyes as a rush of longing swelled in her throat. Why did even the sound of his voice penetrate every last one of her defenses? Her finger hovered over the button controlling the security gate. With a sense of inevitability she released the gate, granting him access.

Was it her imagination, or could she hear his every step on the stairs? Or was that her heartbeat? She combed her fingers through her hair and took a deep, steadying breath before she opened her door to him.

Her knees dipped convulsively as her gaze locked with his. That ever-logical part of her brain warned her she was being foolhardy. That she'd regret it in the morning. But her eyes greedily took in every detail of his handsome face. Every nuance. Every shadow. Every fear.

Was he as afraid as she was? The muscles of his body rippled beneath his denim shirt and lightweight jacket. His jeans clung suggestively to his thighs as he mounted the stairs. Paulina felt woozy with the overpowering desire to be with this man. To know him in the most vulnerable way a woman can know a man.

He stopped on the private landing outside her door, dominating the secluded tile enclosure with his presence in the same way he dominated her mind and her heart. His eyes were dark with need. "I couldn't sleep, so I decided to go for a drive. If you want me to leave, I will..."

Her heart melted along with whatever last-ditch refusal her mind was attempting to compose. Shaking her head, she lifted her arms and closed the space between them in three steps. A sigh escaped her as his arms circled her in a tight embrace, and her mouth joined with his. The heat of him swept over her in a tidal wave, obliterating the coldness penetrating her soles from the tile floor.

She clung to him, her fingers delving into the softness of his hair as their tongues traced the first steps of an erotic dance. She felt his hands slip under her T-shirt. A volley of shivers skated over her skin as he possessively cupped her bare buttocks, then slid his fingers in seductive circles over her hips and rib cage to finally lay claim to her breasts. Paulina arched against the heat of his palms, feeling a responsive inner clenching as his thumbs teased her nipples with exquisite care.

Gil broke their kiss and laid a path of searing kisses down her neck that raised goose bumps on her arms. He tugged impatiently at her T-shirt with one hand, bunching it up as he bent his head to caress her breasts with his tongue, toying with the nubs until they jutted out proudly and she was panting with need. The moist heat of his mouth shattered her. She dug her fingers into his shoulders for support as the shards of her self-control melted into a simmering pool of tension.

There was no going back. She wanted him too much.

The hard planes and edges of his muscled body beckoned her to explore downward. She bypassed the row of silver buttons on his shirt and went straight for his leather belt. She loosened it with trembling hands and unzipped his jeans.

Spurred on by Gil's guttural moan and the thrusting of his hips, she slipped her fingers beneath the band of his briefs and palmed the smoothness of his powerful erection. Lord, he was magnificent, and she hadn't gotten his clothes off yet.

She felt the feathery brush of his fingers on her inner thigh and a jolt of sheer, sweet ecstasy as one finger dipped into her and found a point of intense pleasure.

His touch felt so exquisitely right. She stroked him in return, wanting to give back as much as she got.

Legs quaking from his tender assault, Paulina threw her head back. Her eyes lifted heavenward at the sensations rocketing through her like errant missiles set to explode. Her gaze fell on the brass stairwell light. Gradually, their surroundings registered in her passion-clouded thoughts. *My God, they were on the landing!* Not that anyone could see them from the carriageway below. But still...

"Gil," she whispered, nibbling on his ear, loathing to stop even for an instant. She traced the tip of his erection with her finger, empowered and awed by his straining response. He was so hard. She didn't want anything to break the spell of what was happening between them. "We're not inside my apartment yet."

He lifted his head from her breast, his breath tickling her taut nipple. "I can fix that," he muttered hoarsely. He picked her up and she clung to him, hooking her legs tightly around his waist and nearly going mad at the feel of his maleness so close to the center of her desire.

He kicked her apartment door shut. "Paulina, you feel so good," he said thickly, pounding down the hallway to her bedroom.

An unaccustomed shyness clutched her as he peeled off her T-shirt leaving her naked to his gaze, but it disappeared when she saw the wonder and desire glimmering in the depths of his eyes.

"You're so damn beautiful, Paulina. I want to love you and show you how special you are."

Paulina assumed he meant love in a physical sense, not an emotional sense, but she was beyond clarifying things. Her fingers were already helping him remove his jacket and shirt. Then his jeans and the sexy gray briefs. His arousal surged, warm and ready against her thigh as he joined her on the bed. She scooted closer to him, eager to receive his weight. Eager to receive him inside her.

"Not yet," he said, parting her thighs. He stroked her with a skill that stopped all her objections and turned them into whimpers as she writhed beneath him. He kissed her deeply, tormenting her with the coaxing play of his tongue, while his other hand fondled her breast. Paulina felt the sensations overlap and merge, building steadily in an intensity that could have no end. But she was wrong.

Calling out his name, she grasped his shoulders and hung on tightly as a spasm shuddered through her in a pulsing wave. She kissed him greedily, hungrily, as a second wave hit. Then another and another. And then she went over the edge into a dark abyss.

Her skin was damp with perspiration when she finally opened her eyes and realized Gil was leaning over her, a distinctly proud male smile on his lips. She cupped his face and drew him down to kiss her, closing her eyes so he couldn't see the wonder she felt burgeoning inside her. She and Karl had had a healthy sex life, but it had been nothing like this... Nothing that made her lose consciousness with pleasure.

And if the slow, seductive way Gil was massaging her breasts and whispering promises in her ear was any indication, there was more to come. Her breasts felt full and achy as the restlessness renewed inside her. A restlessness for him. Her hands moved feverishly over the firm, smooth plates of his pectorals and the double ridges of his abs, seeking his maleness. She opened herself to him, urging him inside.

"Wait, sweetheart. Let me protect you first," Gil whispered.

Paulina wasn't sure where the foil packet came from, only that it took seconds that were too agonizingly long for him to sheathe himself. Then finally he pushed her back on the coolness of her sheets and entered her, inch by inch, until Paulina thought she'd go absolutely crazy with wanting him. She arched into him, meeting his powerful thrusts with everything in her. She could feel the tension tightening in the muscles of his back with each forceful thrust, his rhythm escalating. The tension between them built to a perfect sweetness, so fine and hard and tight.

It was too much and too good... Just when Paulina thought she couldn't take it anymore, Gil gave a final thrust and she soared on a crescendo of feeling as Gil shuddered and reached his own climax. She tightened her hold around his waist and pulled his full weight upon her, not yet willing for him to withdraw.

She felt his every breath as his chest rose and fell rapidly. Every thunderous hammer of his heart echoed in her rib cage. Her hair stuck to his damp shoulder, but she didn't care. She kissed his shoulder, tasting the faint saltiness of his skin, then snuggled her chin into the crook of his neck and smiled wryly. Now she knew how Eve must have felt after the first bite of that forbidden fruit. Hungry for more.

THE WEIGHT OF A TREE limb pressed against her chest roused Paulina from sleep. Instinctively, she tried to push it off, but when her fingers came in contact with warm skin and crispy hair she realized Gil's arm was thrown protectively across her and she was in the Garden of Eden. She touched him ever so lightly, not wanting to disturb him but needing to assure herself she wasn't dreaming. That their lovemaking hadn't been a fantasy.

It wasn't. He was real. The scent of their mating clung to her skin and the sheets. Last night was real. Details slowly filtered back to her—along with the sobering knowledge that had it not been for Gil's foresight she would have slept with him without protection.

She turned her head to look at his face, not knowing whether to be grateful to Gil or angry with herself.

His features were obscured by shadow, but as her eyes adjusted to the dark, she was able to make out the contours of his cheeks, the strong edge of his jaw, the bump in his nose. His breath rasped against her bare skin. A stirring of emotion twisted sharp and sweet in her body. She stared at Gil for a long moment, battling the feeling, battling him, trying to deny his tender ministrations had made her so mindless she'd forgotten about birth control. She'd always been extremely careful—paranoid even—during her marriage. But then, truth to tell, she hadn't needed birth control since she and Karl had parted.

She ran her hand over her flat belly and said a quiet prayer of thanks that Gil had saved her from that worry—this time. But boy, oh, boy, every languid, satisfied inch of her body warned her she was still in deep, deep trouble.

Wide-awake now, Paulina slipped out of bed being careful not to disturb Gil. She didn't know how much sleep he'd had lately, but she would bet it wasn't nearly enough. Shivering at the chill in the morning air, she fumbled on the floor for her T-shirt and found it heaped on top of her briefcase on the floor. She pulled her T-shirt over her head, then retrieved her briefcase and Mikey's file and tiptoed into the living room. Work was always her cure for disturbing thoughts.

She turned on the lights, pausing as her gaze fell on the photograph of her and her dad on her wedding day. She stepped closer, wishing her dad were here with her now.

It occurred to her that Gil was much like her father. Gil wouldn't give up searching for Mikey any more than her dad had given up searching for her. Paulina pressed her lips into a thin line. And her father had expected her mother to be content staying at home and raising Paulina. Her mother's second act of independence—her first being to flee to the United States with Paulina—had been to get a job doing clerical work for an insurance company.

Even if Paulina wanted a casual relationship with a man right now—her father had casually dated other women— Gil would not be a suitable candidate. Once they found Mikey, Gil would be searching for a woman to take care of his nephew.

With a small sigh, Paulina piled her briefcase and file on her blanket chest-coffee table, then snuggled into the corner of the couch nearest the reading lamp and pulled a rose wool afghan across her lap. A searching parent had knitted the afghan. Paulina had located Diane Little's five kids in a suburb of Los Angeles the previous year. They had been reunited with their mother and now lived in Windsor, Ontario.

Paulina fingered the checkered pattern in the soft wool and smiled. Sometimes, all it took was a little reminder to get her head straight. She reached for her file, trying to remember where she'd left off reading the night before. With Tweedie? She found her notes about his conversation with Cindy and started to read.

She hadn't got past the third paragraph when two sentences seemed to leap off the page. *"She said a man had given her an ultimatum—was trying to tell her what to do about the baby. I was under the impression she might have to give up her son."*

Paulina drew in a sharp breath as a connection clicked in her brain. She reread the sentences a second time. Was it wishful thinking—or had she been looking at this case from the wrong angle?

Chapter Nine

What if the man Cindy referred to as pressuring her to give up her child was Jean-Luc—not Gil? Paulina's thoughts raced as she explored the possibility. Maybe Jean-Luc didn't want anything to do with another man's son and had encouraged Cindy to give Mikey up for adoption. Jean-Luc probably didn't think anything of abandoning Mikey. Hadn't Robbins said Jean-Luc's father had cleared out when he was three years old?

Everything seemed to fit. Cindy's visits to Elva for counseling. The airplane tickets. Even the travel agent's recollection that Cindy had seemed nervous and had held on to Mikey. But if Cindy wanted to abandon Mikey, why hadn't she left him on Gil's doorstep?

Paulina could think of only one good reason.

She scrambled off the couch and padded down the hall-way. The morning's first rays were streaming into her apartment. "Gil—" Her breath caught in her throat at the sight of him sprawled across her bed, the sheets twisted around his body. She plunked herself down on the foot of her bed and patted his exposed, hairy calf. "Gil, wake up. I've got something to tell you."

He sat up instantly, the sheets and blankets gathered at his waist. His chest was absolutely magnificent. She schooled herself not to let her eyes travel the path of dark hair drifting down his tanned abdomen.

He raked his hands through his disheveled hair, the muscles in his chest rippling and creating yet another distracting temptation.

"Hey, what's up?" he asked sleepily.

His indigo eyes focused and narrowed on her, conducting a lazy surveillance from her shoulders to her ankles. Paulina felt a compulsion to hitch her T-shirt down to cover more of her legs, but what would be the point? He'd seen all of her last night.

She blushed, feeling heat steal over her. Was this the part in casual relationships where you asked how the sex was? Paulina could be frank in many situations, but this was not one of them. Karl had told her he loved her before they'd ever slept together. There was no love between her and Gil. Better she shouldn't say anything.

Instead, she told him her theory that Jean-Luc was the man pressuring Cindy to give up Mikey.

"Wait a minute," Gil said, "I'm not following you. If Cindy wanted to give up Mikey, why didn't she ask me if I'd raise him? I'd already offered to take care of her."

"Because as kind and generous as you are," she said very gently, "you wouldn't give her a lump-sum payment for Mikey, and that's what Jean-Luc was after so they could start a new life together someplace else. That's why Jean-Luc quit his job and Cindy didn't pay the rent. They didn't intend to return."

Gil swore. "So what do you think happened?"

"Well, this is all supposition, but what if Newcombe arranged an illegal adoption for Mikey and something went wrong? Cindy could have changed her mind at the last minute. In Ontario, it's illegal for a birth parent or a third-party intermediary to receive any payment or gift in regard to an adoption. The lawyers themselves only receive established fees approved by the ministry. It's a criminal offense to charge more.'' She paused. ''Of course, there are always ways to get around the law.''

She didn't tell Gil she'd actually been to Newcombe's office and that Newcombe had expressly implied Gil was trying to take Mikey away from Cindy. How clever that seemed now on Newcombe's part. She twitched the rumpled blanket. ''Who'd suspect a respected lawyer of selling babies?'' she said.

Gil's face darkened with anger as he swung his legs off the bed and stood, looking like a warrior rising for battle. ''Well, let's go after the bastard.'' He plucked his watch off her bedside table. ''You think we can reach Robbins at this hour?''

Paulina's mouth went dry. She did her best not to stare at his naked backside. Buns of steel was apropos. ''I d-don't think it would be wise to say anything to Robbins yet.''

Gil swiveled to look at her, his astonishment clearly evident. ''Why not?''

''I think we should get some evidence first. If Newcombe suspects they're on to him, he could destroy his files and they'd never find Mikey. Besides, when the police find Elva Madre, they may learn Cindy arranged the adoption through another third party and only went to Newcombe when she became concerned you'd take her baby away from her before the adoption was complete.''

''But didn't the waitress in the diner refer Cindy to Newcombe? Maybe the waitress is in on it, too?''

Paulina bit her lip. ''I hadn't thought of that. You're right.'' Something niggled on the fringes of her thoughts, but she couldn't call it forward.

The phone rang. Gil reached to answer it, but Paulina leaped off the bed. ''No, I'll get it.'' She stepped beside him, conscious of the bare heat of him. Her voice sounded far too weak as she said hello into the receiver.

"Ms. Stewart, this is Detective Zuker. Detective Robbins asked me to give you an update of the situation. We searched the counselor's house. Nothing incriminating. No baby paraphernalia. Maybe forensics will come up with something. We've got an APB out on Elva Madre a.k.a. Karen Jamieson. We're heading over to the counseling clinic now. Sorry, that's all I've got for now."

"Thank you, Detective. Mr. Boyer will appreciate the information."

"Then I trust you'll give it to him, seeing as how his car was parked outside your apartment for the night."

Paulina froze. Zuker was shrewder than she'd given him credit for. Detective Robbins was probably listening to the call on the other line, hoping she'd trip herself up. "I'm glad we're not the only ones working round the clock on this case, Detective," she said with quiet dignity. She hung up the phone, amazed to see her hand was shaking. So, the police were keeping an eye on Gil's whereabouts. Forewarned was forearmed.

Gil's hands settled on her shoulders, his breath stirring her hair. Paulina started.

"Who was that? Robbins?" he asked.

"In a way." She told him what Zuker said, fighting the impulse to lean back into the alluring heat of Gil's body. "It's obvious they still consider you a suspect. Either that or Robbins thinks we could be holding out on more information and they're keeping a close eye on us."

"They sure got an eyeful last night." Gil pulled her against him and pressed a kiss into the base of her neck. The sensation whisked like a velvet ribbon down her spine. Try as she might, she couldn't summon up the will to resist him. His maleness nudged her buttocks, hard and inviting. "So, what do you suggest we do?" he asked.

Paulina swallowed hard. Darn, he made it difficult to think. She took one of his hands and smiled up at him over her shoulder, feeling like she was fighting a losing battle. "We take a shower and try to figure out a way to set up Newcombe." Her stomach flip-flopped at the answering smile creasing his face and the undisguised desire flaring in his eyes. She tugged on his hand, urging him to follow her. Anticipation made her footsteps light. "I don't suppose you know any expectant mothers who'd be willing to help us?"

RENÉE PILON PUSHED through the door of Joe's Diner and glanced around uneasily, trying to remember Gil's description of the waitress. Red hair, that was it. Unconsciously, she rubbed her enormous belly and sighed. Two more months and she could have her waist back. A ginger-haired woman, arms laden with breakfast specials, headed toward a corner of the diner. That must be her.

Renée waddled after her and took an empty booth in the same section. Pathetic, she reminded herself. She was supposed to act pathetic and discouraged.

The waitress flashed by her, giving her a beaming smile. "I'll be right back, sugar, with a menu and some ice water. Would you like coffee, too? We've got decaf—"

"Decaf will be fine, thanks." Renée's stomach rumbled at the smell of bacon and eggs drifting over from the next table. She'd eaten before Gil called her—now she was hungry again. It wasn't even nine o'clock. She'd never get her waist back if she kept eating like this.

The waitress came back wielding a coffeepot and a glass of water. A menu was tucked under her arm. She told Renée her name was Francine, pronounced the French way, but that was the extent of her accent. It was always hard to tell who was bilingual in Ottawa. Accents weren't evident if the person learned both languages at an early age.

Renée got a good look at the woman. Working on her feet had kept her fit, and her disposition was open and friendly. She reminded Renée of her Aunt Jeannine. *Gil thought this gal was involved in Mikey's disappearance?* Renée would do anything to help her boss find his nephew—as long as it wasn't dangerous. Gil treated his consultants well. Besides, her husband, Lonny, was standing across the street, his eyes peeled on the entrance to the diner. He wouldn't let anything happen to her and the baby.

"You all right, sugar? You look a bit under the weather," Francine said. "Is this your first baby?"

"Yes, my first." She rubbed her stomach. She barely fit in the booth. "I'm fine, just tired. It's hard to find a comfortable position with this big belly. Not that I could sleep anyway. I haven't figured out what to do once the baby comes. My boyfriend took off as soon as he heard I was pregnant."

"It's like that, is it?" Francine made a sympathetic sound. "You're not the first single mother, you know."

"I know. I just—it's so much responsibility. I turned twenty-three two months ago. I didn't even want to think about having a baby until I was in my thirties."

"Don't you have some family who could help you?"

Renée shook her head.

Francine patted her hand. "Well, let's take care of fixin' your appetite. Maybe your troubles won't look so bad on a full stomach."

Renée ordered eggs, brown toast and bacon. She nearly swooned when Francine set her order in front of her. It smelled so good, she nearly forgot the reason she was here.

"Eat hearty, sugar. I'll be back in a few minutes to see if you need anything else."

By the time Francine returned, Renée had cleared her plate and was wondering if she should order more toast.

"There, feel better?" Francine asked, nodding at Renée's empty plate.

"Yes, much. I'm sorry I went on like that about... everything."

"There's nothin' to be sorry about." Francine's tone lowered confidentially. "You know, sugar, I believe things happen for a reason. Now, you might think I'm interferin', but here's the phone number of a lawyer I know." She handed Renée a business card. "He specializes in matchin' up babies with good homes. Couples who can't have children and can't afford those high-priced fertility clinics. Now, I'm not suggesting anything, and I hope you don't take offense, but just take the number. Maybe it would help to talk to him, explore your options. There's no charge for an initial consultation."

Renée stared at the card and tried to gather her scattered thoughts. *Dear God, maybe there was some truth to Gil's crazy theory.* Her voice shook. "Thank you. Do you think he could see me today?"

"There's a phone by the cashier. Help yourself and find out."

Renée hoisted herself out of the booth, nervousness slowing her progress to the phone. It was simple enough to make an appointment. The receptionist informed her Mr. Newcombe would be pleased to see her this afternoon at two.

Renée paid her bill and left Francine a generous tip. As she stepped outside, she felt enormously relieved that Lonny was just where he was supposed to be.

"I'M PLEASED TO MEET YOU, Ms. Pilon," Vern Newcombe said, offering Renée his hand as she waddled into his office. "Please sit down. Could I offer you a glass of water or some juice? My wife was forever thirsty during her pregnancies.''

"No, thank you,'' Renée stammered, feeling flustered. His desk faced the window. She angled a glance at the computer on his desk as she moved toward the proffered chair. He was composing a letter.

"Tell me how I can help you. I understand you were referred to our firm?''

"Yes. A waitress at a diner in the Market referred me—'' Renée broke off. It sounded so tawdry. Which was all the more reason for her to act and sound convincing.

"Ah, that must be Francine Loiselle.''

She waited for him to elaborate on Francine, but he didn't. An uneasy tremor rocked her spine.

"Please, go on,'' he encouraged her. Renée didn't know how to interpret the concerned intensity of his expression. She didn't trust lawyers—especially ones who wore expensive suits. "I—I came to ask some questions about giving my baby up for adoption,'' she said hesitantly.

He rested his elbows on his desk and folded his hands together, steepling his index fingers. "Okay. There are two ways to give a child up for adoption in this province: through the Children's Aid Society and through private adoption. Since you've come to see me, I assume you're considering private adoption?''

She nodded.

His steepled fingers touched his chin. "Well, I've arranged many private adoptions over the years. I have a number of clients on a waiting list for private adoptions— people who can afford to give a child a loving home. Should you decide adoption is the best plan for your baby, you would be able to choose the adoptive family for your child and keep in contact with them if you so desire. There are many more open adoptions these days. Or, if you prefer the arrangement to be anonymous, you'd only be given nonidentifying information about the adopting parents.'' He went on to explain that she could sign consent to the adoption any time after her baby was seven days old, and once she'd signed she'd have twenty-one days to withdraw her consent.

"Have you discussed adoption with the baby's father?" Mr. Newcombe asked.

"No, I haven't spoken to him in six months—since I told him I was pregnant."

"I see. Well, how about I start up a file for you, take some background information and we'll talk again next week? This is an important decision you're facing. There's no need to rush. And you need not concern yourself with paying consultation fees. The fees incurred are paid by the adopting parents."

"All right." Renée swallowed hard, watching his every move as he closed the file he'd been working on and opened a new one. She made up information in response to his questions—she had no intention of keeping the second appointment. Lonny would laugh at the info she'd improvised about the baby's father.

"That should do it," Newcombe said finally. He picked up his phone and asked the receptionist to send someone named Lydia in. Renée glanced in dismay at the pretty blonde who entered the office. Why did most of the women she'd encountered today have waists like fence posts? "This is Lydia Kosak. She's a paralegal and my metaphorical right hand."

Lydia smiled and offered her hand. Her amber eyes lit up with amusement. "It's more like I dot his *i*'s and cross all his *t*'s."

Renée murmured hello and tried to look friendly.

"Lydia will be phoning you early next week," Newcombe added, "to explain the steps involved in a private adoption such as the need for a private social worker to visit you and take a medical and social history.''

Renée nodded vaguely. The interview was nearing its conclusion and she hadn't posed the key question. ''Um, there's one thing I didn't ask,'' she said awkwardly. ''Will I... I mean, private adoption means the birth mother receives some money from the adopting parents to cover her expenses, right? The doctor says I'm retaining water and I might have to take my maternity leave a month before my due date. I haven't been at my job long enough to qualify for maternity benefits.''

''Hmm.'' Newcombe glanced at her sharply, causing her to flush deeply with embarrassment. Then his expression softened. ''I understand that an unexpected pregnancy can create financial stresses, but it's illegal for a birth parent to receive any payment in regard to an adoption. The removal of financial gain from the equation keeps the system focused on what's best for the children involved.''

Renée's disappointment was genuine. It was not the response she knew Gil hoped to hear.

GIL STUCK THE POSTER of Mikey onto the telephone pole with two red thumbtacks and jogged down the sidewalk to the next pole lining Bronson Street. He wanted the neighborhood surrounding Elva Madre's home plastered with posters, in case someone had seen her with Mikey the previous week.

Despite the APB, the police still hadn't tracked down Elva. The counseling clinic had produced Cindy's file, but there was no mention of any counseling sessions after Mikey's birth. The clinic's appointment log confirmed Cindy hadn't booked a session recently.

A co-worker had told the police Elva had gone on holidays to the cottage country. The police had located and searched her cottage, but there was no sign of Elva.

Gil figured it couldn't hurt to cover all the bases—especially in light of what Renée had reported after her visit to Newcombe's office.

Was Newcombe playing it cool? Not taking any chances because of the publicity Cindy's murder had garnered? Gil would find out for certain Tuesday morning. He'd had his best sales rep sell Newcombe's partner, Richard Bullhauser, on a website package. Gil could hardly wait to get his fingers on the law firm's computer system.

The fresh chill of the morning air felt good in his lungs as his strides lengthened. The thumbtacks rattled in rhythm with his pace. At nine-thirty on a Saturday morning, the traffic on the main arterial route was light. Gil stopped, put up another poster and resumed his pace.

The waiting for news was killing him, eating him up from the inside out. God, his parents were staying in his house and he couldn't stand to see the pain in their eyes and hear them voice the questions that Gil wished he had the answers to. Last night, they'd decided to wait another week before setting the date of Cindy's memorial service. Then his parents had asked him where he'd gone so late Thursday night and why hadn't he come home? Gil had lied to them. He'd told them he couldn't sleep, so he'd gone to the office to work because he didn't want to disturb them. How could he tell them he'd slept with the private investigator he'd hired?

They'd think his selfishness was bungling their chances of finding Mikey—just as he'd bungled Ted's last phone call.

Gil sprinted across an intersection. Hell, he couldn't stand to look at himself in the mirror. There was no escaping the fact that none of this would have happened if he'd given Ted seven hundred dollars for those damned truck repairs.

Pulling up short, he dug in his nylon waist pouch for

more tacks. His chest heaved as he inhaled and exhaled deeply. He didn't regret sleeping with Paulina for an instant. And he'd remember that interlude in the shower yesterday morning for the rest of his life. He'd never known soap and conversation could be so mentally and physically stimulating.... They'd even come up with one hell of an idea to set up Newcombe. Paulina put a whole new slant on brainstorming, in Gil's mind.

Gil grinned and broke into a jog again. For a few blessed hours he and Paulina had been as close as a man and a woman were meant to be. For the first time in his life he understood how sacred that intimacy could be. Maybe it was because he'd witnessed death lately, or maybe it was his growing awareness of how unhappy Cindy must have been in her relationship with Ted. Had she turned to Jean-Luc for the intimacy she hadn't gotten from Ted?

Of course, once he and Paulina regrouped in her office, where he'd called Renée, Paulina had been all business. By five o'clock, when she'd ordered him to go home and see his parents, she was back to the handshake nonsense again. Did she really think she was the only one who felt the sparks when their palms met?

He shook his head. What did it matter anyway? Paulina was married to a cause—and Gil had every intention of raising Mikey along with two or three other kids in his house in Kanata. He and Paulina *were* going to part company. Gil just didn't know when.

"ARE YOU NERVOUS?" Gil asked Paulina, taking her hand as he helped her out of his car and they gazed up at the sandstone facade of St. Anne's Church in Hull. Paulina's face was whiter than the austere collar trimming her black print dress. Her fingers were cold.

"A little," she admitted. "Going to a funeral seems a terribly underhanded way of gathering information. At least the fact we found the body gives us a legitimate reason for attending." Her fingers tightened around his, seeking reassurance.

Gil squeezed her fingers back, the prospect of walking into the church seeming less formidable with her beside him. It occurred to him that exactly two months ago he'd attended Ted's funeral. Cindy's funeral would be next week. Gil's body turned to ice.

Paulina's voice tugged him back from the brink of his thoughts. "Keep your eyes open. Robbins is probably here, too. I'm sure he'll get a big kick out of our presence. You can bet he's got someone filming the crowd. Killers like to attend funerals."

"Gee, you are a fun date." Gil had no idea why he'd said that. It was a Freudian slip—or he was cracking up. "Sorry. Poor choice of words."

She gave him a probing look he couldn't interpret. Perhaps didn't want to interpret. They'd made love and he couldn't imagine asking her out on a real date. Dinner and a movie. And yet part of him wondered what it would be like to spend a lifetime with her.

"Let's go inside," she suggested.

They filed through the reporters hounding the church steps.

Paulina felt the solemnity of the occasion filter into her heart the moment she entered the century-old church and saw the closed black coffin surrounded by a bank of purple-and-gold chrysanthemums. A photo of Jean-Luc was placed on an easel. Gil's hand lay firm in her own. She squeezed it gently, as if to say she knew soon he and his family would be laying Cindy to rest.

Fifty mourners turned out for the funeral. Gil was handed a bilingual program that invited family and friends to gather at the home of Alain Valiquette after the service. The service was conducted in French, with the odd bit translated into English. Paulina assumed the woman dressed in black in the front pew was Jean-Luc's mother. Several people shared the pew with her. Other relatives? Friends? During the short service, a young man in his early twenties with a thin face and a sharp nose left the front pew and delivered a eulogy. Even from a distance, his dark eyes appeared swollen. Paulina's French was still in the rudimentary stages, but she recognized the word *ami.* Alain Valiquette had been Jean-Luc's friend. Had Alain met Cindy? she wondered.

There had been no mention of Cindy's name thus far in the ceremony. But then, the family may have preferred it that way, given the media's suggestion that Jean-Luc had murdered Cindy, then committed suicide. Gil seemed to be listening intently.

"Can you understand anything?" she whispered, her shoulder brushing against the solid pillar of his arm. It was oh-so-tempting to continue leaning on him. Bad enough their fingers were still woven together. When had their roles become reversed? When had she started drawing strength from him instead of offering her own?

He glanced down at her and her mouth went dry at the chiseled handsomeness of his face and the penetrating blue of his eyes. Memories of their night together flashed unbidden into her mind. Heat laced through her as her gaze focused on the sensuous shape of his lips. He nodded and mouthed, "I'll tell you later."

Through strength of will, Paulina sat up tall and studied those assembled. How many of them knew of Jean-Luc's relationship with Cindy? She recognized the director from the community center. Robbins and Zuker were in the back of the church.

With a final hymn, the service was over.

Paulina and Gil departed down a side aisle to avoid the line of people forming to offer their condolences to the grieving family. "We'll introduce ourselves at the house, where it's more private," she explained.

Robbins intercepted them at the entrance. "Detective," she said with deference, defiantly keeping hold of Gil's hand. Robbins would think she was trying to hide something if she let go now. Paulina realized, to her surprise, that she was comfortable with this intimacy with Gil.

"Ms. Stewart. Mr. Boyer. Might I have a word with you privately? Some information has come to light concerning Mr. Tweedie that I thought you should be made aware of."

Paulina didn't trust Robbins's smooth, rehearsed voice. She knew his experience told him the obvious suspect usually did it, but Paulina *knew* Gil. Sooner or later, Robbins would change tacks.

"What have you got, Detective?" Gil asked gruffly.

Robbins's gray eyes flicked from Gil to Paulina. "We've interviewed Tweedie again. He claims he was at a home-building event for the homeless in Moose Jaw, Saskatchewan, when the child in Swift Current was kidnapped."

"How far is Moose Jaw from Swift Current?" Paulina asked.

"One hundred and seventy-two kilometers—slightly under a two-hour drive. We're checking into the possibility that he still could have done it. This event lasted a week. He could have left for several hours without being noticed. By the way, there's still no word on Elva Madre yet." He turned to leave, then paused, reaching into the breast pocket of his gray tweed blazer for a pair of dark sunglasses. "Keep in touch, eh?"

"We will, Detective," Paulina replied.

"Do you think he knows we had Renée infiltrate Newcombe's office?" Gil murmured, leaning close to her so that she could smell the spicy aftershave on his jaw.

"No." Paulina watched Robbins conferring with Zuker.

An unsettled feeling shimmied beneath her breastbone. "But you can be sure Robbins will be noting who we talk to at the gathering."

When they were in Gil's car alone, Paulina asked what Alain Valiquette had said during the eulogy.

Gil inserted the key in the ignition and frowned, flicking his finger at the silver football dangling from his key ring.

"He said Jean-Luc was his best friend. They went to school together and partied together. Alain helped Jean-Luc fix up his Mustang. When Madame Deveau was transferred to Quebec City four years ago with her employer, Jean-Luc stayed here. Alain made a joke that they used to lift weights too, but no matter how hard he tried, Alain's muscles never measured up to Jean-Luc's."

"It sounds as though they were good friends."

"Yeah." Gil drew a weary breath and let it out slowly, his massive shoulders rising and falling with the movement. "I want to hate Jean-Luc, but I can't. I'm sorry he's dead. I'm sorry Cindy's gone, too. Maybe they could have been happy together—I don't know." He flicked the football again. It spun wildly on its chain. Gil stared at it, his somber expression reflecting his acquiescence of Cindy's relationship with Jean-Luc. "I just want Mikey back safely."

Paulina let her hand rest on Gil's rock-hard thigh. "I know."

Gil started the car. They drove to the Valiquette residence in contemplative silence. Paulina let Gil take over the introductions to Jean-Luc's mother, since the woman didn't appear to speak English.

"*Je suis desolée…*" Paulina murmured, expressing her sympathy. She felt the petite woman's watery brown gaze upon her as Gil made an explanation. She heard Gil mention Cindy's name, but Madame Deveau shook her head and pressed a lace-trimmed handkerchief to her lips.

"Merci. Excusez-nous," Gil responded.

Paulina felt Gil's hand at her elbow. He drew her aside to a quiet corner of the small bungalow. "I told her we found her son and that you're a private investigator and we're doing what we can to assist the police. She doesn't mind that we're here."

"Good." Paulina fingered the lapel of his black wool suit jacket, unable to keep herself from touching him. "Where'd you learn to speak French like that?"

"Playing hockey and football when I was younger."

"Hmm. I'm impressed."

"You are?"

His arms tightened around her, securing her in a cocoon of warmth and strength.

His lips brushed across her forehead. "Good, because impressing you happens to rank very highly on my list of priorities."

Paulina wasn't sure whether to be alarmed or pleased by his admission. She took a step backward, relieved that he released her easily. "Why don't we try to find Alain?"

Alain was on the back deck staring out at the neatly mown lawn, a bottle of beer clenched in his hand. He swiveled toward them when Gil called his name, his eyes bloodshot.

"It's okay to speak English," Alain said, cutting off Gil's introductions. "You knew Jean-Luc?"

"Actually, we were the ones who discovered his body," Paulina explained. "He'd been dating Gil's sister-in-law Cindy D'Ange—"

"He didn't kill her," Alain said vehemently, his eyes flashing. "He was obsessed with her, but Jean-Luc wouldn't kill her. He wouldn't hurt a baby, either. I told him it was a no-win situation—her with a husband and a kid, but he wouldn't listen to me. He was sure it was all going to work out." He took a long swallow of beer. "You want a beer?" he offered. "There's a cooler in the kitchen—"

"We're fine," Gil said.

"When did that conversation take place?" Paulina asked curiously.

"A few months back, I guess." His words were slurred. Paulina imagined the beer clutched in his hand was not the first he'd had that day. "Jean-Luc banged up his Mustang and brought it into my auto-body shop. All he could talk about was *sa blonde*—how he'd met her at work and fallen in love with her. How this woman was having problems with her husband and was very unhappy, but she was worried about leaving him for Jean-Luc because of the kid." He made a helpless gesture with his free hand. "He was sure it was all going to work out."

Paulina felt guilty for intruding on his grief. "Did you know Cindy's husband died?"

Alain nodded. "*Oui.* I remember Jean-Luc phoning and telling me that. His voice was so strange, I knew something was wrong. I think he felt bad. He wanted the guy— how do you say?—out of the picture? But he wasn't wishing him dead or anything."

"I understand," Gil said tightly. A look passed between the two men.

"Alain, when's the last time you talked to Jean-Luc?" Paulina asked.

Alain fixed his dark eyes on her. "Eleven days ago when he sold me his Mustang."

Chapter Ten

Paulina stared at Alain in amazement, unable to believe her ears. "Jean-Luc sold you his Mustang?" she parroted.

"*Oui*. He wanted a car with four doors because of the baby. I thought it was strange—he loved his Mustang." Alain shook his head, his voice slurred. "I told him he could park it outside my auto-body shop with a sign in the window and he could sell it himself—just like that." He ineffectually tried to snap his fingers. When no sound emerged, he tried a second time, then abandoned the effort.

"But Jean-Luc couldn't wait," he continued. "He'd seen a used car he wanted and the owner told him there were other interested parties. Jean-Luc and I fixed a price. He wanted a cashier's check. He was going that evening *après souper* to finish the deal."

"So, Jean-Luc came to see you a week ago Wednesday to sell you his car?" Paulina clarified, wondering how much she could rely on Alain's inebriated recollections.

"*Oui*, that's what I said." He leaned close to her, his breath reeking of beer. "Why do you repeat back what I say?"

Paulina flushed. "I'm sorry, I didn't mean to." She felt Gil's hand settle protectively on the small of her back, letting her know he was there if she needed him. "What time of day did Jean-Luc come see you?"

Alain's narrow jaw tightened with belligerence. "What difference does it make?"

"A great deal." Paulina touched his shoulder gently. "Someone tried to make it appear that Jean-Luc killed Cindy on Wednesday, then committed suicide on Saturday. You may be the only one who can prove your friend couldn't have killed Cindy."

Alain cursed under his breath and threw his beer bottle into the yard. It hit the grass, bounced and rolled to a halt beneath a hydrangea. "He phoned the night before and said he wanted to come by the shop the next morning early, but I had a big job to finish and told him *midi* would be better. He arrived about then. We went to McDonald's for lunch, then I had a look at his car at the shop."

"What time did he leave?" Paulina asked.

Alain rubbed his bloodshot eyes. "I don't know. Two o'clock, maybe three. We went to the bank to get a certified check."

"Did Jean-Luc mention where Cindy and Mikey were while he was with you?"

"No."

Paulina shared a speculative glance with Gil. Cindy had died between noon and eight that Wednesday evening. Assuming Alain was telling the truth—the surveillance cameras at the restaurant and the bank could confirm that—it would indicate Cindy had died in the early afternoon. Since their flight to Reno left at 7:00 p.m., Paulina figured Cindy and Jean-Luc had probably agreed to meet in the late afternoon and Cindy hadn't shown up as scheduled.

"Wait a minute," Gil said, doubt still evident in his tone. "If Jean-Luc sold you his Mustang, why was he still driving it?"

"I was going to pick up the Mustang after he knew when he could take possession of the new car. He said he'd call me and let me know."

Gil raised a dark brow. "Weren't you worried he was going to stiff you?"

"Even though he's my friend, I'm not stupid. He signed it over to me."

Paulina spotted Zuker rounding the corner of the house. She hooked her arm through Alain's arm, feeling him sway unsteadily on his feet. "Come on, there are a couple of detectives who need to hear what you just told us."

"CAN I BUY YOU DINNER?" Gil asked Paulina as they drove past Parliament Hill. He slowed for a red light, training his gaze toward the Sunday afternoon tourists snapping shots of the majestic Gothic Revival buildings that housed the country's government, to avoid looking at her. He knew she'd say no. But he had to ask.

She responded just as he'd predicted. "I don't think that would be a good idea, Gil."

The light changed. Gil punched the gas pedal and the car surged forward. "Why not?"

"You know why." She paused.

Yes. He knew. She was worried dinner might be the prelude to another night of lovemaking, and she didn't want to encourage him.

Gil risked a glance at her, saw the pale pink of discomfort on her cheeks. The starry quality of her eyes. As his body responded to her beauty, he felt a defeating tightness in his chest he hadn't experienced since he was an adolescent.

Paulina stared at her fingers in her lap. "We haven't really talked about the other night."

He let go of the stick shift to run his knuckles over her stockinged knee. "Regrets?" he asked huskily.

She edged her leg away from him. "N-no."

Gil let out his breath, suddenly aware he'd been holding it. He wasn't sure he could stand the idea of her regretting what had happened between them—not when the experience had profoundly affected him.

"Good," he said. "Me neither. My ego quite enjoyed the part where you cried out my name and fainted."

"Gil!" She blushed an attractive shade of scarlet.

He couldn't resist teasing her. "That's exactly the way you said my name before you collapsed."

Her mouth dropped open, but then she collected herself quickly. "It's *not* going to happen again."

"I know. That's why you're *not* having dinner with me."

He parked down the block from her office. He turned to face her. The golden sunlight lancing through the window picked up the blue highlights in her black hair. For a fraction of a second, her eyes were wide and dubious as she gazed at him. For once, she didn't look completely sure of herself. But he could see the determination stealthily taking over.

"You're absolutely one hundred percent certain you don't want a family someday?" he asked her solemnly.

Paulina sighed. "Gil, I can't answer that question. I don't have a crystal ball that allows me to see into the future. All I can say is that devoting myself to these missing kids is what feels right to me at this stage of my life. My dad had this philosophy that some things are meant to be. I know I was meant to help these kids, but I'm not certain I was meant to have children of my own." She tilted her head and smiled at him, her eyes clear and honest. "Is that the explanation you needed to hear?"

"Yes." Gil smiled back, even though it hurt. He touched her chin with his finger. "Hey, the day isn't a total bust. At least I know for a fact Mikey is Ted's kid. And we found out Jean-Luc probably didn't kill Cindy. The money that Robbins confirmed the police found in Jean-Luc's wallet corroborates your theory that Cindy and

Jean-Luc meant to go off together. It's still confusing, but it gives me hope Mikey's alive and well somewhere. You have my utmost respect, Ms. Stewart—always.''

He leaned closer, his mouth hovering above hers. The dilation of her eyes and the unconscious parting of her lips was a bittersweet victory. "Even if you don't want to sleep with me again." Her pulse fluttered wildly at the base of her slender throat. He placed a kiss on her cheek, nearly groaning aloud at the silken softness of her skin. Why did people always want what they couldn't have—and not want what was theirs for the asking?

She stroked his cheek with the tip of her finger and for a crazy, heart-pounding moment Gil thought she was going to move her lips to join with his.

"Thanks for understanding," she said very softly. "I expect to see you in my office tomorrow so we can go over your strategy for accessing the information in Newcombe's files. Don't forget to keep your ideas legal. You won't be much of a guardian for Mikey from a jail cell." With that, she opened her door and stepped onto the sidewalk, the fullness of her black dress swirling around her slim legs as she slammed the door closed.

Only the fact that he respected her and her choices kept him from escorting her to her door. He watched her walk away, admiring her carriage and her confident, ladylike stride. He hoped someday he'd be married to a nurturing, sexy woman who'd keep him so content he'd never lie awake at night and wonder about Paulina.

PAULINA TOLD HERSELF not to turn and look as she heard Gil drive away. This time he hadn't waited for her to get upstairs. Her blood thrummed unsteadily through her body. She didn't know whether to be relieved or disappointed he hadn't come after her. She supposed she should be relieved. But all she felt was…restless.

She kicked off her high heels the moment she entered her apartment and padded to the refrigerator for a can of ginger ale. Sitting on the couch, she rummaged through her briefcase and came up with a legal pad and her gold pen. Automatically, she wrote the date and time on the top line, then stared at the rest of the page until her thoughts started to flow in an orderly fashion. She quickly noted the details of their attendance at Jean-Luc's funeral, the information Robbins had given them about Elva Madre and Tweedie, and the conversation she and Gil had with Alain.

Paulina twirled her pen pensively. Clearly, Robbins and Zuker had been interested in what Alain had to say. The fact Robbins had never mentioned the money in Jean-Luc's wallet suggested the police had been looking for a killer with a motive much stronger than sixty-five hundred dollars worth of greed right from the start. Which still made Gil their most likely suspect—especially if Robbins had had a chat with Vern Newcombe.

Paulina finished her soft drink. She just hoped Robbins didn't get suspicious of Newcombe and start digging into the activities of his law firm before Gil had a chance to get into the files. Time was of the essence. It was bad enough the earliest appointment Gil could get was Tuesday.

Setting the report aside, Paulina went into her bedroom to change into more comfortable clothes: jeans and a long-sleeved cotton shirt. It was only six o'clock. The rest of the evening stretched out before her. Maybe she'd go for a walk in the Market and have dinner out rather than nuking frozen lasagna. A traitorous voice in her head pointed out that if she hadn't been afraid, she could be having dinner with Gil right now. Maybe laughing and having a good time and anticipating his bringing her home.

Her body tingled at the thought, her breasts aching for the touch of Gil's hands. Paulina closed her eyes as an image of Gil standing naked in her bedroom infiltrated her mind.

The phone rang, startling her. She ran for it, grateful for a distraction of any kind. But even as she answered it, her traitorous heart was hoping it was Gil calling.

The sooner this case was over, the better.

"Paulina, this is Andrea. I'm so glad you're home. I went in-line skating this afternoon and dropped by the post-office box. I think we got a letter on the Bryan Watson case. The return address is from Frankston, Victoria, Australia."

"What? That's great." Paulina's pulse quickened with hope. With the assistance of a friend's fancy computer, she'd concocted a realistic letter about a high-school class reunion, which she'd sent to the parents of Margaret Russell. Margaret had accompanied Oliver Watson when he fled Canada with Bryan twelve years ago. Bryan's mother, Brenda, had learned from a neighbor of her former in-laws that Oliver had married Margaret. "Open it," Paulina urged.

She heard the sound of paper tearing. Andrea's voice shook with excitement. "It says:"

Dear Sue,

I was delighted to receive news of the Brookdale High School class of '72 reunion. You might remember me as Margaret Russell way back then, but I go by the name of Peg Oliver here.

As you can tell by the postmark I'm living in Australia. I work in a tasting room at a vineyard and my husband operates a surf shop. We have four children: two boys and two girls, our youngest being seven now. Unfortunately, I'm unable to attend the October Halloween reunion (such a shame as we don't celebrate Halloween here), but I would like to receive a

copy of the roundup newsletter you mentioned would
be available to those who couldn't be present.

My thoughts will be with you and the festivities on
All Hallows' Eve.

Sincerely,
Margaret Russell

Paulina sank to the pine floor in her bedroom and rested
her forehead on her knees as the shock set in. After all
these years, Brenda was going to be reunited with her son.

"That's all there is to the letter," Andrea said. "Do you
want me to read it again?"

Paulina was trembling too hard to answer.

"Paulina? Are you still there?"

"Yes," she said weakly, wiping at the tears trickling
off her chin. She took a deep, gulping breath. "Look, are
you going to be home for a while? I'll call Brenda and tell
her I'm coming over. I'd like to give her the letter in person. You're welcome to tag along." She glanced down,
noticing the receiver was quivering from the trembling of
her hand. "In fact, I think I'm going to need you to drive."

Andrea laughed. "Sure, boss. Stay there, I'll be over in
twenty minutes. Brenda's going to be thrilled."

Yes. And Paulina hoped with all her heart that Bryan
would be thrilled, too.

PAULINA WAS STILL feeling shaky Monday morning.
Brenda had had a lot to absorb last night. Now she had to
decide how and when she was going to make contact with
Bryan and whether or not she wanted her custody order
enforced. Bryan might never forgive her if she had his
father arrested for kidnapping.

Before Paulina got down to the day's work, she took
Bryan's picture from his file and pinned it on her Found

wall. She stood there, smiling at it for a moment. Some joys were worth savoring.

"You looked pleased with yourself."

She whirled around at the sound of Gil's voice. The sight of him made her heart leap like a skittish lamb noticing a wolf at the edge of a pasture. He wore navy cotton slacks and a designer knit shirt with a golf theme in olive-golds and blue. The blue brought out the indigo of his eyes. Paulina turned away from the shadowed longing and desire she saw reflected there; it too nearly matched her own. Was he thinking about last night, too?

"I am very pleased with myself," she said. "This is my motivation board—my found kids." She straightened Bryan's baby photo as she talked. "I have a ritual of putting up their pictures when a case is solved. This one's Bryan—I've been working on his case for three years and we finally had a breakthrough last night." Paulina shot Gil a brief glance. "He's fourteen years old now."

"Jeez," Gil said. Paulina saw the dark stab of worry register in his expression.

She put her hands on her hips, trying to keep things breezy between them—and away from the fanciful imaginings of what could have happened between them had she given in to temptation and slept with him again. "I fully expect to put Mikey's picture up here someday," she reminded him.

"I know."

"So, let's go over what you plan to do in Newcombe's firm tomorrow." Gil's best salesman had contacted Newcombe's partner Bullhauser and sold him on a special rate for an Internet home page to advertise the firm's services.

Gil sat in her father's chair. "Newcombe's got a spare computer that they are willing to use as a server. Our standard procedure when we set up a home page is to ask for information about the firm such as the letterhead logo, advertising brochures and copies of informative articles they've created that would be interesting for browsers to read. Rob picked up some materials late Friday and I put together an initial design. Setting up the server will take a couple of hours, so they won't notice if I run a program I wrote to search the files. As soon as I get a minute alone, I'll pull up Cindy's file...."

Paulina took notes as he outlined his plan, interrupting him from time to time when he used an unfamiliar term of computerese.

"Don't worry, I'll turn you into a chiphead before you know it," Gil said, with a grin. Paulina didn't doubt it—he had a clear way of explaining things that made it less intimidating to understand.

"Andrea will thank you," she replied dryly, unable to resist the urge to smile back at him. "She's been hinting since she started working for me that the computer in the front office is a dinosaur."

"She's right. What you really need is a—"

"Stop being a salesman. Now what key words were you planning to use in this search utility you were talking about? Maybe we should make a list."

They worked on stratagems right through lunch. Paulina wanted to be certain there was no way Newcombe could figure out someone had been rooting through his system. She also wanted Gil to be aware that Newcombe could have the knowledge and the means to pass these adoptions off as being legal without the adopting parents knowing anything illegal was transpiring. Andrea brought in roast beef sandwiches, coleslaw and coffee at noon. At two, Paulina glanced at her watch and realized she'd wanted to make a few calls about Newcombe and Bullhauser.

She phoned the law offices of Mayheu, O'Connor and Dingwald, hoping Ken Mayheu wasn't out to a late lunch or in court. Newcombe had said he'd played golf with Ken.

"Paulina." Ken Mayheu's boisterous voice carried over the phone line. "This is a pleasure. You know, I was just talking about you to someone last week."

"Really?" Paulina wondered if Newcombe had checked up on her after she'd left his office. "It wouldn't happen to have been a call from Newcombe and Bullhauser, was it?"

"Indeed, Vern's paralegal gave me the third degree. She's practically ready for the courtroom, that one. Not to worry, though, I gave your agency a glowing reference. Lydia probably thought we were sleeping together."

Paulina laughed. Ken had his own style.

"What can I do for you, Paulina? I've got a deposition in twenty minutes."

"Actually, I was hoping you could tell me a bit about Vern Newcombe. I understand you played golf with him recently. You close?"

"That was a tournament for the children's hospital. We've negotiated a few divorce settlements. He's a decent lawyer, well respected within the legal community. He's made a name for himself handling private adoptions, which is interesting because there aren't as many babies being put up for adoption these days. Vern told me most of the adoptions are open and that makes all the difference. The young mothers don't feel so bad if they know they won't completely lose touch with their children. But tell me, why the interest? He hasn't run off with his kids or anything?"

"Oh, no." Paulina didn't even contemplate giving Ken a line. Some players you played straight with—always. "He represented someone in a case I'm involved in. I just wanted to know what kind of person he is, on the off chance it parlays into some work being thrown my way."

Ken harrumphed. "He's not a member of the shark pool, so don't worry about wading in the water."

Paulina laughed, though her heart wasn't in it. "Thank you, that's what I wanted to hear. I knew I could count on your discretion."

"Any time."

She hung up and repeated what she'd learned to Gil. Then she proceeded to call several contacts she had in other law firms. Receptionists were the custodians of the grapevine and knew all the juiciest tidbits. Forty-five minutes later, Paulina finished her last call and rubbed her bleary eyes. Her late-night meeting with Brenda, combined with the restless images of Gil disturbing her sleep, was catching up with her. It didn't help having him within arm's length all day. She blinked and told herself that if she had the strength to say no last night, then she'd have the strength to continue saying no until Gil was completely out of her life. Why did that thought make her feel depressed rather than relieved?

"Well, that's it," she said tightly. "Newcombe has a sterling reputation. His wife is a former model. He's got three kids and a golden retriever, and he plays squash. Oh, and his favorite charity is the Children's Hospital of Eastern Ontario."

Gil flexed his shoulders. Paulina could hear the tension crackling through his muscles. "Not exactly the profile of a baby racketeer," he said grimly.

"On the contrary, Gil. His sterling reputation could be a perfect foil."

Chapter Eleven

Gil was pumped, prepared to give the performance of a lifetime for Mikey. He took the pregame jitters rampaging through his gut as he stepped into the law offices of Newcombe and Bullhauser as being a good sign. He always performed well under pressure. He'd already lost the police tail that had been on him when he left the house this morning—or at least he hoped he had. Paulina had told him he was probably being followed, and she was right.

For a moment, as he gave the receptionist his name, he wondered if Paulina felt like this when she went into one of those story routines she did. It occurred to him that it took an enormous strength of will and confidence to carry off what she did.

But then, he'd already concluded she was special. More special than any woman he'd ever met. The thought of her lying naked and pliant in his arms...and wanting him, made his chest swell.

He shoved the notion away. If anything could crack his concentration, it was Paulina.

"I'm Richard Bullhauser. How do you do?"

"Fine, sir. I'm Gilbert Boyer, president of Working Solutions, Inc." Bullhauser gave no sign of recognition with his name. "Your appointment was originally with one of my consultants—Rob Smalley," Gil continued. "But his wife is experiencing complications with her pregnancy, so I'm filling in for him. I hope it's not an inconvenience."

"Not at all."

Gil shook the lawyer's proffered hand and sized him up. His hand felt soft and fleshy. Middle age and a desk job were affecting the man hard, making inroads on his hairline and padding his waist. But Gil liked the frankness he saw in Bullhauser's dark brown eyes. This man made the money decisions.

"I'll be setting up your web server and home pages this morning," Gil explained. "It won't be accessible from the Net until the phone company installs your Internet connection, but you'll be able to use it internally until then. Now, why don't you tell me about your current system?"

Gil listened intently as the lawyer showed him around the office. There were five networked computers: one in Newcombe's office, one in Bullhauser's office, one at the receptionist's desk, one at the paralegal's workstation and the spare in an empty cubicle beside the paralegal's workstation. Gil's glance into Newcombe's office was far too brief. Bullhauser told him his partner was in court this morning.

The tour ended at the empty cubicle where the spare computer sat on a desk. "How long will the installation take?" the lawyer asked. "I'll be on a conference call for part of the morning, so I won't be available to answer questions."

"Approximately three hours," Gil replied. "It's fairly straightforward, but things never go as smoothly as one would like."

"Well, Lydia's at the courthouse filing papers, but she should be back soon. If you have a question or a problem and my office door is closed, see her."

"Okay. Are your files encrypted?" Gil asked.

Bullhauser chuckled. "We're not that technologically advanced."

"What is the password to your database?"

"*Mediation.* We'll be changing it after you're done."

Gil set his briefcase on the desk and sat down. He booted up the computer and double clicked the hard disk icon.

Bullhauser took a moment to explain the main folders used by the firm, then patted Gil on the shoulder and wished him luck.

Once he was certain he was alone, Gil opened his briefcase and inserted a diskette into the computer. Then he opened Newcombe's folder. The files were listed in a hyphenated code. He chose "Find..." from the File menu and typed in Cindy's name. Her file appeared on screen and he realized the code consisted of the first three letters of the client's last name, a file number and the year. He wondered why the law firm didn't make use of the computer's capability for long file names and list the client's name in full. Was the code for privacy?

Aware of the passage of time, Gil scanned the contents of Cindy's file quickly. Disbelief slammed a numbing blow to his heart when he read that Cindy had originally approached Newcombe about putting Mikey up for adoption, then changed her mind when she learned there was no money in it. Newcombe noted Cindy seemed confused and highly unstable. He felt any decision she made about putting her baby up for adoption would be made under duress. He advised her to seek counseling to help her deal with Ted's death and being a single parent.

Gil frowned. Perspiration clung to his body in a clammy film. This wasn't what he'd expected to find.

His frown deepened as he scanned the notes for Cindy's second appointment; they concerned Ted's estate. Ted had died without a will. At her last appointment, she'd asked

Newcombe whether it was possible her brother-in-law could get custody of her baby.

Gil copied the file onto his diskette. Were he and Paulina on the wrong track with Newcombe? Or was this file for appearances and Newcombe had other hidden files detailing his illegal adoptions? Gil performed a file content search using Mikey's name. Cindy's file was the only one that appeared in the search list.

Had nothing more come up because Newcombe took the precaution of not referring to the children who were put up for adoption by name? Gil remembered Paulina had said that Mikey might be referred to in the files as a male born April 19.

Trying not to be deterred, Gil initiated the program he'd written the night before to search for and copy files that contained selected key word occurrences. He'd designed it to run in the background and copy the output onto the hard disk while he set up the server. Then he immersed himself in the complexities of installing the software. The law firm was going to receive exactly what it had paid for.

Two hours later, Gil swore softly under his breath as he tried to copy the output file onto his diskette. The file was too big. His search criteria had been too general and he was picking up too much data. And the system he was working on didn't have the tools he needed to adjust the program. He'd have to do a manual search.

This time he did a search for "adoption." He whistled at the number of files in the resultant list. Were these all couples who'd come to Newcombe to arrange private adoptions? Gil saved a copy of the list on his diskette. Then he rose and checked to make sure the paralegal wasn't in her workstation. As far as he knew, she hadn't returned from the courthouse. Gil risked printing off a hard copy on the printer in her station so he could use it as a cross-referencing tool to narrow his search.

A key word search for "infant male" produced another list of forty or so files on the screen. Gil ticked them off against the master "adoptions" list. Next he tried Mikey's birthdate: April 19. A dozen file names appeared, Cindy's among them. But none of the remaining eleven file names was on the master list.

Undaunted, Gil examined the file names he'd ticked off on the master list. At first glance, he thought he could safely eliminate any of the files with years other than the current year, then he questioned his logic. The year in the file number probably referred to when the client originally approached the firm. Some of these couples could have been on a waiting list for years. It could take a long time to examine each of these files separately. More time than he had.

What he needed was an index. If Newcombe didn't mention the child's name in the individual adoption files maybe he kept a separate reference list or an index indicating which child had been placed with which parents. Gil picked up a pencil and ran his gaze over the file names printed on the master adoption list, circling the names that differed from the hyphenated code. There was nothing obviously labeled Index. But what was this file labeled CNSFA? Gil opened the file. It was a list. He nearly laughed at the irony of the title: Clients Not Suited For Adoption. Paulina had thought Newcombe's sterling reputation was a cover for illegal activities. Was this Newcombe's attempt at being deliberately clever?

The list detailed couples whom Newcombe had turned away for various reasons because he felt the adoptions would likely not be approved by the Ministry of Community and Social Services. Gil copied the list onto his diskette. Maybe Newcombe had sold Mikey to one of these couples and didn't dare keep any incriminating records on his hard disk—especially when anyone in the office might stumble upon the information. Could Newcombe have the information on a diskette stashed somewhere in his office?

Gil glanced at his watch. He'd been at it two hours and forty minutes. He had no idea what time the paralegal would make an appearance—and he still hadn't done a search on Francine Loiselle's name. Bingo, three general disbursement files appeared on the screen.

Gil found it interesting that Newcombe and Bullhauser had sent her two pricey gift baskets as tokens of appreciation since the beginning of the year. One February 5, the other August 16—a few days after Cindy's first appointment. Francine had received five other gifts of flowers, chocolates and a painting in the other disbursement files for previous years. He pressed his lips together tightly. Just how many people had she referred to the firm? Unfortunately, there were no file reference notations on the disbursement records to indicate which clients had been referred to the firm by Francine. Still, the firm must be profiting handsomely from her referrals if they could afford to send her one hundred and seventy-five dollars' worth of fruit.

Keeping a vigilant ear attuned to the sound of approaching footsteps, he methodically started pulling up the infant male adoption files that were ticked on his master list—checking the age of the infant and the dates of the placement with the adopting parents. It looked as though there was no other way he could do this now, but one at a time.

"ALL RIGHT, BRENDA, I'll let you know when I'm free to leave town," Paulina assured her client and hung up the phone. She'd been talking with Brenda most of the morning. Paulina glanced at her watch and went into the reception area. She cleared her throat to get Andrea's attention. "Has Gil called?"

Andrea glanced up from the invoice she was processing

into the dinosaur. "No. If he had, I would have let you know." She cocked her head and regarded Paulina intently. "Are you okay? I've never seen you so jumpy."

"Of course I'm jumpy. One of my clients is doing my job for me and another of my clients wants me to fly off to Australia with her for two weeks."

"Are you sure that's it?" Skepticism gleamed in Andrea's black eyes. "It's none of my business, but you and Gil seem kind of tight. Can't say I blame you. That man has a body to die for, and he's smart and handsome, too."

Paulina flushed. Great, she'd trained Andrea so well, her intern was capable of reading her. "You left out he wants a wife at home." Paulina felt a hollowness in her chest. "First rule of investigating, Andrea, don't expect to lead a normal life."

"I don't know. That contradicts your second rule—where there's a will, there's a way. Besides, I think you'd deal with life with Gil the same way you deal with everything else. Head-on."

"Thanks for the vote of confidence, Andrea. But you don't understand. Gil wants a family and the thought of having a baby petrifies me. I've never envisioned myself as being a mother. I didn't even play with dolls when I was a little girl."

Paulina expected Andrea to be shocked or at least puzzled. Didn't every woman want to have a baby eventually? But her friend was unruffled, her gaze steady and nonjudgmental.

"You know, Paulina, lots of couples stay happily married—my parents among them. I think you, of all people, would probably find motherhood and a family life very fulfilling."

Paulina's chin jutted out. "How do you figure that?"

Andrea's cheeks turned bright pink, but her gaze didn't

waver. "It would make up for all the things you missed out on while you were growing up without your dad."

"Well, if that were the case, Karl and I would still be married and raising a couple of kids, by now."

"Maybe you didn't have enough trust in your relationship with Karl to have children with him."

Paulina stared at Andrea for a moment, unable to deny the ring of truth to her comment. She still remembered the icy tremor of alarm that had shot through her when Karl had told her he wanted her to have *his* child. Not their baby. *His* child. And she had no reason to believe Gil would be any different than Karl in that respect. Paulina couldn't live up to Gil's expectations any more than she could live up to Karl's. Could she?

No. And there was nothing wrong with her life such as it was. Her work gave her a wonderful sense of fulfillment. She'd done the right thing in telling Gil it was unlikely babies would ever figure in her future.

She rapped her knuckles on Andrea's desk. "Enough of this idle chitchat," she said briskly. "Since Gil hasn't called, I'm going to lunch. There's a certain waitress I'd like to talk to without my handsome shadow present."

Her handsome shadow. As Paulina walked to the diner, she had the discomposing presentiment she'd forever think of Gil as her handsome shadow. Some people made an impression on you that lasted a lifetime, even when you didn't want them to. Paulina straightened her shoulders, trying to exert some logic over the tumultuous feelings growing in her heart. This constant dwelling on Gil was inappropriate to her purpose of finding Mikey—and interviewing Francine Loiselle.

If Francine was working today.

The lunch crowd formed a line past the door. Paulina spotted the gregarious, ginger-haired waitress through the window while she waited her turn to be seated. A twenty-dollar bill slipped to the hostess ensured her a booth in Francine's section.

But Francine took one look at Paulina and the waitress's friendly smile literally fell from her face. "I'll get someone else to wait on you," she said thinly.

"Please don't," Paulina implored. "I was hoping we could speak privately without my client present."

"Hmph!" Francine snorted as she wiped off the soiled table with a damp rag and set out fresh silverware. "That's not bloody likely." Then, almost as an afterthought, she added, "Are you really a private investigator?"

"Yes, I am. I want to find Mikey and get to the truth of Cindy's death—and I think you can help me." Paulina noted Francine's hand trembled as she picked up the rag. Paulina had the distinct impression something was weighing heavily on the woman's mind. The black fringe of her eyelashes emphasized the uneasiness mottling her crystal blue eyes. Was she feeling guilty she'd referred Cindy to Vern Newcombe?

"Since you bothered to come over here," Francine began hesitantly, lowering her voice. "Do you think it's possible your client killed her? Cindy told me plain as day he wanted her baby."

Paulina's heart rebelled vehemently at the suggestion. It took every ounce of her self-control not to let her true emotions show as she rested her elbows on the table and leaned forward in a conspiratorial manner. "That's exactly why I came to see you. Did you know Cindy's boyfriend was also killed?"

"You mean her old man in that car accident?"

Paulina shook her head. "No, Cindy apparently had something going on the side with a French-Canadian named Jean-Luc Deveau while she was still living with Ted. I don't know if you've seen the news lately, but Deveau was found dead last Wednesday night. He'd been murdered, and whoever did it tried to make it look like a suicide. Fortunately, the police weren't fooled.''

Francine's face turned whiter than bone china.

So Francine hadn't known about Jean-Luc. "I'm thinking it's possible that my client killed them both," Paulina went on, trying to ignore the uproar the traitorous statements caused in her heart and her conscience. Not on her life did she believe Gil would harm Cindy. "You seem to think so, too. Did Cindy mention anything else about her brother-in-law that might help me figure out what really happened the day she was killed?"

"No, not that I recall."

"She didn't mention she'd be seeing him later that day?"

Francine shook her head, her lips glued together.

"Did Cindy say he'd actually threatened her? You know, when his brother died, Mr. Boyer offered to pay child support for Mikey in exchange for visitation rights. Quite a substantial amount actually. Not many men take family responsibility that seriously. It makes you wonder what would push a man like that to kill." Paulina paused slightly.

Francine didn't offer an opinion. She stood there quaking like an aspen leaf.

Paulina narrowed her gaze, convinced the waitress knew more than she was telling. "Maybe he killed them because he found out Mikey wasn't his brother's child," she speculated, just to witness Francine's reaction. "Though I can't imagine him harming an infant. But then, what would he do with him? He wouldn't want to raise a child that wasn't his brother's."

"I'm sure Mikey was Ted's son," Francine blurted out.

Paulina raised an eyebrow, but she didn't question how Francine could be so certain. "Hmm," she replied. "Then the only plausible theory is that my client killed Jean-Luc and Cindy because he found out they were leaving town with Mikey. If that's the case, it means Mikey will miraculously reappear one day in a public place. I'd hate to see Mr. Boyer get away with murder. I'm sure you would, too, seeing as how friendly you were with Cindy.''

Was Paulina mistaken—or were there tears gathering in Francine's eyes? Paulina touched the waitress's arm, aware of the activity of the busy restaurant around them. ''There's obviously something bothering you. When do you finish your shift today? Maybe we could go someplace and talk.''

Francine took a step backward as though Paulina's touch had scalded her. ''I get off at two, but I can't meet you. I h-have an appointment.''

''Maybe another time?'' Paulina suggested.

''I've already told you and the police everything I know.''

''Miss?'' a man called from two booths over, waving his arm in the air to get Francine's attention. ''Could I have the check please?''

''I have to go. Did you want to order?''

Paulina asked for a tuna melt with a garden salad on the side and a ginger ale. When Francine had scurried away, Paulina glanced at her watch and started calculating. It was a quarter to one. She should have just enough time to eat lunch and fetch her car before Francine finished at two. Paulina doubted Francine actually had an appointment, but even if Francine went straight home, Paulina might get more out of the waitress by approaching her in the privacy of her own home.

There was no doubt her presence at the diner made Francine extremely nervous. The waitress delivered Paulina's meal ten minutes later with obvious agitation. Paulina decided not to press her further for the moment. When Francine came around with the check, Paulina handed the woman her business card. "Please call me if you remember something that might help me find Mikey—or Cindy's killer."

Francine seemed reluctant to take it. Her lashes concealed her eyes as she glanced at it for a long moment, before tucking it into the pocket of her apron. "Don't count on it," she warned, her tone bordering on the aggressive side. Then she turned back to her tables.

Paulina paid the cashier and hastened into the street. The familiar hand of instinct pressing on her spine told her the opportunity to follow Francine was too good to pass up.

"MR. BOYER?"

Gil instinctively deleted the file on the screen at the sound of his name and swiveled around in the cubicle. Newcombe's receptionist was smiling at him, an inviting, flirtatious smile. The sensual, evocative fragrance drifting into his nostrils told him she'd freshened her perfume just before she'd walked down the hall.

"Yes? Janine, isn't it?" he said cordially.

Janine's plump cheeks reddened. "Um, I just came to let you know that Lydia has been detained at the courthouse. Mr. Bullhauser told me she was to assist you, if necessary."

"That's all right. I'm managing fine on my own," Gil replied. "It's just time-consuming."

"I'm going to lunch now and I'll be back in an hour…" She hesitated, her gaze flicking over him. "Would you care to join me?"

"I appreciate the invitation, Janine, but I don't normally eat lunch. It breaks my concentration when I'm working."

Disappointment flickered in her dark eyes. "All right, then. Mr. Bullhauser is still tied up with that conference call in his office and doesn't wish to be disturbed."

"I'll leave him a note if I finish before you return."

Gil waited until he heard the outer office door click, then he checked the hallway. Bullhauser's office door was closed. So was Newcombe's. Janine hadn't mentioned it, but Gil thought Newcombe hadn't returned from the courthouse, either.

Now was his opportunity to get inside Newcombe's office. The man was smart. So far, Gil hadn't found any incriminating files on the hard drive, but he was willing to bet Newcombe might have something on a backup diskette hidden in his office.

Gil stepped into the hallway. The carpeting absorbed the sound of his footsteps as he approached Newcombe's office. Even if he couldn't find a backup diskette, he'd learned something about the adoption process while pulling up the individual files that could give them a new angle in finding Mikey. Each adoption file had contained a report from a private social worker stating the suitability of the adoptive parents. The name of the social worker was always the same: Susan Clark-Fitzhugh. Maybe this woman had done a similar report for Mikey.

Gil took a deep breath, gripped the brass doorknob and turned.

Damn, the door was locked.

The receptionist must have locked it. Was there a key to Newcombe's office in Janine's desk?

Gil strode into the reception area. Paulina would blow her top if she knew he was contemplating entering the lawyer's locked office, but Paulina wasn't here...and she didn't have to know.

And Mikey needed to be rescued.

One by one, Gil eased open the three drawers in the receptionist's desk. Janine was an extremely organized woman. Every paper clip and Post-it pad was in its proper place. He found a bottle of perfume in the bottom drawer, but no keys.

Now what was he going to do? He couldn't exactly kick Newcombe's office door in; Bullhauser might notice.

Gil's gaze fell on the pink message book near the phone and a smile curved his mouth. This surely was an opportunity Paulina couldn't object to. He glanced over his shoulder at Bullhauser's office. The door was still closed. Without a second thought, Gil thumbed through the messages. Maybe Newcombe had been making contact with the adopting parents—someone on that list of unsuitable prospects.

A name caught his attention. Francine Loiselle called Lydia the Wednesday morning after Cindy's body was found. The message read: *Urgent, please call back ASAP.*

Gil frowned.

He continued to scan the pages. His heart dropped to his stomach when he found two messages from Jean-Luc to Lydia dated the Friday after Cindy was killed. Gil checked the time of the calls—10:00 a.m. and 3:00 p.m.

Why were Jean-Luc and Francine contacting Lydia— and not Newcombe?

Gil felt a stab of suspicion embed in his chest. He had a pretty good idea why Lydia had suddenly been detained. He positioned the message book precisely the way he'd found it. Just where the hell was Lydia hiding Mikey?

Gil wasn't sure, but he knew the most logical place to start looking.

Chapter Twelve

Gil hadn't phoned yet. Paulina nervously tapped her fingers on the steering wheel, her eyes glued to the entrance to Joe's Diner. She'd been hoping Andrea would have news for her when she'd returned from lunch to get her car, but no such luck. She wondered if that meant Gil hadn't found anything to indicate Newcombe was involved in illegal activities. Could she be wrong about Newcombe?

Paulina moistened her lips. It was more likely Gil had found out something incriminating about Newcombe and had gone off on his own to recover Mikey, which had been her chief fear about letting him go into Newcombe's office in the first place. That, and the fact two people were already dead.

For all his size and strength, Gil's muscles couldn't stop a bullet from penetrating his stubborn hide. Jean-Luc was proof of that.

Paulina's stomach lurched. If anything happened to Gil, she'd never forgive herself. Why hadn't the darn man phoned?

A horn tooted and Paulina glanced over her left shoulder. A blue-green Honda was coveting her parking spot. Paulina waved the Honda to go on.

Her gaze darted back to the diner and she adjusted the bill of her Lynx baseball cap. With the cap on and a pair of dark sunglasses, she wasn't worried about Francine recognizing her via the rearview mirror.

Paulina didn't have long to wait. At seven minutes after two, Francine emerged from the diner and headed south toward York Street where Paulina was parked in a three-hour-maximum metered lot. Paulina felt her heartbeat accelerate as she tipped her head down and pretended to reach over for something in the glove box. She waited a few seconds then glanced up again. Francine was down the block heading west toward Sussex Drive, her turquoise bowling shirt making her an easy mark. There was a large all-day parking lot on Sussex. Was that where Francine was headed?

Telling herself to play it cool, Paulina backed out of her spot, made a U-turn and crept down the street as though searching for a parking space. Ahead of her, Francine crossed Sussex and veered toward the lot. Paulina pulled into a loading zone at the end of York Street to watch and wait as Francine retrieved her car. Paulina groaned out loud when a bakery truck stopped at the light, obscuring her view.

"Come on, get out of the way," she urged, straining her neck to see. The truck made a slow right turn. Where the heck was Francine?

Was she driving one of the two cars lined up at the pay booth?

"Hallelujah," Paulina muttered, spotting the ginger blur of the woman's distinctive hairstyle behind the wheel of a red Ford Escort.

Paulina experienced a few tense moments waiting for the light to change as Francine zipped out of the parking lot and headed south on Sussex Drive. The second the light turned green Paulina made a hasty left turn after her.

She tailed Francine's progress onto Wellington Street, holding her breath as she squeaked through several amber lights and one glaring red light. Francine passed the Parliament Buildings and the Supreme Court of Canada before she turned south onto Lyon Street. Minutes later, Francine turned west onto Somerset Street. Traffic thinned, but Somerset was a main route that had changed names twice. Paulina stayed well back, not worried Francine would suspect she was being followed.

Then Francine turned south onto Island Park Drive, the beautifully landscaped emerald necklace linking the Central Experimental Farm to the Champlain Bridge. Seconds later, she whipped onto a side street in a wealthy neighborhood of Cape Cod, modernist and Tudor homes. Could a diner waitress afford to live in this neighborhood?

Paulina's palms were sweaty on the wheel. It was harder to tail someone on deserted streets. She deliberately signaled and drew to the side of the road, watching as Francine continued down Geneva Street and made a left turn. As soon as the red car disappeared from her sight, Paulina pulled away from the curb and put on a burst of speed. She reached the street where Francine had turned in time to see the car head north on another side street three blocks up.

Had Francine suspected she was being followed?

Paulina braked when she reached the intersection where Francine had made her last turn and peered down Iona Street, frowning. Francine was parking at the far end of the block. Paulina continued straight through the intersection and parked. Tossing the baseball cap and sunglasses aside, she grabbed her purse and jumped out of her car. As she rounded the corner, she saw Francine walking up the asphalt drive of a large Tudor-style home. Francine hadn't parked in the driveway. Did that mean she was visiting someone?

Paulina increased her pace as the bulk of a cedar hedge blocked Francine from her view. She wanted to be in a position to see who answered the door, but to Paulina's surprise, Francine didn't approach the front entrance. Instead, the waitress skirted around the north side of the building.

Curious, Paulina kept her eyes trained on the Tudor house as she hurried down the sidewalk. The house was well maintained; the stucco freshly painted, the landscaping professionally done. *Could this be Newcombe's home? But wouldn't Newcombe be at his office this time of day?*

Maybe, Paulina acknowledged, she was chasing a red herring.

Still, she noted the address as she passed the house, then spotted a salmon paving-stone walkway that Francine must have followed to the backyard.

When she reached the corner, Paulina crossed the street and made a beeline for the same walkway. The narrow path was shady and bordered with blue hostas. Paulina took pains not to let her heels tap on the pavers. As she neared the arbor at the end of the path, she heard the murmur of voices in the rear yard. Clearly, Francine was speaking to a man.

Paulina wasn't close enough to make out any distinct words, but the anxious shrill to Francine's tone suggested this might be a conversation worth overhearing.

Fortunately, Francine hadn't closed the gate properly which allowed Paulina to ease it open and slip into the yard without making a sound. She just hoped a dog wouldn't suddenly appear and announce her presence. Paulina stepped behind a tall, columnar juniper and peered around it, trying to locate Francine. The voices were louder now and appeared to be coming from a screen porch on the rear of the house. A dense shrubbery bed softened the projection of the porch into the yard and provided a verdant wall of privacy for the homeowners.

Her heart pounding with caution, Paulina crept across

the thick, green lawn as close as she dared to the screen porch and concealed herself behind the purple foliage of a sand cherry.

"I don't care—I want out," she heard Francine say.

Out of what? Paulina wondered, though with a keen sense of certainty she thought she already knew. Her afternoon was growing more interesting by the second.

"Don't be ridiculous, Francine. You're overreacting," the man replied, trying to placate her. Paulina listened carefully to the man's voice, trying to recognize a characteristic of it that she could attribute to Newcombe. But then, she'd only met the lawyer once.

"Overreacting? Two people are dead. I didn't mind helping women find good homes for their babies, but I draw the line at murder."

Paulina froze as the sour taste of bile rose in her throat. She clamped her hand over her mouth.

"Francine, you gotta believe me. We didn't have anything to do with Cindy's murder. Her money-grubbing boyfriend obviously killed her. We paid Cindy fair and square when she delivered the baby. What happened to her when she got back to her boyfriend has nothin' to do with us. They must have had a fight. There was somethin' strange about him, anyway, if you ask me."

"You're lying. The police on the news said Jean-Luc didn't kill himself. He was murdered."

"So? Maybe they sold the baby to cover a drug debt."

"I don't buy that, either. We both know the truth."

"Ah, the truth. Are you suggesting I bumped them both off?" The man laughed softly, almost dangerously.

Francine didn't reply.

Paulina felt a clammy shiver of alarm inch up her spine. This man had a rough edge that seemed out of sync with Newcombe's measured shrewdness. She cast a wary eye at the distance remaining between her hiding spot and the porch. Could she get close enough to get an ID on the man?

She edged her way through the shrub bed toward a two-meter-high golden cedar strategically suited to her purpose.

"Do I have to remind you, Francine, that we've got fifty thousand riding on this deal? We'll deliver the baby as soon as the publicity dies down. Two weeks from now everyone will have forgotten about Cindy's death."

"We're going to get caught," Francine insisted. "A lady P.I. has been nosing around. She came to the diner today asking questions."

"Did you tell her anything?"

"No, of course not, but—"

"Well, then, there's nothin' to worry about. Lydia's got everything all figured out. She even checked up on this P.I. you're talkin' about. She's set things up so Newcombe will take the fall if anyone gets wise to our operation."

Lydia?

An image of the confident blond paralegal working in Newcombe's office flashed in Paulina's mind. Anyone smart enough and cocky enough to use an ethical lawyer's sterling reputation to camouflage her illegal activities would be instantly concerned about having a computer expert having access to the law firm's electronic files. An impending sense of doom shifted ominously onto Paulina's shoulders.

Gil was still at Newcombe's office, where presumably Lydia was, too. At any moment, Lydia could link Gil's name to the work the firm was conducting on Ted's estate. With one warning phone call to this man, Mikey could be whisked away so fast the police could never recover him.

Paulina whirled around and examined the leaded casement windows studding the half-timbered wall of the house. Was Mikey somewhere inside? Maybe she should ascertain he was in the house and use a neighbor's phone to call the police.

She took an uncertain step toward the house and cringed as the branch of a lilac caught on her skirt pocket and caused a faint rustling of leaves. Paulina unhooked the branch and dropped to her knees in the moist earth, her heart hammering in her ears.

The conversation had ceased in the screen porch. Had they heard her? The lilac's straggly foliage provided scant coverage. The dark blue of her suit would give her away if anyone bothered to look.

Suddenly, Francine spoke again. "Fine, I'm getting out of here."

Panic clawed at Paulina's skin. She glanced around, searching for a better hiding place. A row of winterberry shrubs defined the edge of the bed against the house. In a crouched position, she headed for the row, hoping there would be room to conceal herself behind it.

The screen door screeched open. Paulina dove over the shrubs, her eyes widening in dismay at the river stones forming a wide band around the perimeter of the wall. She was going to make noise....

Pain shot through her as she landed with a thud and the rocks cracked together like marbles. Her arms and shins stung where her skin had laid down skid marks on the stones.

"Doug, there's someone back there!" Francine's panic-stricken voice rang out like a call to arms. "I think it's that private investigator. She must have followed me from the diner. I *knew* we were going to get caught."

Paulina scrambled to her feet and ran toward the gate. She had to get out on the street where she'd have a better chance of attracting attention and getting help. Doug had killed two people. He wouldn't hesitate to kill her. The stones impeded her flight, sucking at her heels. She cried out as her left heel sank into a crevice and her ankle wrenched. She braced her palm against the house and kept on moving, using the wall as a crutch.

From the corner of her eye, she could see the man racing around the shrub bed to intercept her flight. He blocked her path and reached behind him, pulling a black semi-automatic pistol from the waistband of his jeans.

"Hold it right there, lady," he barked.

Paulina halted, her breath coming in gasps as she stared down the nose of the gun.

IT WAS THE STRANGEST sensation, but Gil felt an invisible hand settle on his right shoulder, guiding him as he sat down at the computer and accessed the law firm's personnel files. Gil pulled Lydia Kosak's file onto the screen and scanned it for the paralegal's address. She lived on Iona Street in Ottawa. The street didn't sound familiar, but he had a map in his car. He'd find it.

He was about to print a copy of the file to take with him—the information on Lydia might prove useful—when he felt an insistent pressure on his right shoulder that held him firmly down in his chair.

What about emergency contacts?

Gil wasn't sure how or why that suggestion came to him just then, but it was a damn good one. Lydia would need someone to care for Mikey while she was at work. Who better than her next of kin—or a close friend?

He printed the file and quit the program. Then retrieved the hard copy from the printer in Lydia's workstation. Lydia's emergency contact was a Doug Clark. Gil frowned and kneaded his forehead. The name sounded vaguely familiar. Where had he read it earlier? Which adoption file? Should he go back into the files and look up the last name Clark?

The pressure in his right shoulder twinged again.

Clark-Fitzhugh.

That was it. Susan Clark-Fitzhugh, the *social worker*, Gil realized in a flash, rolling his shoulder to ease the twinge in the muscle. He'd been sitting most of the day and was getting stiff. Could Doug Clark be any relation to the private social worker who conducted the home studies for the adoptions Newcombe handled?

Everything was starting to make a lot more sense. Gil reached for the phone on Lydia's desk to call Paulina, then changed his mind. He'd learned from observing Paulina in action that phone calls were too easily traced. He dialed his office instead and asked his secretary to relay a message to Paulina's office that he'd be calling her from his car phone in a few minutes. "Tell Paulina it's important," Gil said curtly.

Gil wrote Bullhauser a note explaining he'd finished the installation and would call in the morning. Then Gil turned off the computer and collected his briefcase. The spasm in his shoulder muscle seemed to have transferred to his back. Now he felt an odd prodding sensation in his scapula, as if someone were poking him with a finger.

Gil didn't need further urging. He hustled across the lobby of Barrister House as soon as the elevator door released him, then sprinted down the block to his car. There wasn't a cloud in the blue, Indian summer sky, but Gil felt an inexplicable anxiety overshadow him.

"LET HER GO, DOUG," Francine said, her voice shaking.

"Shut up, Francine! I'll handle this," Doug snarled. He pointed the nose of the gun inches from Paulina's belly. "Didn't anyone ever tell you snooping isn't good for your health?" His menacing tone made Paulina's skin prickle.

Paulina glanced from the waitress's pale face to Doug's cold, hard eyes and tested her weight on her twisted ankle.

A knife of panic sliced the ripples of pain throbbing through her body. She could run, maybe.

But not far.

Kicking the gun from his hand was out of the question.

Paulina focused on Doug, centering herself to attack. He was about six foot one. His bristle buzz cut and washboard physique suggested he'd spent time in the military. He held the gun as though he enjoyed the power it granted.

"You might want to rethink this decision," she said. "My office knows I'm here. I called in the address from my car phone. You'll have a little trouble explaining that to the police."

"Nice try, but your car doesn't have a phone. Lydia and I checked out your operation. You don't pull in enough income to warrant costly expenditures." His thick lips spread into a sickening smile on his broad face. "I think we can eliminate you from this scenario, no problem. The police will think your client did you in for figuring out he knocked off Jean-Luc and Cindy."

"There's been enough killing," Francine insisted. In the periphery of her vision, Paulina saw a blur of turquoise as Francine made a grab for the gun.

Paulina screamed, trying to distract Doug as he lifted his left arm and backhanded Francine. Leaning to the right, Paulina drove her right arm to the left and slapped the gun from his hand. It fell to the rocks with a clatter while she slammed the heel of her right hand into his nose. Doug grunted and instinctively clutched his nose.

Paulina used the precious second gained to reach down and grab a rock, her breath exhaling in a controlled rush as she wielded it toward his head, focusing all her strength and power into the movement. For Mikey's sake, she had to escape.

Doug high-blocked her thrust and countered with a roundhouse blow to her head. Paulina raised her left arm in a desperate attempt to deflect the blow, but was a split second too late. His hand connected with her temple, shattering her thoughts into a million black pieces. Paulina was vaguely aware that the stone she was holding hit the ground just before she did.

The fall knocked the breath from her lungs and Paulina lay there stunned as darkness engulfed her.

She tried to lift her head and peer into the dark, but her head felt so strange and heavy. Two hands brutally seized her shoulders and yanked her upward.

"Come on, Francine," she heard Doug say. "Give me a hand or I'll kill you next."

Chapter Thirteen

Tape. Duct tape.

Doug said it was in the junk drawer in the kitchen. The second drawer from the sink. Francine put a trembling hand on the drawer and pulled it open, staring blindly at a jumble of batteries, elastic bands and poker chips. Her heart thumped in her chest like a bird trying to escape from a cage.

Oh, man, what was she going to do? Lydia would be here any minute and Doug was going to kill that lady P.I.—if she wasn't dead already. Francine had helped Doug carry Paulina to the screen porch where they'd laid her on the floor.

Doug had paged Lydia to tell her what was up, but Francine had no idea what they planned to do because Doug had sent her into the garage for rope to tie Paulina's feet. All Doug had told her was that Lydia would be here soon.

Francine closed her eyes. There were many things in her life she wasn't proud of. Sometimes you got backed into a corner and you had to do what was necessary to survive. She'd been doing those young women a favor—helping them out in a difficult time. She knew what it was like to be pregnant and alone and worried enough about how to feed herself…much less raise a baby. Somewhere in southern Ontario Francine had a nineteen-year-old son.

As far as she was concerned, she'd done the kid a favor giving him a mother and a father who could pay for nice things like a university education. Folks like that had children who became doctors and teachers and engineers. It was a better life than she could have provided in the dingy run-down apartments she'd lived in over the years.

When she got up in the morning and faced herself in the mirror, her conscience was crystal clear.

But this…

No matter how hard she tried, Francine couldn't get Cindy out of her mind. She'd been scared that Wednesday morning facing the prospect of handing her baby over to strangers. Francine had seen it and scurried away, thinking of her own cut of the money and the trip to Barbados she was planning and how it was best for everyone. With time, Cindy would get over the loss and be glad for the money that was getting her back on her feet.

Killing had never been part of the arrangement. At least she knew Mikey was being well cared for—wherever Doug and Lydia had him stashed.

Francine sucked in an unsteady breath. If she didn't help Doug, he'd kill her. Things didn't get any simpler than that.

She spotted the duct tape crammed in the rear of the drawer and wiggled it free. Reluctantly, she grabbed a pair of scissors, too. They'd need something to cut the tape with.

You have no choice, she told herself firmly as dread clumped in an indigestible lump in her stomach. She nudged the drawer closed with her hip and whirled around toward the arched opening that connected with the family room.

Then she saw the wall-mounted telephone on the right side of the archway and remembered the card she had in her back pocket. Something about the lady P.I.'s manner had made Francine transfer Paulina's business card from her apron pocket to her jeans when she'd finished her shift. Francine threw an apprehensive glance through the family room toward the screen porch. She could see the back of Doug's head where he was seated in an iron lounge chair, keeping a close eye on Paulina.

Setting the duct tape and scissors down quietly on the glistening ceramic countertop, Francine withdrew the card from her pocket and eased the receiver from its cradle.

Maybe she still had a choice, after all.

"GOOD AFTERNOON. Stewart Investigations, how may I help you?" Andrea answered the phone pleasantly, hoping Mr. Boyer was finally getting around to calling. Paulina had been uncustomarily anxious about him when she'd returned from lunch and there'd been no message from him. That phone call from his secretary ten minutes ago had spooked Andrea. Why was he relaying messages?

Andrea wasn't looking forward to telling him that Paulina wasn't available at the moment and she had no idea where her boss was or when she'd be back.

"Hi, you don't know me," a woman's voice whispered, sounding theatrical.

"I would if you could tell me your name," Andrea quipped, suppressing a smile. Answering the phone around here was never boring.

"There's no time for that," the woman replied, urgency straddling her tone. "Your lady P.I.'s in trouble, they're gonna kill her—"

Andrea snapped to attention. "Who's going to kill her?" she demanded firmly, concentrating on the woman's voice and the background noises. She could hear something—a man's voice, but it sounded muffled. "Where are you calling from? Tell me so I can help you," Andrea said, her pen poised over a message pad.

The line went dead.

"Hello?" Andrea gaped in stunned dismay at the telephone. Had Paulina followed that waitress and got into trouble? Or was this some kind of a prank? What should she do? What would Paulina do?

Anxiety pinched Andrea's heart as she punched in *69 and jotted down the phone number of the last party that had called. She quickly dialed the phone company's service number which provides the *name behind the number* for customers, but the operator informed her it was an unpublished listing and the information was not available.

Andrea tucked her hair behind her ears and told herself to stay calm and think. *The library.* She should phone the library and see if someone in the research section could cross match an address with the phone number in the city directory. Andrea flipped through the card file on her desk for the Ottawa Public Library's phone number.

She'd just given the researcher the phone number when the second phone line rang. Andrea put the researcher on hold and answered line two. "Stewart Investigations, may I help you?" she said, praying the woman had called back. Or even better, that it would be Paulina reporting in.

"Andrea, this is Gil. Put Paulina on."

"I can't, Gil. She's not here. She went to Joe's Diner to talk to that waitress and decided to follow her home. She hasn't checked in since she left and I think she's in trouble. I got a call a few minutes ago from a woman who told me someone was planning to kill Paulina."

She heard Gil swear.

Andrea told him what the woman had said verbatim.

"They?" Gil said. "That must mean—"

"Hold on," Andrea said, suddenly remembering she had the researcher on line one. "I've got the library on the other line checking out the number."

Gil pulled his car off the roadway and spent the longest

thirty seconds of his life waiting for Andrea to come back on the line. The worry in her voice had been unmistakable. Gil felt as if a wall of offensive linesmen were using him to wipe their cleats. Had Paulina followed Francine to Lydia's place?

Andrea returned. "Gil, there's no match."

That wasn't the news Gil wanted to hear. "What's the number?" he demanded. He reached onto the passenger seat and scanned Lydia's personnel file. Andrea read out Lydia's home number, digit by digit. "Listen, Andrea," he said, "I have a hunch the paralegal, Lydia Kosak, is behind the illegal adoptions. She lives with someone named Doug Clark." He gave her the exact address on Iona Street.

Gil pulled out into traffic with a squeal of tires. "Phone Robbins and Zuker and tell them to get there ASAP. I think Mikey could be there—or with some social worker named Susan Clark-Fitzhugh, whom I suspect is related to Doug Clark. I'm on my way to Lydia's address now. Call me back as soon as you've gotten through to Zuker."

"Gil, you shouldn't go in there. It could be danger—"

"Just phone the police," he growled and promptly hung up. He settled both hands on the wheel and pressed the gas pedal to the floor, terrified that once again he'd arrive too late.

A RUMBLING JARRED Paulina awake. It took her a moment to realize the noise wasn't generated in the darkness in her head, but was instead the mechanical grind of an automatic garage-door opener. From beneath lowered lashes, she noticed the light shift from pitch-black to shadowed daylight. She heard the purr of a car motor and felt the motion of a vehicle between the sensations of pain registering in pounding waves throughout her body. Every inch of her

felt bruised and sore as though she'd been battered by a
methodical maniac.

Details came to her consciousness as she took stock of
her predicament.

She was seated in the first rear passenger seat of a minivan, her head propped against a window. From the sound
of the voices talking sporadically, she realized Lydia had
joined them and was driving the minivan. Paulina tilted
her head back slightly, changing her viewing angle through
the veil of her lashes. The slight shift of position caused
new waves of pain to slam inside her skull like a punishing
fist. Lydia's ponytail curled like a yellow ribbon down the
back of the driver's seat. A haze of turquoise told Paulina
that Francine was seated in the right front passenger seat.
The occasional sniffling sound coming from behind her
suggested Doug was in the back seat.

Either Doug had postnasal drip or she'd connected sol-
idly with his nose. Paulina wished her aim had been more
precise with that rock. She could have avoided this car trip
altogether.

The interior of the van was burgundy. The windows
were tinted black, which explained why someone had
thought there'd be no harm in slapping a piece of tape
over her mouth. Her hands were bound together at the
wrists with duct tape.

She grimaced, flattered good ol' Doug was worried
about her hands.

Paulina drew a calming breath through her nostrils,
struggling against the upsurge of panic running riot in her
chest. She tried ever so carefully to move her legs, feeling
the bite of rope slide against her nylons at her ankles. Her
right ankle had swollen so badly she couldn't slide her
heel down into her shoe—not that she'd want to put any
pressure on that ankle.

She was incapacitated and surrounded. Things couldn't get any worse.

"Where are we going?" she heard Francine demand. "I think I have a right to know what I'm involved in."

"To Gatineau Park. We'll dump her there and no one will be the wiser," Lydia replied, her voice ringing with confidence. "You have a specific spot in mind, Doug?"

"Nah, we'll just drive until we find a secluded place. This time of year, there's all kinds of people driving through the park watchin' the leaves change." Doug cleared his throat noisily. "We don't want her turning up any time soon. But I was thinkin', once it's done I'll clean the gun and then slip it inside Cindy's brother-in-law's car along with this little lady's car keys after I move her car tonight. That should keep the police busy and keep the brother-in-law off our backs. I don't think he'll go hiring any more private investigators. So, stop worrying, Francine. We've got it covered."

Paulina glanced through her lashes out the window, trying to determine their location. They were on Island Park Drive, presumably heading for the Champlain Bridge which spanned the Ottawa River, linking the provinces of Quebec and Ontario. The Gatineau Park was on the Quebec side of the river.

"I wish I'd never laid eyes on Cindy," Francine mumbled.

"You and me both," Lydia replied. "We've been operating without a hiccup. Then along comes Cindy. None of this would have happened if she hadn't changed her mind about the adoption at the last minute and Jean-Luc had bought my story about her screwing us both and running off on her own with the baby. Jean-Luc thought Cindy had pocketed her percentage and left him high and dry. Can you believe that jerk waited for me outside the firm and demanded a cut of the money?"

"I never met him. Cindy mentioned him, of course," Francine commented, "but he doesn't sound like much of a prince."

Lydia snorted. "He was not very smart, either. But Doug took care of him. He's good at covering my behind."

"You got that right, sweetheart," Doug piped up in a lascivious tone. "And that's a sweet, little behind you've got. I like covering it every chance I get—and you love every minute of it."

"You bet I do, hard stuff."

Paulina thought she was going to be sick. None of these people knew anything about love. Not the commitment-forever kind of love. Not Gil's kind of love. The only thing they knew was that it was a valuable commodity when it came to couples who were desperate enough to pay anything to have a child.

Gil.

A picture of him formed in her mind, comforting her with the haziness of a fond dream that she couldn't completely recall.

Lydia hadn't mentioned Gil's being at Newcombe and Bullhauser today. Maybe that meant he was safe for a while—at least until the gun linking him to her murder was recovered by the police. That, Paulina thought miserably, would make Robbins's day.

And the idea of Gil facing such a battle on his own gnawed at her heart. If her life had been different, Gil would have been exactly the kind of man she'd want to fall in love with. Successful. Caring. Sure of himself. Now that she was minutes away from being killed, she could admit to herself that Gil challenged her heart in a way Karl never had.

She'd fallen in love with Karl over a period of months, as she'd gotten to appreciate his intelligence and skill as an RCMP officer. The fact her father knew Karl well and approved of him had heightened his appeal. Paulina had thought Karl was a blue knight in uniform; the perfect mate for her, considering her interests. But there had been none of the wild, instantaneous craziness—the tumultuous warring with desire that she felt whenever she was near Gil. That deep-rooted feeling of knowing it wasn't right, but not giving a damn anyway. Was that how Cindy had felt when she was with Jean-Luc?

Cindy hadn't had the strength of mind to withstand the wants of her body. But at least she'd possessed the strength to stand up for her baby. Paulina was convinced Edison Tweedie had given Cindy the reassurance she needed to fight to keep her baby.

Paulina wasn't going down without a fight, either. Once they got her to the secondary location, she was dead meat anyway.

Through her lashes, Paulina saw the two neat rows of white globe lights that ornamented the bridge like pearls on a tarnished silver bracelet.

She had to act fast or she'd lose her chance.

She had a lot of children to live for—who needed her. And there was the very pleasant thought of seeing Gil's face when he was reunited with Mikey.

The bridge was narrow and two-laned; a corridor filled with witnesses if Paulina could find a way to attract attention. She inhaled and exhaled deeply, gathering her strength. The bridge leap-frogged over three islands. If she was going to try anything, better to do it over open water before they hit the first island.

Adrenaline enhanced her courage as she lurched forward and grabbed hold of Lydia's ponytail, jerking hard to the right as she fell to her knees. Her sore ankle throbbed in protest to the sudden pressure of her body weight. Shards of agonizing pain vibrated through her shins, but Paulina was beyond caring.

Lydia let out an unearthly scream. The minivan swerved and jumped the curb. Her balance precarious, Paulina mulishly held her grip. The deafening roar of an explosion—like hundreds of paper bags bursting at once—drowned out Lydia's cries. Paulina felt a stinging sensation rip through her side as the minivan crashed into the low black iron guardrail.

That bastard had shot her... she realized in stunned disbelief.

With a screech of crumpling metal, the van tilted and slowly flipped over into the river below.

Paulina tumbled around inside the interior of the van like a rag doll in a clothes dryer. Something hard prodded her in the shoulder as she was flung against the side passenger door, then gave way with a grating sound as she slid across the ceiling.

At least, she wasn't going to die in isolation, she thought fleetingly as her head smacked against a window with a dull thump and she saw a kaleidoscope of colors. Her mother and Gil would be spared the agony of wondering where she was and what had happened to her.

Then, blessedly, Paulina didn't feel anything at all.

Chapter Fourteen

"Where the hell are your men, Zuker?" Gil barked into the receiver of his car phone from the intersection of Island Park Drive and the Ottawa River Parkway. "They're heading onto the Champlain Bridge." Sweat beaded his forehead and trickled down his temples. The light changed to green and Gil surged ahead with the other traffic. He was seven cars behind the burgundy minivan that had left Lydia's house minutes ago.

After he'd checked out Paulina's abandoned car—hoping to find a note of some kind—he'd driven down Iona Street to Lydia's house on the corner. He'd been making a rapid U-turn on the cross street when the garage door had opened and the van had shot out.

"Don't worry," Zuker responded in a conciliatory tone. "They won't make it across the bridge. The Aylmer police will stop them on the other side. The OCP will close off this end. They'll be boxed in. Robbins is en route."

"You're damn lucky I saw them leaving the house," Gil groused. He didn't feel lucky at all. His heart was riddled with fear, knowing Paulina must be in that minivan—maybe dead.

Was Mikey in the van, too?

"Hang in there, Mr. Boyer, it'll be over soon. We've

dispatched two cars to the house, in case Mikey's there. Just stay out of the way and let us handle it.''

In the distance, Gil heard the faint wail of sirens and muttered a word of thanks.

Please let her be alive, he prayed silently, hugging the bumper of the station wagon in front of him. His knuckles glowed bone white on the receiver.

The seconds ticked like hours. Gil's mouth dropped open in horror as he saw the van veer suddenly, jump the curb and clip the right guardrail.

His heart vaulted from his chest as with a slow surrealism the van somersaulted over the rail and plunged to the rapids below.

Gil's mind went blank with petrifying fear—for Paulina and Mikey.

"Oh, God, they're in the river!" he shouted at Zuker, bringing his car to a screeching halt. Gil flung open his door heedless to the traffic around him. His legs couldn't seem to move fast enough as he sprinted to the rail, legs and arms pumping. The van bobbed and swayed with the current, the heavier front end sinking fast.

Gil didn't think twice. He aimed for a patch of blue water and jumped, hoping he wouldn't hit a rock.

PAULINA REALIZED she wasn't dead. If she were, why was someone ripping her mouth off her face and tugging insistently on her arms?

"We have to get out of here or we'll drown," a woman's shrill voice clamored in her brain. "The water's coming in."

Paulina forced her eyes open. Cold water lapped at her body, numbing her pain. She was lying on the floor of the minivan. Francine was bending over her. The side passenger door was open about eight inches and bright sunlight beamed through the gap, turning Francine's hairstyle into a glowing ginger beehive. Blood dripped from a cut on Francine's cheek. The minivan lurched and swirled around, jostling them as if they were on a dizzying ride at a fair. The nose of the vehicle was going down, forcing the rear up. The water level was rising fast.

Something sharp dug into her wrists. Francine was jabbing at the duct tape with her long fingernails.

"I got the rope off your legs, but I can't get the tape," Francine wailed. "Oh, my God, you're bleeding bad. I can't believe he shot you."

Paulina glanced down at her right hip. She could see blood seeping through her suit, but she didn't feel any pain.

"Can you swim?" Francine asked, helping Paulina up onto her knees.

Paulina nodded and moved her lips weakly. "Yes. I can float."

"Good. I'll help you, if you need it."

Francine squeezed through the narrow space toward the rear side passenger door.

The van swung around suddenly in the current and Paulina teetered, instinctively propping her arms against the back of the driver's seat for support. She glanced anxiously at Lydia, who was hunched over the wheel, one arm hanging limply.

Francine grabbed the handle of the door and tried to push it open, grunting with the effort. She didn't quite make it and the door slid down again. "Damn!"

Doug moaned from somewhere in the back of the van, but Paulina couldn't see him.

Terror lanced through Paulina's heart. She had no idea where the gun was, but she had no intention of hanging around to find out. Her mind was still trying to deal with the fact that the blood on her clothes belonged to her. Maybe if she lived through this she was going to call her mother. They hadn't talked since Mother's Day—and Paulina had only phoned then because despite her mother's disapproval of Paulina's work, Sarah was still her mother. Hand-sewn Halloween costumes, countless Girl Scout meetings and her college education still counted for something.

"Try again, Francine. I'll help," Paulina whispered in desperation. Crawling forward on her knees, she wedged her body against the front passenger seat. Then she braced her good leg on the door as Francine pushed it up. This time the door caught and locked in place. Francine helped Paulina to stand and they slid into the water.

The shock of the river's chilly embrace overwhelmed her for an instant. Until the will to survive took over. Paulina made a few hurried butterfly kicks, scooping at the water with her arms to get clear of the minivan. Then she went into a dead man's float to conserve her energy. The current carried her downstream. She'd always assumed the river was shallow here—there were parts of the river where people constructed rock pile sculptures for the viewing pleasure of the bridge commuters—but she couldn't touch bottom. The bank wasn't that far away, but battling the current to get there would require more energy than she had. She'd never felt so tired in her life. Or so cold—except for the patch of warmth on her right hip. Was she losing a lot of blood?

Francine splashed beside her doing a breaststroke. "It's all right, sugar," she said. "We made it. Try to hang on. Help's on the way—I hear sirens."

Paulina put her head in the water to rest, then pulled herself up for a nice, easy breath. "Do you see D-doug and Lydia?" she gasped as water sprayed into her mouth.

Francine's eyes widened, her hair plastered around her face. She turned her head to look at the minivan. "No, but who cares about them? They get what they deserve. I never meant for you to—''

Paulina lost the tail end of Francine's sentence as she lowered her face back into the water. Staying alive became her main concern. She blew her breath out steadily through her nose, then lifted her head above water again and gulped a breath of air. Fatigue invaded her muscles. Paulina wasn't sure how much longer she could go on. Francine was still talking, her voice an unintelligible jumble in Paulina's mind.

Paulina thought she must be going into shock because Francine's voice was altering—sounding unmistakably like Gil's. Up, breathe, down, rest. Up, breathe, down, rest. She tried so hard to persevere, knowing rescue couldn't be far away. Her body felt unbearably heavy, as if she'd snagged a lead weight and it was dragging her down. She desperately wanted to lay her head down in the water and rest—just for a minute.

''Paulina!'' Gil's voice practically bellowed in her ear, making her lift her head from the water, take another breath. ''I'm coming, sweetheart. Hang on.''

Was she hallucinating?

Paulina slipped below the surface of the water. With a superhuman effort, she pulled herself back up again—like a child pulling on her father's coattails. To her disbelieving eyes, a man was cutting through the water straight toward them. His arms moving at a furious pace.

Francine let out a whoop. ''Now that's what I call a *prince*.''

Paulina wholeheartedly agreed as Gil reached her. She quickly reassured him that Mikey hadn't been in the minivan, then let herself rest in his arms.

GIL GAZED DOWN at the battered figure sleeping in the hospital bed and hardly recognized her. Paulina's pale skin was mottled with a mass of bruises that made him wince. One side of her head was red and swollen, ugly purple colorings streaking her face. And beneath that sickly yellow hospital gown, he knew a dressing covered a gunshot wound. A graze, the doctor had called it. But the thought of how close it could have been sent Gil's stomach churning unsteadily.

He was still trembling from the shock of seeing her go over that bridge.

She had a minor concussion, a sprained ankle, abrasions and contusions, but she'd be all right. They just wanted to keep her in hospital overnight for observation.

His Paulina was the worse for wear, but still alive.

Lydia and Doug hadn't been so lucky—she'd died instantly and Doug had drowned before the police could save him.

Love, gratitude and guilt mingled in Gil's heart. Paulina was one hell of a woman. She'd risked her life to find Mikey. Gil loved her and respected her in a way he had never thought possible. The feeling was so fragile, like the blown-glass figurines his mother collected, that he was afraid to embrace it for long for fear it would shatter. He didn't know many men who had the guts to do what she had done to save herself. When he'd caught hold of her in the river, he'd been so exultant at finding her alive, he'd wanted to gather her to him. To keep her safe and close to his heart so he wouldn't feel so damn vulnerable.

Zuker and Robbins reassured him the police were all over Lydia's house. They were confident they'd find some kind of records, which would tell them exactly where Mikey was, but they would have to act with the utmost caution so as not to endanger him. Gil just had to be patient and let them do their job.

Gil pulled a chair close to the bed. Hitching up the back-to-front hospital gowns a nurse had given him to wear until

his parents arrived with dry clothes, he sat down and
warmed Paulina's cold, slender hand with his own. Here
was as good a place to wait as any.

PAULINA OPENED HER eyes to the muted morning light and
groaned. *How could it hurt to open your eyelids?* Then her
gaze fell upon Gil dozing in the chair beside her bed and
she forgot all about the pain as she absorbed every detail
of his appearance—the bump on his nose, the curl of his
dark lashes against the strong curve of his cheeks, the
shape of his lips—and felt grateful for the opportunity to
do so.

He'd found her. She didn't know how he'd done it—
the details were foggy in her mind. She didn't even remember being transported to the hospital. She *did* remember Gil had been with her all that time. She'd heard him
arguing with a nurse or a doctor, insisting that he stay in
the room with her. She smiled, the muscles in her face
twinging with pain. Of course, he'd won. She recalled trying to warn the nurse or the doctor that it was pointless to
argue with him; he was a darn, stubborn man. But it came
out as a weak, mewling sound and she hadn't the strength
to repeat herself.

She was just so very glad he was here. And that he
seemed none the worse for wear for his swim in the river.

She looked at him for a long time, finding the way he'd
managed to squeeze his massive frame into the vinyl chair
by hunching his shoulders around his ears oddly endearing.
He was wearing jeans. A black T-shirt stretched snugly
across his broad chest. His hands rested loosely—one
across the ridged muscles of his abdomen, the other dangling over the arm of the chair. Paulina found the fine,
dark, swirling hair on his arms sexy in the extreme, making
her want to crawl out of the hospital bed and plunk herself
down in the cradle of his lap, where she could feel those

arms tighten around her and experience the magic of his kiss. Memories of their lovemaking blanketed the soreness in her body with a fusion of downy heat.

She sighed and closed her eyes, shielding herself from temptation.

"I'll TAKE GOOD CARE of her," Gil promised the doctor, who was signing Paulina's release papers.

"See that you do," the doctor responded. "Check her pupils every hour and her mental status. If she falls asleep and you can't rouse her, there's something serious going on and we'll need to do another CT scan. Try to rest the ankle—keep her off it for at least a day. It should be feeling normal in a week or so." The doctor winked at Paulina. "Take it easy in those high heels."

"Gil, you don't have to do this," Paulina said, looking visibly annoyed while he helped her out of bed and into a wheelchair. She winced as he cupped her elbows to keep her from putting any weight on her bad ankle. "You're not responsible for me—"

"You got hurt working for me—that makes me responsible," he said firmly, dismissing her argument.

"It's not particularly wise to go around making statements like that," she grumbled, gingerly lifting each leg—clad in rose-colored sweats that Andrea had brought by for Paulina's trip home—and setting it in a footrest. "Andrea will be happy to baby-sit me. She said so."

"You can't expect her to hold down the fort at your agency and look after you, too," he commented dryly. "You already sent her off to gather Mikey's file together and stock the kitchen for your convalescence."

"But Gil," she said patiently, "you're a *client*."

He didn't miss the inflection of her tone, the resolute reestablishment of boundaries. "Not anymore." His hands tightened on the handles of the wheelchair as he pushed it forward. "As of this moment, you're fired."

She snorted.

Gil couldn't figure out what she was so bent out of shape about—unless she was worried he might have to assist her with personal intimacies like dressing and bathing. Andrea had helped Paulina dress this morning. Gil didn't know whether to be irritated or flattered. They'd made love, for goodness' sake. Whether she wanted him near or not, every centimeter of her silken body was indelibly inscribed in his memory.

"I could take you to my house instead until we hear more from the police," he offered. "My mom's got nursing experience. Maybe you'd feel more comfortable having a woman look after you." The elevator button pinged and the massive doors slid open, allowing them entrance.

"That's very sweet, Gil, but your mother already has her hands full with your dad. Besides, my apartment is closer to the police station. With luck, Robbins and Zuker will ferret out Mikey's location by the end of the day."

"Well, then, it looks like you're stuck with me."

She sighed audibly. "Yes, I guess so."

Gil wasn't the least bit sure how to interpret that sigh either.

THE DARN MAN INSISTED on carrying her upstairs and over the threshold to her apartment. Andrea was there waiting, holding the door open for them. Paulina didn't know whether it was heaven or hell to be held so firmly against him. She hurt everywhere her body made contact with his, but snuggling her head under his chin and inhaling the sexy, male scent of his skin while his heart pounded steadily beneath her ear was pure bliss.

She gritted her teeth as Gil carried her down the hall to her bedroom and laid her on the bed, propping a pillow beneath her sprained ankle. The gentleness of his touch sent a frisson of awareness through her body. Paulina was all too cognizant that he'd made love to her on this bed. In this room. No wonder Eve couldn't resist the apple when it was constantly within her reach.

"You cold?" he asked, his indigo eyes flashing with concern.

"N-no," she stammered.

"Are you sure? You're shivering." He put his hand on her forehead to test her temperature and Paulina nearly leaped out of her skin.

Andrea entered the room carrying a plastic tub of water, her steps slow and mincing. "I thought you'd like to clean up after that dip in the river," she said cheerfully. "It won't be as good as a bath, but maybe we'll try that tomorrow."

"You're a lifesaver, Andrea," Paulina muttered, feeling slightly hysterical.

"You don't have a fever," Gil said, frowning down at her. He leaned closer and looked into her eyes, his face inches from hers. "Your pupils look all right."

Paulina batted him away. "I'm fine, really." She turned her gaze on Andrea, who was setting the tub of water on the bed table. "After I freshen up, I want you to take notes while Gil tells us what he found out yesterday at Newcombe's office. Maybe we can assist the police in finding Mikey."

Gil put his hands on his hips. "I distinctly remember firing you about forty minutes ago."

She smiled at him sweetly, feeling her facial muscles contort in a smile that must be hideous to be viewed. "Fired or no, I don't quit until the job is done." *Besides, the sooner the police found Mikey, the sooner her life would revert to normal—minus Gil Boyer.*

"You are unbelievably stubborn. Do you know that?" Gil asked, shaking his head.

"That's the pot calling the kettle black."

"You were almost killed—"

Andrea put two fingers in her mouth and let loose an ear-piercing whistle. "Okay, that's enough you two." Paulina stared at her friend in amazement. Andrea playfully tapped Gil's chest. "Trust me on this, Big Guy. This is your cue to exit gracefully and give Paulina some privacy. There's coffee on the stove and Danish on the counter. Help yourself."

Gil looked ready to object, then set his mouth in a firm, disapproving line.

Paulina breathed a sigh of relief when Andrea shut the door firmly behind him. "Thanks, pal." She rested her eyes, enjoying the temporary reprieve from Gil. But a muffled snicker made her eyes snap open. Andrea was leaning against the door, laughing her head off.

"I don't see what's so funny," Paulina muttered sourly.

"Don't you?" Andrea snorted. "I find it remarkable how someone who's astutely intuitive with other people can be incredibly blind when it comes to her own life."

Paulina clenched fistfuls of her duvet cover in her hands. "I'm not blind. I'm just being smart."

"Hmm." Andrea didn't sound convinced, but she managed to keep a straight face.

"Let's just get the bath over with quickly, okay? I can't think about anything else but getting Mikey home safe and sound."

THE PHONE RANG at 3:47 p.m. Gil picked up the extension in the living-room on the first ring, hoping the noise wouldn't disturb Paulina. Fatigue had finally conquered her pigheaded determination forty minutes earlier and she'd fallen asleep with her cute scraped-up nose still buried in Mikey's file. Gil had moved the file to the far side of the bed so she'd be more comfortable.

"Mr. Boyer, this is Detective Robbins. How is Ms. Stewart doing?"

"Fine. She's too stubborn to let a few bruises stop her for long."

"I'm glad to hear it, because we believe we've got a fix on your nephew's location."

Gil's heart stopped. "You found him? Are you sure?"

"As sure as we can be until we access the house. We found a diskette at Lydia's home with her records on it. We've interviewed the couple who were adopting Mikey. They haven't received the child. Lydia had told them the birth mother needed additional time because there'd been a death in the family." Robbins cleared his throat. "So, based on your suggestion, we probed into Susan Clark-Fitzhugh's background. Turns out she's Doug Clark's sister. We put some surveillance on her house. One of our men just called in. Says they spotted her in a window with a light-haired baby in her arms. According to her neighbors, Clark-Fitzhugh doesn't have any children. She and her husband keep to themselves. We got a call in to the Children's Aid Society—they're sending a social worker so we can go in. I've dispatched a car to meet you. I thought you and Ms. Stewart might like to be present."

"Of course we want to be there," Gil stated adamantly.

"I thought so. But under no circumstances are you to approach your nephew. In a situation like this, his identity will have to be positively established. He'll be placed in a foster home in the meantime."

A foster home? Gil swallowed a frustrated protest. He couldn't believe that after all he'd been through to find Mikey, he was going to be denied access to him—even temporarily. This sounded so crazy. "When can I bring him home?" he asked.

Robbins paused awkwardly, making Gil's anxiety escalate. "A social worker will explain the procedure once we have Mikey in protective custody. Our immediate concern is to recover the child. The car should be arriving any minute."

Gil hung up the phone. He hoped Robbins wasn't inferring he might not be granted custody of Mikey. A mushroom cloud of elation overshadowed this new worry as he quickly called his parents with the news, then sailed down the hallway to Paulina's bedroom. He crept to the side of her old-fashioned iron bed and gazed down at her sleeping form. His heart expanded with the love he had for her until his chest ached. Her hair was black as night against the lavender pillow slip. She was still wearing the pink sweats—due either to modesty or her habit of being prepared to go at a moment's notice. Though she was black-and-blue from head to toe, Gil thought she'd never looked more beautiful to him.

Damn, he wanted to kiss her!

And this was probably his last chance. He kneeled on the gleaming oak floor and tenderly brushed a kiss onto a patch of white skin on her forehead that had escaped bruising. She stirred in her sleep, moving in a sensuous way that made him long to stretch out beside her and feel every silken contour of her body molded against him.

"Paulina, wake up," he whispered, daring a second kiss. The scent of her silken skin lingered on his lips as her eyelids fluttered open.

Instant wariness settled in her eyes.

But even the knowledge that she didn't want him couldn't dampen his joy at knowing Mikey would soon be with him.

"You're taking this concussion business seriously, aren't you?" she said grumpily. "It's bad enough they woke me up at the hospital every hour. How are my pupils?''

"Beautiful," he said with unabashed enthusiasm, barely giving them a glance. He was grinning so hard he thought his face would crack. He braced his forearms on the edge of the bed, fortifying himself against the fearsome sight of her bruised face sporting an arctic frown.

"Gil—"

"The police think they've found Mikey," he announced, dropping his bomb. "They're sending a car for us."

"Really? That's wonderful!" She threw back the duvet that covered her slender body and hooked her arms around his shoulders, making him catch his breath in surprise. "Let's go," she said. "I'm ready."

"What? Like this?" Gil asked, settling his hands obediently around her waist. "Don't you want a shoe for your good foot?" Knowing Mikey would soon be safe and having Paulina this close and smiling at him was a powerful aphrodisiac. He counted to five slowly and reminded himself that Paulina had thrown her arms around him to demand that he carry her—not kiss her.

"Why bother with a shoe when you're going to carry me anyway?" she pointed out pragmatically. "Now, who phoned? I want to know exactly what they said."

"Robbins phoned..." Gil lost track of his sentence as he lifted her easily into his arms, his senses completely scrambled by the drugging warmth of the silken-sweet woman's body cradled against his ribs. She was so adept at ignoring the attraction that crackled like a match striking flint when they were together. At pretending it didn't exist even when her nipples hardened into telltale buttons beneath her sweatshirt.

But he couldn't ignore it. His heart was racing at ninety miles an hour. It was all he could do not to let her shift down to his hips—to let his body communicate what words could not.

"Did he say where Mikey was?" Paulina asked, tilting her chin up to see him. Her lips were so agonizingly close...

Gil drew his gaze away. His legs felt weak. He aimed for the door and tried to concentrate on Mikey. How could he look at Mikey every day for the rest of his life and not think of Paulina? Of what she'd done for them both?

"Mikey's at Susan Clark-Fitzhugh's home," he managed to say.

"Where does she live? Do the police know if anyone else was involved?" Her questions came at him faster than he could compute responses.

Gil struggled to make his mind function, to respect her wishes and keep their relationship on a professional level. But as he carried her down the hall, he couldn't help wishing she was peppering him with celebratory kisses rather than questions.

Chapter Fifteen

"Nervous?" Paulina asked Gil, gripping his fingers as they sat in the back seat of an unmarked police car and watched Robbins direct a swarm of officers to surround the tan brick bungalow situated at the end of a quiet cul-de-sac in Nepean.

Gil's gaze was trained on the house. "On tenterhooks. What if he isn't there—or it's some other baby?"

Paulina squeezed his fingers. "He'll be there," she said, wondering what it was about Gil that made her utter rash promises. "You and Mikey are meant to be together."

His eyes shifted, dark and curious, to her briefly. "How do you know that?"

Paulina shrugged and immediately regretted the movement because a razor-edged pain slashed through her aching shoulders. But she was more concerned about the emotional wounds this case was inflicting on her than the physical ones. "I just know."

"Do you have any other predictions for the future, Ms. Stewart?"

His question appeared innocuous, but Paulina sensed a trap. She had the uncomfortable notion he was asking if she could see a tall, dark and handsome man with indigo eyes in her future. The inference was there that he hoped she'd somehow changed her mind because it would make *him* happy. But his wording remained vague enough that she'd appear paranoid if she addressed that issue directly. Maybe *she* was being paranoid. Gil didn't strike her as being the kind of man who'd settle for less than he wanted. He was driving her crazy.

She rubbed her temples to soothe her frazzled wits. He was still waiting for an answer. She kept her voice carefully neutral. "Sorry, that's the extent of my psychic abilities."

She darted a sideways glance at him. His lips were pressed together in a thin, accepting line. The police were entering the dwelling.

Paulina craned her neck forward and felt Gil's fingers stiffen in her own. Time stood still, the seconds stretching into what must have only been a few minutes but felt like an eternity. Gil's sharp intake of breath echoed in her heart as an officer appeared on the front steps and motioned for the social worker from the Children's Aid Society to enter the house.

"That's it—he's there!" Gil said thickly. "Please, God, let it be Mikey."

Paulina added a silent prayer of her own and pressed her left hand to her mouth to suppress the hope rising in her heart like a geyser on the verge of spouting. She saw a movement in the doorway. Then the social worker walked out of the house, holding a plump, downy-haired infant on her hip.

Paulina's eyes watered and spilled over.

"It's him! Oh, God, Mikey—" Gil's jubilant cry broke off abruptly. She saw tears trace his cheek as he released her hand and fumbled for the door latch, but the officer who stood guard outside the car sent him a warning look. "Damn!" Gil slammed his hand in a futile gesture against the glass.

Paulina watched, her heart locked in a vise, as Robbins

conferred with the social worker. Was he inquiring which foster home Mikey would be sent to? With a choked sob, Paulina scooted across the seat as Gil's rigid shoulders heaved beneath his gray flannel shirt. She pressed her mouth against the rock-hard muscles in a kiss meant to comfort, and locked her arms around his waist. It seemed so unfair the police wouldn't let Gil see Mikey, much less hold him. "It's okay," she whispered, "you'll have him in your arms soon. Didn't I tell you some things were meant to be?"

He nodded as a shudder racked through him.

Paulina raised her head and looked out the window. Her mouth dropped open in surprise and gratitude. Robbins was escorting the social worker and Mikey straight toward them! "Gil, look!"

So Robbins had a heart, after all. The detective motioned to the uniformed officer to open the door for Gil.

"I'm not supposed to do this," he cautioned Gil, "but I have kids of my own. Just a quick hug."

Paulina thought she would never forget the way Gil's arms tenderly circled Mikey and drew him next to his heart. Tears blurred her vision as Gil planted a kiss on Mikey's forehead and murmured thickly, "Oh, buddy, am I glad to see you." Mikey gurgled and bestowed his uncle with a wide-eyed smile that was truly adorable. These two guys belonged together. Paulina wiped her damp palm on her sweatshirt and leaned out of the police car to tweak Mikey's toe, feeling emotionally gratified by the brief contact. Mikey looked healthy and well cared for—any parent's joy.

Already the social worker was reaching out for Mikey. Gil reluctantly handed him over and Mikey started to whimper. "You're going to go with this nice lady here for a few days, buddy," Gil explained, reassuring him, "but pretty soon I'll bring you home for good. I promise."

Paulina reached for Gil's hand as he rejoined her in the back seat, holding it tightly as Mikey was loaded into another car and driven away.

Finally, it was over. She could post Mikey's picture on her Found wall and take up where she'd left off on her other cases.

So, why, then—despite her cataclysmic relief at Mikey's being found alive and well—did she feel so scared? Paulina had no time to examine the feeling. A woman, presumably Susan Clark-Fitzhugh, was led out of the house in handcuffs, and Zuker came to join them in the police car.

Gil ran a hand through his hair. "What happens now?" he quietly asked the two detectives. He looked haggard and tired. But Paulina could see the steel of his strong will beneath the exhaustion.

"A sample of Mikey's DNA will be compared with samples saved from Cindy's autopsy," Robbins explained. "Once his identity is established, it's a question of you proving to the Children's Aid Society that you're capable of caring for him. A social worker will contact you tomorrow and set up an appointment. The process usually takes two to three weeks—provided there are no countermotions for custody."

Gil nodded. "Good. Thank you."

"No. *Thank you,* Mr. Boyer," Robbins replied with candid frankness. "As cops, we don't like citizens poking their noses in our work, but there's no question that we might not have found your nephew if you hadn't hired Ms. Stewart."

Paulina hoped her bruises concealed the blush this unexpected praise brought to her cheeks.

"And you deserve all the credit for saving Ms. Stewart's life yesterday," Robbins went on. "Lydia Kosak and her boyfriend, Doug Clark, had been operating right under her boss's nose—culling clients from his reject list and matching them up with mothers willing to sell a five-dollar charm bracelet to the adopting parents for fifteen grand.

"That dame even had contacts in government offices provide her with legitimate birth certificates," Zuker added. "We'll be investigating that for some time to come. The RCMP will launch a parallel investigation."

Robbins loosened his tie. "The deal with Susan Clark-Fitzhugh was that she could work off the price of a child by providing this service for them. Apparently, she was supposed to receive the next child. She doesn't know about Doug yet. Her husband works for Statistics Canada, we're not sure of the extent of his involvement. We had another team pick him up at work."

"Did Francine Loiselle give a statement?" Paulina asked. "I heard Lydia and Doug admit to Francine that they killed Cindy and Jean-Luc."

"We got Ms. Loiselle's statement to that effect."

Paulina frowned. "What's going to happen to her? She didn't know anything about the killings. My intern told me that Francine called my office and said I was in danger. I couldn't have gotten out of that minivan without her help." Just the mention of her narrow escape yesterday made Paulina shudder.

"She'll be charged with conspiracy to commit abduction, but she'll probably be allowed to plea-bargain in exchange for testifying against Clark-Fitzhugh."

"At least that ties everything up," Paulina said.

Zuker grinned. "Not quite. Elva Madre arrived home from her holiday this afternoon and found one of our men waiting for her. She disclosed that Cindy had phoned her to discuss giving Mikey up for adoption. Apparently, Cindy's new boyfriend didn't want the baby and he didn't think Cindy was a very good mother. Elva told Cindy she had to do what was best for herself and her baby. She suggested Cindy needed to decide if her new boyfriend was the type of man she really wanted to spend the rest of her life with.''

Zuker paused. "When you approached her, Ms. Stewart, Elva was worried her advice had sent Cindy to her death. She needed time to think things out. We had trouble finding her because she'd gone to stay at a friend's cottage.''

"So Cindy made up the story about her mother watching the baby for the travel agent's benefit," Paulina mused.

"That's what we think," Zuker glanced at Robbins for confirmation. "And it turns out Ed Tweedie's alibi was solid for the day that infant was abducted in Swift Current. His car had broken down and it sat in a repair shop for three days waiting for parts while he was at the home-building event. He had no means of transportation.''

"I'm glad to hear that," Paulina murmured, feeling the fatigue sweeping back into her battered body in the wake of elation. "He tried to help Cindy. Not too many people these days would take the time to listen to a troubled stranger." She blinked tiredly, longing to be home in her own bed. She was *not* going to fall asleep in front of these two detectives.

Gil's arm settled around her shoulders, propping her up.

"I think Ms. Stewart's had enough excitement," he told the detectives.

Paulina smothered a smile. For once—and probably because her defenses were low and she was too bushed to object—she admitted to herself it was nice to have a man looking after her.

PAULINA HUNG UP THE PHONE in her darkened bedroom and let the small miracle of her phone conversation with her mother settle into her heart. Her mouth curved into a tremulous smile as she hugged her knees tightly to her chest. She'd been terrified she was just setting herself up for more hurt by trying to extend the olive branch, but her mother had actually agreed to come to Ottawa in November to celebrate her fiftieth birthday. Would wonders never cease?

She lifted her head as a light knock sounded on her door.

"You okay?" Gil asked, swinging her door inward. "I heard your voice." The light from the hallway silhouetted his massive form, making him more of a shadow man than ever.

Paulina sniffed at the analogy and wiped her tear-dampened cheeks on the knees of her sweatpants as he walked around the foot of her bed, the light from the hallway illuminating his path. "I called my mom. I told her I wanted to make peace."

His hand gently cupped her head.

"Ah, and did you?" he asked.

"Yes."

"I'm glad." His voice took on a husky tinge that rippled softly over her skin. "I want you to be happy, Paulina."

She gazed up at his silhouette in the dark. He'd invaded her life so completely. She wouldn't be able to go to bed at night for a long time without thinking of him. He'd be like a shadow, hovering in the back of her mind. Tomorrow she had to send him back to his life. He had plans to make for Mikey's arrival. "I want you to be happy, too, Gil," she said wistfully.

He cleared his throat. "Are you hungry? I made dinner."

"I'm starving."

"Come here, then." He reached for her and she needed no second invitation to be picked up and held by him—if even for the twenty seconds it took for him to carry her down the hall.

Her stomach growled at the appetizing scents of pasta and garlic wafting from her compact kitchen. She gasped as Gil carried her into the living room. The room was bathed in candlelight from her emergency supply of candles for power outages. He'd pushed the round oak table that served as a dining table close to the window and two white candles were nestled in crystal candlestick holders, twin flames flickering like stars. He'd dug a damask tablecloth and cloth napkins from her cupboards. There was even a vase filled with a dozen fresh red roses on the table and a bottle of red wine breathing on the table. Two steaming plates of fettuccine with a mushroom-and-cream sauce and fresh garden salads were set out along with crisp rounds of baguette. Paulina had no idea how he'd accomplished this feat so quickly, but it was pretty impressive.

He set her down in a chair. Paulina had to mentally tell herself to unhook her arms from around his neck.

"What's this?" she asked, not quite trusting herself to speak.

Gil smiled wryly at the tremor of panic in her voice and wondered how to answer her question. He knew she was worried the flowers and the candles were a romantic overture. "This is a celebration for a job well done," he said quietly.

"Oh." She fingered the stem of her wineglass. Was she relieved? Disappointed?

God, he couldn't tell. Did it matter?

His chest contracted with a pain that was dull and bittersweet. He loved her. And he'd bet his consulting firm that the stubbornly independent woman who was studiously avoiding meeting his eyes, cared about him, too. More than she was willing to admit.

Maybe even loved him.

Gil sat down and reached for the bottle of burgundy. He filled her glass, watching her covertly. She'd kissed him in the police car today. He could point to the exact spot where her lips had pressed against his shoulder. She'd kissed him of her own accord. Maybe she hadn't even realized she'd done it, but Gil knew the gesture came from her heart. There was an undeniable connection between them. And a powerful amount of sexual attraction.

But they were both smart enough to know that love and great sex weren't the only ingredients in a recipe for marital happiness. Gil needed a wife who could be a mother to his nephew and Paulina had different needs just now.

Gil couldn't fault her for her choices. Without her gift and talent, he wouldn't have Mikey. Tomorrow he'd face the challenge of convincing the authorities he could properly raise his nephew. Surely they couldn't turn him down. No amount of procedural red tape was going to stop Gil from bringing Mikey home at last.

Gil filled his glass, the gentle gurgle of the wine emptying into the crystal goblet the only sound. He set the bottle on the table and raised his glass to her. "I'd like to make a toast."

Paulina's starry eyes lifted and locked with his, the raw honesty in them cutting him to the heart.

"Uh-oh," she said teasingly, "you're not trying to butter me up so I'll pare down your bill, are you? If you are, it won't work."

"I'd never dream of it. You're worth every penny— even if you do interrupt toasts." He feigned a menacing frown at her, then started over, emotion creeping into his words. "Thank you for bringing Mikey back into my life. I wish you as much success with all your cases—just try to stay away from bridges and minivans."

"I promise," she said with a laugh and drew a cross over her heart with her finger.

A pleasing *ting* rang out as their wineglasses touched. Gil took a sip and swallowed.

"I have a toast myself," Paulina said. "To Gil—who's

already proven he has what it takes to be a father. Mikey's a lucky kid to have you in his life."

Gil had to bite his tongue to keep from adding spontaneously, *There's room for you, if you ever change your mind.*

They drank again. Then Paulina picked up her fork and speared a piece of romaine lettuce. "I hate to admit it, but you were a good partner. You caught on fast."

"Does that mean you're going to refund me the extra money I paid you to let me tag along?" Gil asked.

"No way. To quote you, 'You're worth every penny.'"

They ate their meal, sending teasing barbs at one another across the table.

"Absolutely delicious," Paulina proclaimed when she'd cleared her plate and Gil was working on second helpings. "I had no idea you could cook."

"If you're as big as I am, feeding yourself is a prime concern. But my recipe base is limited."

She patted her stomach in appreciation and leaned back in her chair. "This was fun. A good way to say goodbye."

The happiness of the evening slipped away from Gil like the high after a hard-won game when reality filtered back in. She'd kicked the door shut on his feelings for her. His gaze flew to her face, trying to read her thoughts. It was time to knuckle down, focus on the long-term goals, nobly accept defeat. "Is it good-bye already?" he asked, trying to keep his voice light.

She nodded, her gray eyes solemn. "You've got to prepare for Mikey's homecoming. And I've got to pack my bags for Australia. I'll be gone for a couple of weeks."

"But you can't even walk," Gil protested.

She waved her hand at him. "I'll manage. I called Andrea before I talked to my mother. She'll take over for you at eight tomorrow morning."

Gil looked at her, knowing she was right. But a part of him rebelled at the prospect. He'd never believed in the concept of soul mates, but Paulina understood him in a way no one else ever had. He'd miss that. "I'll miss you," he said softly.

She reached out and covered his hand with her own. "I'll miss you, too."

"Can I kiss you good-bye?" he asked.

Her eyes widened and Gil saw the pulse leap at the base of her throat above the ribbed neckline of her sweatshirt. His own pulse accelerated when he saw her mouth curve into a smile. Even with the bruises on her face, the smile was undeniably sexy.

"Actually, I was hoping you'd do more than that..." she responded breathlessly.

Was she now? Gil grinned and drew her hand to his lips. He was definitely up for a memorable farewell. He circled her pinkie with his tongue, then suckled gently, savoring the taste of her. Heat banked in the center of his body. He took her ring finger into his mouth, stroking it with his tongue. Then he closed his lips and drew her finger, slowly and provocatively, out of his mouth. Paulina moaned in response.

Oh, yes, he'd make their last night together as memorable as their first. "It'll be a pleasure, *Ms. Stewart*," he promised, caught between the ecstasy of having her one more time and the agony of knowing it would be the last.

Beneath the table, he felt her bare toes brush up his leg. "I'm counting on it, *Gil*."

Chapter Sixteen

Gil paced the length of the foyer, stopped and looked out the beveled-glass sidelight framing the front door for what felt like the one hundredth time. Anticipation crested high in his chest and seemed to fill the house. Where was the social worker? After twenty-two anxiety-ridden days of filling out forms, interviews and making preparations, Mikey was finally coming home today.

And they were seventeen minutes late.

Gil's knees trembled as he resumed his pacing. He could hear his mother and Mrs. McTavish, the Scottish nanny he'd hired, fussing upstairs in Mikey's nursery. His father was out in the garage putting the finishing touches on a special woodworking project he was making for Mikey's homecoming.

Gil pressed his face to the window again. A green sedan was pulling into the driveway, its horn sounding twice. *Mikey!*

"Mom! Dad!" Gil bellowed happily at the top of his lungs. "He's here. Mikey's home!" He heard his mother's excited cry from upstairs as he tore open the front door. A wide grin split his face as he nimbly ran down the front walk. His dad was maneuvering his wheelchair from the garage, a brightly painted puppy pull toy in his lap. Gil beamed at his dad as the social worker unfastened Mikey from his car seat.

Mikey's legs wiggled enthusiastically as she lifted him free and passed him to Gil. "Here's your son, Mr. Boyer."

Gil felt the tears smart in his eyes as he cradled his son in his arms. Holding Mikey was like holding a wiggling bundle of love and hope, and so much more. Gil only wished a starry-eyed private investigator could be here with them to share the moment.

"Hey, Boss, mind if I come in? I want to discuss my maternity leave."

Gil glanced up from the computer screen in his office and waved at Renée to enter, which she did slowly, hampered by the weight and size of the baby she carried. A gift bag dangled from her wrist.

"How are you feeling?" he asked with concern, smothering a yawn as she lowered herself into one of his spare chairs. He knew she'd had a checkup yesterday.

"Enormous," she stated bluntly. "I have a strong dislike for slender women, but I understand that's normal. The doctor says everything's fine. Another three or four weeks and I'll be falling asleep at my desk just like you." She fluffed up her short, spiky bangs. "How's fatherhood treating you?"

"It's only been three days," Gil said, with a grin. "An eventful three days—or maybe I should say an eventful three nights. Mikey's a night owl and Mrs. McTavish made it clear when I hired her that I was on night shift." Gil yawned again. "It would be easier if I were married."

"Why? So your wife could get up in the middle of the night with him?" Renée rolled her eyes. "This may rock the foundation of your being, but I've got a news flash for you. Men are just as capable of taking care of babies as women." She rubbed her stomach. "Lonny's going to stay home and take care of our baby for the first year. We decided it was important for one of us to be there with our child, and from a financial standpoint it makes more sense for me to continue working, because I earn more than him."

Gil didn't know what to say; he was too stunned to speak. Lonny wrote a sports column for the *Ottawa Citizen. He* was staying home?

She plopped the gift bag on his desk. "This is for you. I bought one for Lonny, too."

"Thanks." Gil peeked in the bag and withdrew a book tied with a blue satin ribbon.

"There's everything you need to know in there about taking care of a baby. And I assure you, not once does it say only a woman can do this—with the exception of breast feeding. But Mikey's on a bottle, anyway."

Gil flushed. He'd heard of couples working part-time and sharing the child-care load, but he'd never actually met a stay-at-home dad. Thank God he had the resources to hire a nanny for Mikey. But he still considered Mrs. McTavish a less-than-perfect temporary solution.

He fingered the thick book, unconvinced it could wipe away the uncertainty that had coursed through him last night when Mikey had awakened at three and cried for an hour and forty-five minutes. Gil had tried everything— changing his diaper, giving him a bottle, walking him, even singing to him. Exhausted and out of ideas, he'd piled the pillows against his headboard and settled back, with Mikey tucked securely against his chest—and just held him. Mikey had gradually calmed down, snuffling his little nose against Gil's shoulder in the same way Gil had seen him nosing against Cindy. Gil wondered if Mikey was crying because he missed Cindy.

It made Gil all the more certain Mikey needed a mother. But for some reason, Gil had no enthusiasm for beginning

a wife hunt. Three weeks had passed since he and Paulina
had said good-bye. The heat of the passion they'd shared
that night still lingered in him, warming him whenever
something triggered a thought of Paulina. For a fleeting
instant, he allowed himself to wonder how she was and
what she was doing. Had she returned from Australia?

God, he missed her. Missed the intimacy of their teasing. Missed the intimacy of their joined hands. Their joined
bodies.

He'd received a bill from her office, but there'd been
no other form of communication. Gil knew there wouldn't
be. He had to focus on the present and future. Paulina was
a seductive memory belonging to the past.

He smiled at Renée and searched his mind, trying to
remember what they'd been talking about. Her maternity
leave. Oh, yeah, he wished Lonny a lot of luck. Renée's
husband had no idea what was in store for him.

IT FELT STRANGE TO BE in her office again after two weeks
away. Strange to think it was spring in Australia while a
few stray snowflakes drifted down from the Ottawa skies.
Paulina shifted restlessly in her chair. The walls that had
been her main source of happiness for years, now seemed
somehow confining as she weeded her way through the
paperwork that had piled up on her desk in her absence.
Of course, it didn't help that she found herself glancing
frequently toward her office door—half expecting a certain
handsome shadow to materialize.

Paulina shook her head at her wishful thinking and
skimmed the last page of Brenda Watson's final report.
She gave the document a satisfied pat. A fairly happy ending—all things considered. Paulina got weepy just thinking
about it. It hadn't taken Brenda long to realize she couldn't
uproot Bryan from his family and friends. Especially when
Bryan had always believed Peg to be his mother. Brenda

and Will were eventually able to reach an agreement that would allow Bryan to visit her at Christmas.

Paulina put the report in the Out basket and reluctantly reached for the next task requiring her attention: the final report Andrea had submitted to Gil along with a bill for investigative services. She sighed as she reviewed Andrea's report. It was excellent work. Thorough and concise. Gil had sent a check by return mail, paying the account in full.

The case should be over. Closed.

Paulina smoothed her hand over the pages in the file as though she expected Gil's warmth and personality to flow into her palm. She should instruct Andrea to stick a red dot on the corner of the folder and file it, but she couldn't. Not just yet. A crazy thought had hit her in Australia as she lay awake listening to the ocean pounding on the shore. Paulina knew she had to pursue it before she declared the case officially closed.

But following up the lead would mean she might have to see Gil again. Her heart quivered at the possibility.

She chewed on her lower lip, grappling with the decision. Was it possible she was using the case as an excuse because she couldn't let go of Gil? Regardless of her feelings for Gil, the hit-and-run driver who'd killed Ted Boyer was still at large. And anyway, it was just a hunch.

Paulina searched through the file for the notes of her conversation with Jean-Luc's buddy Alain Valiquette. What was it Alain had said about doing some bodywork on Jean-Luc's car? It might be a coincidence but...she checked the date of Ted's death. A thread of instinct looped into a double knot in her stomach. She knew she was poking her nose where it didn't belong, but her conscience wouldn't let her leave it alone. She picked up the phone and called Robbins.

PAULINA'S PHONE CALL in late November caught Gil completely by surprise. She wanted to see him? His fingers were so damp and sweaty with sudden nervousness, the portable phone nearly slipped from his grasp onto the sofa where he'd been changing Mikey's diaper.

"When would be convenient for me to drop by?" she asked with uncustomary shyness.

"Anytime. I'll be home all day," he told her, as Mikey cooed up at him and rolled onto his tummy, his knees moving like tiny pistons. Gil grabbed him to keep him from falling off the edge of the couch and held on tight. "There's someone here who'd like to meet you," he puffed with exertion as Mikey tried to squirm free.

"I'm looking forward to it. I'll see you soon."

Gil hung up, slightly mystified, a current of excitement electrifying his gut. He couldn't fathom the reason for Paulina's unexpected request to drop by on a Saturday. Was she missing him as much as he missed her?

Hope bloomed in his heart despite the logical protestations of his mind. Maybe she felt as though a piece of her was irretrievably gone, too. Gil had given her a part of himself that last night, when he'd been buried so deep inside the sweet essence of her that he'd literally shattered with the wonder of it. He went rigid just thinking about the way she'd locked her legs around him and wouldn't let him withdraw. They'd lain together, panting and damp with perspiration, until he'd swelled in her again and the hot, insatiable need to be one with her took complete possession of his body and his soul. And he'd walked out of her apartment the next morning knowing he'd never see her again—unless by accident.

Maybe she just wanted to see Mikey.

Who cared what the reason was? What mattered was she was coming. He hoisted Mikey into the air like an airplane. Mikey chortled with glee.

"Okay, buddy, we gotta hit the showers and wash your breakfast off your face. We have a lady visitor to impress. Rule number one about women—they like men to look good and smell good." He gave Mikey a jiggle of air turbulence as they headed for the staircase. Mikey waved his arms and cooed for more. Gil complied, feeling his love for his nephew circle his heart with a glowing warmth. "Whatever you do, buddy, don't drool on her. Women hate that. Just play it cool and look cute. I'll do the talking."

Mikey turned his head and looked at Gil, his fine gold eyebrows arched up as though questioning his uncle's sanity.

Gil chuckled. "Yeah, buddy, I'm crazy. But at least I'll know I gave it my best shot."

THE FIRST VISIBLE SIGN that Gil's house now contained a family sat on the front steps wearing a crooked grin and a sooty, shrunken cap. Paulina was sure the rotting jack-o'-lantern was laughing at her as she marched up the steps, juggling a stack of gaily wrapped gifts for Mikey in her arms. Her legs shook as she freed a finger to press the doorbell. Her mouth felt as though she'd swallowed sand. Why was she so nervous?

All she had to do was tell Gil who killed Ted, admire Mikey and leave. Piece of cake. And yet, she was scared to death.

The door swung open and her gaze locked on Gil, then onto the smiling baby in his arms. Her chin dropped in adoration as an invisible hand gave a strong tug on her heartstrings. Mikey was wearing a blue velour sleeper with a football insignia on the knees. His butter-gold curls were rakishly mussed. His pale blue eyes had a shy, trusting innocence that melted her insides. Pride that she'd played a hand in determining his fate curved her lips into a broad smile.

"God, I love my job," she squeaked over the lump in her throat, unable to take her eyes off Mikey and his dimpled smile. Mikey blinked back at her as though he wondered what all the fuss was about.

"I love your job, too," Gil said quietly, his arms tightening reflexively around Mikey. "You look good. The bruises are gone."

Paulina nodded, feeling a blush creep over her cheeks as she took stock of Gil's jeans and his Ottawa Rough Riders sweatshirt with the sleeves pushed casually up to his elbows, and finally slanted her gaze to his clean-shaven face. She caught the discreet scent of his cologne as she tumbled into the dazzling trap of Gil's eyes. Longing pierced her like a serrated blade.

"Mikey looks right at home in your arms," she said softly. For a fraction of a second, she felt insanely envious of the little cherub. She struggled to get a mental grip on herself. She was here to finish a job. Nothing more.

He pulled the door open wider, looking ill at ease. "Come in. You're always welcome in this house."

"I brought a few things for Mikey," she said awkwardly, stepping into the foyer. She set the presents down on a table and shrugged out of her leather jacket, turning to hang it on the wrought iron hall tree. Her heart gave a painful squeeze at the presence of a pink woman's cardigan suspended from another hook. *It was hand knitted.*

Paulina told herself it was none of her business that Gil had a woman's sweater in his house. It probably belonged to his mother. *Or* he'd lost no time in finding a mother for Mikey, in which case she should be happy for him. She knew exactly how quickly a woman could fall in love with a man like Gil.

Considerably subdued, Paulina gathered her packages

and followed Gil into the living room. She joined him and Mikey on the sofa, noticing that Gil's decor had changed significantly. A baby swing sat in the corner of the living room. Toys were piled in a playpen. And the dining room had been transformed into a handsomely furnished office. Paulina wondered what other changes had taken place in Gil's life.

This was too hard. She should have let Robbins tell Gil about Ted.

"I see you've been busy redecorating," she said tartly.

"Yeah. I hired a live-in nanny to help out. Mrs. Mc-Tavish is a nice, grandmotherly-type Scottish nanny, but I'm the only familiar face Mikey has left, so I want to be around him as much as possible. My parents couldn't stay here indefinitely. This home-office concept is working out better than I expected."

So, the feminine pink sweater belonged to a grandmotherly nanny. Paulina felt ridiculously relieved.

Mikey leaned forward in Gil's arms and patted at the boxes Paulina held against her chest like a shield. Gil lifted one off the top of the pile and let Mikey chew on it. "I see you've been busy shopping." He pointed at the signature gold sticker of a baby boutique, which secured the gift card in place. He read the gift card, then set it aside with a brief thank-you and concentrated on helping Mikey unwrap the package. It was a mother rubber duck and duckling.

"Sorry, there weren't any uncle ducks," she joked, desperately wanting to break the awkwardness that was becoming stickier than peanut butter.

"This'll do."

She talked her way through the other gifts—the stacking rings, the books, the stroller activity toy with gadgets to twist and turn and poke at and the child-size football.

Mikey started to gnaw on a sheet of wrapping paper and Gil cleared it away, his fingers sure and loving.

Paulina closed her eyes briefly. Her lap felt terribly empty. The presents she and her mother had so carefully selected last night were all unwrapped. She felt miniature warm fists pummeling her thigh.

"That's Mikey's way of thanking you," Gil teased, pride in his voice.

"His manners need a little work," Paulina said, laughing. Mikey cocked his head up at her at the sound of her voice and she stroked one of his hands. It felt softer than goose down. "C-could I hold him?" she asked, surprising herself.

"Help yourself," Gil muttered wryly.

She could feel his eyes on her as she inched her fingers around Mikey's plump trunk and planted him in her lap. He was a lot heavier than she imagined, but he smelled divine—of shampoo and baby powder. And his toothless, drippy smile was irresistible. Paulina dropped a kiss on his buttery curls as he explored the flowers dotting her sweater. Mikey made a happy, babbling sound like he enjoyed having perfect strangers kiss him.

Gil cleared his throat, his tone brusque. "What brings you here, Paulina?"

Paulina glanced at him quickly, her heart racing with uncertainty as she tried to decipher the tone of his question. His eyes were veiled, shadowing her from his thoughts. But he seemed to be waiting for an explanation. Was he somehow worried she'd come to throw herself at him?

She lowered her gaze. "There's something I need to tell you about Ted."

"Ah, so this is about the case." He stood up and took Mikey from her. Then he walked across the room and put Mikey in the swing.

Paulina stared at Gil's implacable broad shoulders and

hugged her arms around her. Without Mikey's chubby, busy warmth, she felt alone and vulnerable. It had been a mistake to come. The bond of friendship and intimacy that had woven her and Gil together was already fraying thin.

The swing cranked back and forth as Gil went to stand near the green marble fireplace and rested his elbow on the mantel. "What about Ted?" he asked.

"I've identified the driver who killed him."

She heard Gil draw in a sharp breath.

"It was Jean-Luc," she went on quietly. "Remember his friend Alain mentioned he'd done some bodywork on Jean-Luc's Mustang?"

Gil nodded.

"I asked Robbins to have the police lab run some tests. The paint fragments removed from Ted's body match the paint on Jean-Luc's Mustang."

Jean-Luc killed Ted. Gil swore softly under his breath, trying to absorb the shock of Paulina's announcement. Relief at finally knowing the truth twined with anger at the man who'd destroyed his family. Gil's gaze settled on a pewter-framed photograph of Ted, Cindy and Mikey, taken in the hospital the day of Mikey's birth.

Gil couldn't change what had happened. But there was some comfort to be had in the knowledge that Ted and Cindy would live on in Mikey. Gil silently promised his brother and sister-in-law that Mikey would never lack for love or attention.

Behind him, Gil was aware that Paulina was sitting quietly on the couch, her back taut, her hands folded in her lap. Now, of course, he understood what prompted her visit. He understood the gifts for Mikey and the thin veneer of tension covering her features that made her cheeks look like they were sculpted out of ice: duty. Her sense of duty required she deliver this bad news that anyone with an ounce of compassion could see had to be delivered in person.

The realization demolished the tenuous hopes he'd built in anticipation of her visit like an errant wind sweeping through a house of cards.

Gil swallowed the disappointment rising in his throat and glanced at the swing. Mikey's eyelids were drooping. The kid had kept to his half of the plan; he was looking cute and he'd kept the drooling to a minimum.

"Considering that Jean-Luc tried to sell Mikey, I guess I'm not surprised he'd resort to murder," Gil said finally, keeping his face turned from her. It was easier not to look at her, not to remind himself how beautiful she was, how much he wanted her in his life and Mikey's life. How much he needed her. Panic trembled through him. "Just add your time to my final bill."

"Your final bill has already been paid in full."

What did she mean? He swiveled to look at her, wanting to pierce the artificial veneer concealing her emotions. "It was only half what I was expecting. No offense, but your math is way off."

She tilted her dark head to one side and met his gaze head-on. Gil noticed with regret that the stars were gone from her eyes. She looked...bleak.

Paulina tried valiantly to hide what was in her heart. She couldn't exactly tell him that you don't overcharge someone you love. And she did love him. Being in the same room with him reinforced the fact. Which was all the more reason she should leave before this got any more awkward. At least her mother was in town this week, so she wouldn't have to go home to a depressingly empty apartment. "My math isn't off," she said firmly, closing the subject.

She rose from the couch hating the fact that her knees wobbled, undermining the dignity she was struggling hard to maintain. "I should be going now. Mikey looks like he needs to be tucked into bed."

Gil nodded, saying nothing.

There was nothing left to say between them, anyway; they understood each other perfectly. The irony of it left a bad taste in her mouth.

Though he walked beside her to the door, Paulina felt as if he was miles from her. He reached for her russet leather jacket, holding it for her as she slid her arms into the sleeves. Her nerve endings went on alert when his fingers rested for a fraction of a second on her shoulders, then dulled with discontent as he turned and opened the door.

A brisk November wind blew through the foyer, teasing at a lock of his dark hair as she struggled to come up with a word of farewell other than good-bye, which conjured up painful images of them making love. She finally held out her hand and whispered, "Take care."

"I will." His large hand engulfed hers. Paulina felt the warmth of him blaze a pathway through her veins all the way to her heart. She tried to withdraw her fingers to break the connection.

To her surprise, he resisted, keeping a secure grip on her. "Here's the deal, Ms. Stewart," he said quickly. "I love you. I love who you are and what you do. And I want to be with you. I want to look at you across the breakfast table every morning and think to myself that the best damn private investigator in the world is my wife." His fingers squeezed hers. "I would never try to keep you from performing your job. Mikey's *my* responsibility. I stay home with him. I take care of him. I don't mind you flitting off to parts unknown at a moment's notice. I can live with your life-style as long as I know in my heart you're coming home to me, that I mean as much to you as you do to me. You're so damn significant to me it scares me."

He drew a ragged breath. "Hell, Paulina, I want to marry you. But if the idea of marriage frightens you, I'll settle for a lifetime affair."

Paulina's throat was so strained with checked emotions she couldn't speak. The sacrifices Gil was prepared to make stunned her. Did he truly love her that much? Then she thought of Mikey. As generous as Gil's offer was…she couldn't deprive Mikey of a real mother. A hot tear coursed down her cheek. "N-no, Gil. It just wouldn't work."

His expression fell and he dropped her hand as though she'd slapped him. She saw him grapple for his composure and her heart folded in two. *He didn't understand… It wasn't fair that he be the one to make all the sacrifices. He needed a partner in every sense of the word.*

She cupped his cheeks in her palms, her voice quivering as she tried to explain. "I love you, but Mikey needs two parents, who have *his* best interests at heart. If this is going to work, I want equal opportunity hugs with Mikey. So, how about we compromise and share office space in the house? Maybe if you get me on line I can keep my agency functioning without having to be there every—"

He stopped her with a kiss that whisked the breath from her lungs and made her think it was time they christened his bed upstairs. His heart pounded against hers, the two patterns combining into a turbulent rhythm. Paulina kicked the front door closed with her foot and nixed the bed. The couch was much closer, and as an added bonus, they wouldn't have to disturb Mikey. Gil's fingers kneaded her back as if he were trying to assure himself she was real.

"How do you feel about getting married by Tuesday while my mother's still in town?" she asked breathlessly, breaking the kiss. Not that she thought her mother wouldn't come back for her wedding. They'd rekindled their relationship over the last few days. Sarah would eagerly embrace a grandchild and a son-in-law.

"I'll marry you any day, any time," Gil said huskily, wreaking a fiery assault of kisses on Paulina's neck. "But what made you change your mind? You seemed so sure."

"You," she murmured, shivering with delight as a patch of goose bumps rose along her spine. "And my dad." The prospect of being an instant mother didn't seem nearly so scary knowing Gil would be with her every step of the way. In fact, it seemed downright exhilarating.

His tongue touched the lobe of her ear. "Your dad?"

"Mmm-hmm. He taught me that some things were meant to be...and *you* convinced me that being with you and Mikey was one of them."

Gil chuckled low in his throat and lifted her against him, so she could feel the strength of his arousal against her belly. "And I'll keep on convincing you for the rest of your life."

Paulina gave a blissful sigh and locked her legs around him. She trusted him to keep his word. And she planned to enjoy every minute of it. Particularly the part where they worked on a sister for Mikey.

HARLEQUIN®

INTRIGUE®

43 Light St.

Outside, it looks like a charming old building near the Baltimore waterfront, but inside lurks danger...and romance.

"First lady of suspense" **REBECCA YORK** returns with

FATHER AND CHILD

No other woman could do the job—just Elizabeth Egan. But how could Zeke Chambers ask her to marry him in name only and to put her life on the line in a dangerous rescue mission? Zeke had no choice—and he had the best of reasons: he had to save the life of his daughter—the daughter he never knew.

Don't miss #437 FATHER AND CHILD, coming to you in October 1997—only from Rebecca York and Harlequin Intrigue!

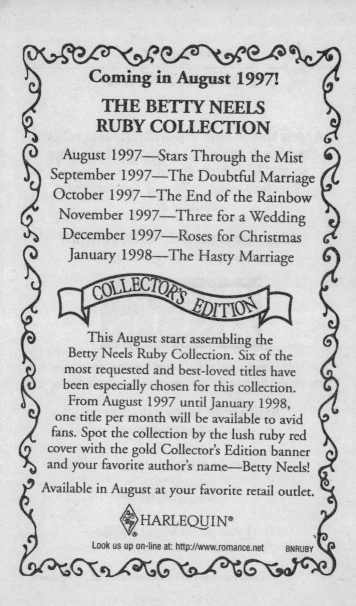

Coming in August 1997!

THE BETTY NEELS
RUBY COLLECTION

COLLECTOR'S EDITION

This August start assembling the
Betty Neels Ruby Collection. Six of the
most requested and best-loved titles have
been especially chosen for this collection.
From August 1997 until January 1998,
one title per month will be available to avid
fans. Spot the collection by the lush ruby red
cover with the gold Collector's Edition banner
and your favorite author's name—Betty Neels!

Available in August at your favorite retail outlet.

HARLEQUIN®

HARLEQUIN®

I N T R I G U E ®

Angels should have wings and flowing robes—
not black jeans and leather jackets. They
should be chubby cherubs or wizened old
specters—not virile and muscular and
sinfully sexy.

Then again, the AVENGING ANGELS
aren't your average angels!

One of the most popular Harlequin Intrigue miniseries. And
now they're back—with two extraspecial angels just for you!

#440 ANGEL WITH AN ATTITUDE
by Carly Bishop
October 1997

#443 A REAL ANGEL
by Cassie Miles
November 1997

Don't miss the AVENGING ANGELS—
they're the sexiest angels this side of heaven!

HARLEQUIN®

I N T R I G U E®

You meet a man. He's so appealing,
so sexy. He's your soul mate, the man
you've waited your whole life to find.
But you get the sense he's hiding
something...and it's not just
his feelings....

You meet some of the sexiest and most secretive men
in the HIDDEN IDENTITY series. These men may talk
a good game, but their kisses never lie! Find out who
the real men are in HIDDEN IDENTITY!

Don't miss the next exciting title:

#434 BEN'S WIFE
by Charlotte Douglas
September 1997

Don't miss any of the exciting HIDDEN IDENTITY
stories—only from Harlequin Intrigue!

HARLEQUIN®

I N T R I G U E®

COMING NEXT MONTH

#437 FATHER AND CHILD by Rebecca York
43 Light St.
Zeke Chambers needed a wife in 24 hours. But could he ask
Elizabeth Egan, the woman he secretly loved, to marry him for a
pretense, to put her life in danger? But Zeke had no choice: He had
to save the life of the child he just found out he had.

#438 LITTLE GIRL LOST by Adrianne Lee
Her Protector
After a fiery crash five years ago, Jane Dolan and her infant daughter
were given a new beginning and new memories. So how could she
believe reporter Chad Ryker's claims that her family is in hiding and
that her precious daughter isn't her child?

#439 BEFORE THE FALL by Patricia Rosemoor
Seven Sins
Wrongly indicted, Angela Dragon is out to find who framed her—
even if that means confronting the mob…and escaping a dimple-
flashing bounty hunter. Mitch Kaminsky has problems of his own:
When Angela learns the truth, will she still want him, or will pride
keep them apart?

#440 ANGEL WITH AN ATTITUDE by Carly Bishop
Avenging Angels
To mother an orphaned baby, Angelo's one true love Isobel had
turned mortal. Now with a killer on her trail, Isobel needed
protection, and Angelo could trust no one with her life. He'd let her
down once before; he wasn't about to lose sight of her again.

AVAILABLE THIS MONTH:

Look us up on-line at: http://www.romance.net

FORTUNE COOKIE

Breathtaking romance is predicted in your future with Harlequin's newest collection: Fortune Cookie.

Three of your favorite Harlequin authors, Janice Kaiser, Margaret St. George and M.J. Rodgers will regale you with the romantic adventures of three heroines who are promised fame, fortune, danger and intrigue when they crack open their fortune cookies on a fateful night at a Chinese restaurant.

Join in the adventure with your own personalized fortune, inserted in every book!

Don't miss this exciting new collection!

Available in September wherever Harlequin books are sold.

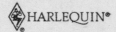

HARLEQUIN®